CAN I TRUST YOU?

CAN I TRUST YOU?

ROB GITTINS

This edition produced in Great Britain in 2023

by Hobeck Books Limited, 24 Brookside Business Park, Stone, Staffordshire
ST15 0RZ

www.hobeck.net

Copyright © Rob Gittins 2023

A CIP catalogue for this book is available from the British Library.

ISBN 978-1-913-793-21-1 (pbk)

ISBN 978-1-913-793-22-8 (ebook)

Cover design by Jayne Mapp Design

Printed and bound in Great Britain

ARE YOU A THRILLER SEEKER?

Hobeck Books is an independent publisher of crime, thrillers and suspense fiction and we have one aim – to bring you the books you want to read.

For more details about our books, our authors and our plans, plus the chance to download free novellas, sign up for our newsletter at **www.hobeck.net**.

You can also find us on Twitter **@hobeckbooks** or on Facebook **www.facebook.com/hobeckbooks10**.

For William Jones
'Wil Sir Fôn'
A brilliant writer, a genius storyteller, and a great friend

Twenty years ago, his daughter vanished.
He was the last person to see her.

Twenty years to the day, a second girl vanishes.
He's the last person to see her too.

PROLOGUE

TWENTY YEARS AGO

TRUST. They always say it, and it's true. Once it's gone, it's gone.

The young girl stared out over the water for a moment, then rose to her feet, damp sand clinging to her jeans. Stray sounds echoed around as she walked towards the waves. Looming up out of the darkness, she glimpsed the indistinct form of an old, disused, lighthouse. In days gone by she'd dreamt of swimming out to it. But now there were just her metronome-like steps, pressing her forward, pushing her on.

The sea was always there. Sometimes it was so close to the shore she could reach down from the harbour wall and touch it. Sometimes, like now, it was out on the horizon, waiting to make its return. But in a world where few certainties still existed, the sea remained.

She could trust that at least.

Which was when she heard it.

From behind.

The sound of someone approaching.

PART ONE

PART ONE

CHAPTER 1
PRESENT DAY

HER EYES ARE the first thing I see; they always are. And as I stare at them, that all too familiar ache begins deep inside. I don't even see the simple caption that accompanies the image on my phone, but I don't need to. Donna, my ex-wife, posts the same picture with the same caption on this same day every year.

I look up and stare, unseeing, out of the window, and for a moment, as the estuary and all the old familiar sights flash past, I focus on them. It's displacement activity, I know.

I watch the cockle pickers out on the beds, moving away from a small semi-circle of Land Rovers waiting to take their sand-sodden sacks back to the shore, for transportation on to a local market.

I watch the fishermen in their small boats out in the bay searching for bass.

I look across at the surfers plunging into the water, praying for a sudden Atlantic swell.

I look up at the ruined castle watching over it all from a hill in the distance.

But it doesn't do any good. And for a moment, as the ache spreads, intensifying all the while, I can't catch my breath. It's as if I've been physically punched. I will myself not to look at that photo again, but I do, just as Donna probably promises herself she won't post it every year, but she always does, because not to would seem like a betrayal. Neither of us needs this visual reminder that it's now twenty years to the day that our teenage daughter, Cara, walked out of our house and never returned, twenty years since she disappeared into a void she's inhabited ever since, a void that immediately and inevitably claimed us too. But Donna still posts it anyway.

The train jerks away from the last station before my home station, the end of the small branch line. For a moment – more displacement activity – I try to remember what's in the fridge. Should I stop in the town or the small convenience store and garage closer to home and pick up something?

Images of the small, rented cottage I've lived in for the past years swim before me, a house that's never remotely resembled anything like a home. But I know Donna feels much the same about our old house, the one we made into a home for ourselves and our daughter and which ceased to be that the moment she disappeared. Then I look back at the image on my phone and into Cara's eyes again.

In the early years a few well-intentioned souls would call into the bookshop on anniversaries such as these and steer the conversation, cautiously, round to Donna's posts. A couple confessed themselves rocked to suddenly stumble on the image like that, feeling much as I'm feeling right now, as if someone had landed a low blow to their gut. One asked if this was Donna's way of keeping Cara's memory alive. I was getting used to dealing with all sorts of inanity and insensitivity, and tried to bite back the bile I could now feel rising in my throat. But perhaps the look on my face was enough, because the asker of the question suddenly decided he could live without the first edition, second printing of the collected poems of one of our finest local poets, replaced the Vernon Watkins collection on the counter and left.

I stared after him long after the ring of the shop bell faded into silence. Did he really think we needed a reminder? Did he seriously imagine we'd need some aid to memory to keep our daughter alive in our minds?

Somewhere ahead, a couple of recently boarded passengers are swaying down the train looking for seats. I hear a voice, and for a moment I don't know where it's coming from. Then I look up to see a female train guard smiling down at me, a little puzzled, before asking again whether she's checked my ticket.

I smile back, apologetic, a silent acknowledgement of my distraction, and rummage in my bag, taking out the copy of the Janet Frame volume I've just sold before retrieving the small ticket from an inside pocket where I always keep it. The guard stamps it, as behind her and further down the carriage I see the two recently embarked passengers now settling themselves into their seats – a man and a woman; the woman fussing over a small baby in a buggy, the baby letting out a protesting cry before settling back to sleep again.

That always happens on this date, too. Everything seems magnified somehow. The cry of a child returns the cries of our own child at that age, although in truth anything can trigger it off. Laughter from a group of teens, a hissed argument between a harassed mother and a truculent child, a stray shout of hello or goodbye as a girl walks towards or away from a friend.

After mine and Donna's break-up another well-meaning friend told us a story her mother had once told her. Relationships are like plates, she'd always said. A swift and clean break scythes the plate in half, but the two pieces will still fit together. It won't ever be the same, but it will still look like and can still function as a plate. Smash that plate into a thousand pieces, inflict upon it destruction by a thousand cuts, and those pieces will never knit together again.

I understood what she was saying, of course. If this split is going to happen, if you really are going to heap misfortune onto calamity by separating just when the pair of you must need each the most, then do it quickly and as painlessly as possible. Don't damn, beyond any possibility of repair, all you might have had before. But it was a fond hope. Some tragedies fuse those left behind, forge an unbreakable bond. For others it's the opposite. The very sight of those left behind only makes an absence ever more clamorous with each minute spent in the other's company. And in the end, there's only one way out.

Another voice breaks in, someone asking if anyone's sitting on the seat opposite, and I realise the book I've just taken out of my bag is lying there. I mumble another apology and, still unseeing, pick it up as my fellow passenger sits down in the newly vacated space, then force myself to concentrate on the front cover, before opening it up and scanning the first page.

Finding a book like this is one of the reasons I've remained in my old trade. Janet Frame's *The Lagoon* was the author's first book, published by the Caxton Press in her native New Zealand in 1951. The copy I'm holding is a first edition, first impression of her first collection of short stories in its original blue cloth-backed grey and blue patterned boards. The dust jacket, the edges and the boards are lightly foxed, but it's still an excellent copy with only minor loss to the foot of the spine.

At the time of its publication, Janet Frame was a patient at the country's Seacliff psychiatric hospital. She'd been scheduled to undergo a lobotomy, but the book's receipt of the Hubert Church Award, one of New Zealand's most prestigious literary prizes, led to its cancellation. It was probably the starkest example I'd ever come across of a book literally saving someone's mind.

A collector in the US called just this morning to bid for it, a companion to the other Frame he owned, a first edition of her debut novel, *Owls Do Cry*. I sold a copy myself last year and can still see in my mind's eye the stunning jacket designed by Dennis Beytagh. We talked for over an hour about the stories before agreeing on a price, just over two thousand pounds. It was a welcome moment of good fortune, but today it feels like good fortune rendered laceratingly bittersweet.

A voice comes over the tannoy, announcing our arrival at the final station on our journey in a few minutes time and asking that all passengers check their belongings before leaving the train. I place the Frame, still open, down on the table, check for my car keys and pick up my coat from the seat beside me. For one last time, and unable to help myself once again, I look at the picture of Cara on my phone, hoping no one sees the sudden tears I'm now blinking back, praying they won't actually run down my cheeks.

All around people are now beginning to stand, retrieving bags, coats, shopping. I look up to check on which platform the train's arriving – there's a choice of two, one involving a small walk from the rear entrance to the nearby car park, the other a detour over the rail tracks. But I don't see which platform the driver's been directed to this evening and I don't see the other passengers either.

Across the small table, Cara is watching me.

For a moment, sound ceases. For that same moment it's as if all the air's been sucked out of the world. I stare at my daughter as she stares back at me, the eyes I've been looking at just the moment before in that photo made real, and they're her eyes, they're Cara's eyes. I'd know them, I'd know her, anywhere.

And in a daze, and acting almost on autopilot, I reach out my hand and touch her.

CHAPTER 2
TWENTY YEARS AGO

I'VE MADE ALL the usual arrangements; ID verification has been completed and proof of funds forwarded. My solicitor, Patrick, will be doing the in-person bidding on my behalf and I've advised him of my maximum bid in case the phone connection fails – which has been known to happen on a few, much-lamented, occasions in the past. All that remains now is to find out how much of the forty thousand pounds I've allotted to this particular purchase I'll actually need to spend. The next twenty or so minutes will tell.

Which is when my personal mobile pulses with a text alert. I look across at Donna to see if she can answer it for me, but she's already returned to the kitchen, leaving me alone in the sitting room, my work phone in front of me. Donna knows better than to disturb me once an auction's underway. I glance at my daughter's name on the display. Cara really should know better too, but she's out at a party tonight. I still remember my own teenage years well enough to know that probably takes precedence over everything.

Quickly, I open the text.

Dad, a few people are going back to Jools's house, is it OK if I go too and stay?

I call out. 'Donna.'

She appears a moment later and I show her the text, keeping

an ear open for anything from the auction house. It's due to start in five minutes and already I can feel a hubbub beginning in the meeting room some five thousand miles or so away from where I'm sitting right now.

Donna hesitates as she reads, then shrugs, the silent signal clear. Why not? Cara's eighteen; in one sense we should be grateful she's even consulted us. A voice breaks in on my speakerphone – Patrick checking the connection.

The volume I'm bidding on is one I've tracked for the last two months. In 1924, the French publishers Three Mountains Press released *In Our Time*, a collection of short stories by Ernest Hemingway. Only three hundred copies were printed during its initial run, but there was an issue. The frontispiece was a woodcut portrait of Hemingway, which was found to have bled through to the next page during printing. Consequently, only one hundred and seventy copies were sold, with the remaining copies given away to family and friends. Very few copies now remain, and when one surfaced, in Istanbul, last year it sold for just shy of forty thousand pounds. Six months ago, another copy was discovered in Arizona, which is where Patrick is right now.

My mobile pulses again; another text from Cara, perhaps uneasy about the ongoing silence.

I'll text you when we get there and call in the morning.

I smile, memories of similar teenage rites of passage washing before my eyes, then glance at the clock. Less than three minutes before the auction's due to start.

'Do you want to text back?'

I hold out the mobile, but Donna shakes her head.

'Just tell her it's fine.'

Donna turns and heads away again, and I pause for a moment, a little unsettled. Work's been crazy lately, one auction after another, lots of distractions – along with a spectacular piece of work-related misfortune I really don't want to think about right now, but I've still registered a strange atmosphere in the house lately. As if Donna and Cara are walking around each other on eggshells. I type a quick text back to Cara.

Have a lovely time and speak in the morning.

The hubbub on the speakerphone is louder now, but I've learnt not to take too much notice of that. Telephone bids are going to be the norm at this sort of auction. It's possible that Patrick might even be a rarity, and that few physical bidders will be in the actual room itself. In these cases, auction houses have been known to pack the floor with employees to create artificial excitement to try and stimulate the bidding. Then the auction begins. Dimly, I'm aware of our front door opening and Donna heading outside, probably for a walk. She knows only too well how wrapped up I get once these things start.

Then a breathless twenty minutes follows, at the end of which I have the answer to my question. I've spent all my allotted sum and another couple of thousand pounds on top. But I have the Hemingway. The next three hours are spent on the resulting paperwork, after which I collapse into bed.

———

I don't sleep, of course, not properly anyway. I never do. The buzz of the auction – and the thrill of the biggest purchase I've completed after that spectacular piece of recent misfortune – puts paid to that. I walk out of the house, much like Donna did a short time ago. I think I go for a drive too, but half an hour later I can't remember actually doing so or where I went. I finally fall asleep about three in the morning, but then – a couple of hours later – I wake and get out of bed as a sudden thought strikes me.

I check my personal mobile but there's no text from Cara, letting us know she's back in Jools's house as promised. I hesitate a moment before deciding she's probably forgotten. I'd have been more than likely to do the same myself at her age.

A couple of hours later I'm heading out of the house as Donna stirs. I check if she's heard from Cara, and there it is again. That slight tensing of the shoulders as I mention her name, but she shakes her head. But then my assistant in the bookshop, Mark, texts with the first of the enquiries that are already rolling in regarding our new acquisition and I head down to the bookshop.

An hour passes as I compile all the details and Mark prepares a trade release. I check my phone again. It's now ten o'clock and still nothing from Cara. I look across at Mark and ask if he went to the party last night too. Cara and Mark have been seeing each other in a semi-serious way. Up to a couple of months ago anyway.

Mark just looks up at me, puzzled.

'What party?'

CHAPTER 3
PRESENT DAY

IT'S like coming up out of a deep dive, breaking the surface for air. Donna has always been passionate about wild swimming, rain or shine, summer or winter, and occasionally, very occasionally, I'd join her, braving the almost intolerable cold. And that moment when you kick out your legs and your head comes back up into the air feels just like this. As if suddenly everything's in the sharpest, clearest focus.

A face I've not seen before is the first one I register. A face staring at me from behind a catering trolley, a woman in her forties with red hair, a badge fixed to her lapel, sporting a name I can't read.

'Excuse me, are you OK?'

I nod back, then realise she's not actually talking to me. She's talking to the girl still sitting opposite, and as I look back at her I realise my hand is still on her arm. The girl's just staring at me, the world coming back more and more into focus all the while, and I now realise other people in the carriage are staring at me too, including the young family with the baby.

I snatch back my hand as, behind the lady with the trolley, another face appears, that of the female guard who checked my ticket a few moments ago, the one who was smiling indulgently at me as I hadn't seemed to see her, but she's not smiling now. She's eyeing me as warily as everyone else.

'Sorry—'

I stop, have no idea what to say for a moment. For her part the young girl, who I can now see can't be much older than her late teens, is still just staring at me and she's not Cara, of course she isn't. How could she be? I've just reached out and touched a total stranger on a train.

What is that, assault? Is that why the female guard's taking her phone out of her pocket? Am I about to be reported or something? Behind the guard, and framed in the doorway connecting the two carriages of the train, I now see someone else – a man dressed in some sort of security guard's uniform, who's also eyeing me very darkly.

I glance at the girl again, trying to get my raging emotions back under some sort of control.

'I thought…'

I stop again. Looking out of the window, I see we've paused at a signal, waiting for another train to leave the station ahead. I now have a few – a very few – moments to try and put this at least halfway right.

'I thought you were someone else. I'm really sorry.' I tail off, helpless. 'It's been a long day.'

All eyes, including mine, are now on the girl, as if the whole carriage is waiting to take their cue from her. What will she say? What will she do? And for a moment longer there's still silence, but then a hesitant smile plays on her lips, and she nods back.

'It's OK. Forget it.'

All around the carriage, the same faces stare at me now, their expressions telling me more eloquently than words alone could manage that they're not quite as forgiving of a middle-aged man who's just reached out to touch a teenage girl on a train.

And behind the trolley lady and the female guard and the young man in the security uniform, I catch something else: a click and a small flash as if someone, not the guard, has just taken a picture, but I can't see for sure through the press of wary, if not positively hostile faces before me. Maybe someone's recognised me. Maybe I'm going to wake up tomorrow to find that one of my fellow travellers has posted a picture on social media. The latest instalment in the unsavoury adventures of the local oddball.

The train is still paused at the signal and suddenly I stand – I can't stay there, not in that carriage, not now. Nodding silent and grateful thanks at the girl, I stumble towards the toilet at the other end of the carriage, away from all those other staring eyes, exhaling a silent sigh of relief as the doors glide shut behind me.

I stare into the mirror for a moment as a low babble of voices breaks out in the carriage behind, an inquest probably taking place into all they've just seen. Maybe the train staff are checking on the girl, making sure she really is OK, that she really is happy, in her own words, to just forget about all this.

I reach out and turn on the tap, splashing water on my face, and for a moment I wish I was back with Donna on one of her wild swims, under that ice cold water, everything else driven from my mind but the simple objective of surviving in inhospitable depths. Then I close my eyes as the train jerks back into motion, the final station now in sight.

My mobile pulses and I look at it, already knowing what it will be. Sure enough, the usual message from Donna is displayed on the screen.

You OK?

It's another of her regular rituals on this most difficult of days. She posts that picture of Cara, then she'll text me that simple question, but she won't wait for an answer. Now Donna will retreat from the world for a day or so, closing the curtains, disconnecting her phone, not even looking at her laptop, cocooning herself with her memories until the world turns again and she can emerge back into the light.

I look up at the door. I don't actually want to go back out into the carriage. Like Donna, I want to stay here in this small space for as long as I can, but that's impossible, of course. Taking a deep breath, I press the button to unlock the door and it slides back. No one's outside, and as I head back into the carriage, I see that the young girl is also nowhere to be seen. The lady with the trolley is still there doing some sort of stock-take, but the female guard and the young security officer are gone now too. I pick up the Frame, still open on the table, and slide it into my bag, but as I do so I stop. On the open page in front of me, I see an inscription scrawled in pencil.

Can I Trust You?

I just stare at it for a moment. I always check for marks or inscriptions, anything that might impact a book's value, but somehow, I seem to have missed this one. And what's even stranger is that inscriptions are usually on the front few pages or on the inside of the cover, not a few pages into the text like this. It could be an annotation of course, but at first glance I can't see what in the text it might be referencing. But there's no time to pursue that now, aside from making a mental note to alert the purchaser to a mark I seem to have missed.

I replace the volume in my bag and head for the nearest exit, where, her back to me, I can see the young girl waiting to get off.

CHAPTER 4
TWENTY YEARS AGO

ONE HOUR LATER, all the formalities have been concluded. The deposit for the Hemingway and the auction house fee have been deducted from the holding account I've supplied. The legal pack and contract have been forwarded on. And there's still nothing from Cara.

I debate whether to text, but then call instead, and her answerphone cuts in after just two rings, which is odd. Her phone usually rings out a good few times before I hear her voice telling me to leave a message.

'Maybe she's turned it off.'

Mark joins me at the reception desk, a few early customers already milling around, holidaymakers for the most part.

I nod, reflecting again that if I was at a party, I'd probably have turned my phone off too.

'Or the battery's died, or she's put it in DND mode.'

'DND?'

'Do Not Disturb.'

I stare at him.'Can you do that?'

He nods.

'It's easy enough to get round it though. Call her three times, back-to-back, and it overrides it. It's an emergency thing'

Swiftly, I do as instructed. But there's still nothing. So, I hit another number instead and a moment or so later, Donna's voice wafts down the line, removing another possibility, that perhaps it's my phone at fault.

I plunge straight in. 'She's probably just sleeping off a hangover, I know – but there's still nothing from Cara and she's not answering her phone.'

One of the early customers approaches the desk, a large volume – an early Harry Potter – in hand, and Mark moves to serve him.

'Have you got a number for Jools?'

Donna sounds puzzled.

'She was at the party too, wasn't she?'

I nod. 'Cara was going back to hers.'

'So, she's probably still sleeping it off as well.'

From the desk, Mark – now ringing up the sale but clearly listening at the same time – cuts in.

'I've got Jools's number.'

He takes out his mobile and shares the contact. I press on the name and the phone rings. But that's all it does. It just rings out, and this time no answer service cuts in.

I look at the clock. It's now ten a.m. Which is still very early if you've just pulled an all-nighter. But it's really not like Cara not to text or call when she said she would.

I stare at my phone for a moment longer.

Then I tell Mark to look after the shop for a short while.

CHAPTER 5
PRESENT DAY

UP AND DOWN the train the doors hiss open. I've hung back in the space the tannoy announcer always calls a vestibule, anxious for all too obvious reasons not to crowd the girl I can still see ahead waiting to get off. I don't know if the small line of people queueing behind are watching me, because, that brief sighting aside, I keep my eyes firmly fixed to the floor. I see that the girl's now wearing a brightly coloured scarf, but that's all I register. I very much avoid any sort of eye contact with her or with anyone.

I sense rather than see her move off the train, which has been directed tonight onto the nearest platform to the car park, for which I proffer heartfelt, if silent, thanks. Disembarking on the other platform would have meant my virtually stalking her across the tracks.

I file in among the rest of the passengers and, keeping my head down, cut through a small gate that leads onto a staff car park and from there onto a larger public car park in the shadow of a newly erected footbridge. I press the security fob on my car key and two flashing lights sanction my approach, illuminating the only other car parked there, an older vehicle in a more dimly lit section, avoided by most locals as it's prone to flooding. I can't see the young girl now, but I am aware of a few of my fellow passengers making their way over the footbridge above me towards the town. Maybe she's among them. Again, for all too obvious reasons, I don't stand and stare.

For a moment I just wait by my car, letting the events of the last few minutes wash over me. And it's strange, and I have no idea why, but I feel that if I'd had chance to explain properly, then she would have understood what had just happened and why. Or maybe that's me trying to put the best spin on things. Wishful thinking.

Feeling my breathing beginning to slow to something approximating normal again, but still not able to actually get in my car and drive away, I look out at the lights of the town at the bridge now fast emptying of travellers, then back towards the station where the train is being moved to the sidings, probably to be cleaned.

Which is when, suddenly, I hear her.

'Two hours?'

Almost involuntarily, I turn. The young girl is facing away from me, looking up a slight incline that leads from the station to the main road. Usually there's a couple of taxis parked there waiting for fares, but this evening there aren't any. As I keep watching she leans into her phone, her voice wafting across the car park towards me again.

'You've really nothing sooner?'

I turn back, open the car and put my bag on a rear seat before closing it and walking round to the driver's door. This really is none of my business. Then I hear her again.

'Well, what about buses?'

I can't hear the response on the other end of the line, but I don't need to. The last bus leaves just before eight in the evening and we're a good hour or so past that now. And it's obviously what she's just been told, because her voice, now sounding more anxious, cuts across once again.

'I need to get to Carmel. How far is that to walk?'

I pause again. I know exactly how far it is: around three to four miles. A good hour or more at this time of night, along largely unlit roads leading to a small collection of houses. It's also one of the routes I take to reach my cottage further along the coast.

I remain where I am for a moment, half-in, half-out of the car, and now I'm telling myself that this is crazy. I can't even begin to think what I'm thinking right now. Even if all that's just happened on that train hadn't happened at all, if I could rewind time and wipe it, how could I even consider offering a young girl, albeit a stranded young girl, a lift to what seems to be her final stop on her journey tonight? And if I did, what young girl, even if she was stranded, would dream of accepting it?

I get into the car, put my keys into the ignition and make to pull the door after me, when her voice wafts across from the station entrance once more.

'OK, OK, thank you.'

And it's the tone. The note of resigned desperation. The realisation that she's now in for a cold long wait outside a deserted rail station for a taxi that may not come at all. And, suddenly, I see them again. I see her eyes as I looked into them those few minutes ago. And while they're not Cara's eyes, they are the eyes of a young girl who must be around my daughter's age the last time I saw her. And what would I do, how would I feel if it was Cara standing there? How would I feel if I knew it was in some well-disposed soul's gift to help her?

I turn round in my seat and look across at her, still alone outside the station entrance, still facing away from me. Because I know, despite everything that's just happened, that I am well-disposed. I am not some madman who spends his time touching strange girls in train carriages; there is an explanation for all that happened even if she'll never know what it is. But I'm still only too aware that what I really should do right now is turn the key in front of me, start the engine and go home.

A few moments later I'm back out of my car and walking across the car park towards her.

She's facing away from me, still looking up that small incline, her phone still in hand, almost as if willing a taxi to appear by magic. And in the moment before I speak, I find myself wishing the same, because I could then just turn away, perhaps without her even seeing me. But no taxi appears. And a moment later, I call out.

'Excuse me.'

The girl turns and I put my hands up, almost in a surrender gesture, deliberately keeping myself at a safe distance from her all the time. Behind, I can now see a couple of other stray souls exiting the station entrance. Thank God it's not just me and her out there.

'I just wanted to say sorry. Again. Honestly, I really do feel so bad about all that.'

She just keeps looking at me, and I take a quick, deep breath.

'And look, please feel free to say no – I really wouldn't blame you – but I heard you just now on the phone, trying to get hold of a taxi, asking about buses?' Sudden panic overtakes me. 'I wasn't listening. I was just in the car park, that's all.'

I stop. Dimly, I'm conscious of someone else coming out of the small gate set into the fence on the platform I exited those few moments before and pausing as they look across at us. But with the young girl still just staring at me, I plough on.

'I live just beyond Carmel. It's on my way home. It's a ten-minute drive, if that.'

I take another deep breath.

'I wondered if you'd like a lift?'

And suddenly it's as if I'm back on that train again. I have that same sense of the world holding its breath as I wait for her answer.

'As I say, I'd totally understand if you'd rather not.'

Now I can see the figure who's emerged from the gate, and it's the lady manning the catering trolley, who must have finished checking her stock and is presumably on her way home now herself. But she's clearly recognised me, and she's registered the young girl again too, and she's watching us.

For a moment I don't think the girl's going to answer, that she's just going to keep on staring at me until I turn and head back to my car. But then she nods.

'Thanks.'

She reaches down, hitches up a small rucksack from the pavement and fastens it in place over her shoulder, taking care not to snag it on her kaleidoscope-coloured scarf, and then we both head for my car. Out of the corner of my eye I see the trolley lady from the train, now smoking a cigarette, her eyes seeming to burn into my back.

I make for the boot to open it so the girl can put her rucksack inside, but she shakes her head, clutching onto the straps as if it's some sort of comfort blanket.

'I'll keep it with me.'

I nod back. We get into the car, and with the keys in the ignition where I left them, I start the engine. I look around, can't help myself, searching for the trolley lady, but I don't see her now.

But I do catch sight of another figure hurrying past us as I pull out of the car park. The young girl's absorbed in her mobile by now and she doesn't see him, but it's the man from the train, the man dressed in what looked to be a security guard's uniform, the man who was watching me along with everyone else. He's almost running now, towards the old car parked in that more dimly lit section of the car park.

A stray overhead light captures him in a momentary flash, and I can see his face contorted in what looks like fury.

CHAPTER 6
TWENTY YEARS AGO

TWENTY MINUTES after leaving the bookshop, I park my car on a grassy bank leading down to the sea. A few dog walkers are out on the sands, but I can't see anyone else.

Then, tucked into a steep cliff at the far eastern edge of the beach, I see a few dim shapes: a couple of figures huddled together by an outcrop of rocks, some other figures beyond them prone on the sand. I walk over, trying to look casual, desperately trying to think up some innocent-sounding reason why I might be passing this out-of-the-way location, only too aware of the tongue-lashing I'm about to get from my daughter if one of those dim shapes does turn out to be her, and she realises I'm checking up on her.

The smell of stale weed hangs in the air as I approach. I dodge a few stray bottles dotted here and there in the sand. Still trying to look as if I'm a simple stroller out on a walk, I check each of the post-party casualties as I pass, but I can see instantly that none of them is Cara.

Then I see another prone figure, lying further out on the sand. The returning tide is beginning to approach, and I know these tides. When they turn, they turn quickly. I hurry over. Whoever that is, be it Cara or someone else, they really can't stay there, particularly in what looks to be a semi-comatose state. But as I hurry over, the figure – a teenage boy, I can now see – is already struggling to his feet, aware now himself of the lapping water. I attempt a greeting, but the eyes that turn my way are blank, bewildered, and when I ask, hesitantly, about Cara, show him a picture of her on my phone, he looks even more blank, even more bewildered. I don't know what planet he's on right now, but wherever it is he's still quite clearly up there. He doesn't look as if he'd recognise himself if I held up a mirror instead of my phone, so I turn away as he stumbles back towards his equally spaced-out companions still huddled by the outcrop of rock.

I check my watch. It's now gone eleven a.m. I look at my phone again. I've got reception, albeit only just, but there have been no calls, messages or texts, meaning Cara still hasn't been in touch. And Donna would definitely have phoned me to let me know if she'd been in touch with her.

I look at the dim figures a hundred or so metres away. Then again, I'd lay odds that none of them will have contacted their parents this morning either. Some might have promised to do so, but – and like Cara too, in all probability – have simply forgotten.

Which is when it happens. I get the strangest sense of déjà vu, as if I've been here, standing on this very same spot and recently too, but that's nonsense, of course. It's a combination of the buzz of last night's auction and too few hours' sleep, probably.

I look back out over the water. It seems tempting enough now in the warm morning light, but it must have looked irresistible last night. Those lapping waves, kids high on a cocktail of drink and soft drugs. So irresistible, and so dangerous.

I check my watch again, but then tell myself I'm just panicking unnecessarily. It's still early.

CHAPTER 7
PRESENT DAY

IT'S the strangest of feelings. Not as strange, admittedly, as looking up on a train to see your daughter who's been missing for the previous twenty years looking back at you, but it's still pretty well out there.

The young girl's sitting next to me, absorbed, or pretending to be absorbed, by her phone. And for a moment it's like time has stood still, as if I am actually back twenty years again, because it's exactly what Cara used to do in the few months before she disappeared. She'd get in the car, and we'd set off somewhere, to school, to the shops, to see one of her friends, and instantly the phone would come out and she'd start messaging. And that would be that. For the rest of the trip, long or short, I'd get nothing out of her save a series of non-committal grunts.

Unless – a new thought now strikes me – my new and unexpected companion is just taking some simple precautions. Maybe she's texting whoever she's travelling to meet to tell them she's in some stranger's car, giving them the registration number; she could easily have memorised it as she approached. And now I think about it, I hope she is, because that would be sensible. Streetwise. The sort of thing I'd hope Cara would have done in similar circumstances.

She looks up from her phone and stares out of the window. I clear my throat, nervous, and make a stab at conversation.

'We're no more than a couple of minutes away.'

She nods but doesn't reply.

'There's not much traffic. There never is on this stretch of road.'

Still, there's no response.

'We're a bit off the beaten track so even now, in the season, we don't get that many holidaymakers.'

I tail off, resigned to spending the rest of the short journey in silence, but then, suddenly, out it comes.

'What's your name?'

I pause, more than a little ambushed by that.

'Axel.'

She nods, and for a moment I think she's going to go back to her phone, but then she puts it down on her lap and looks out of the window again. We're now passing one of the local quays, and dim shapes can be seen outside the nearby Boat Club; coracle men about to head down to the river, carrying their black, round, single seater crafts on their heads, setting off for a night in pursuit of the local delicacy, a sea trout locally called sewin.

I clear my throat, cautious again. I wouldn't have asked before, but it's as if she's just given me permission.

'And what's yours?'

She doesn't seem to hear me, and for a moment I don't know whether to ask again. Maybe she's giving some silent signal that she doesn't want to answer. Then, equally suddenly, she answers.

'Penny.'

From out of nowhere as she replies, an image flashes in front of my eyes. The Frame volume, that strange inscription that I'd missed, that pencilled question.

Can I Trust You?

I pause, wondering for a moment. Did I miss that? Or was it added later? Perhaps by Penny when I was away from my seat, when I was locked in the toilet, not wanting to re-emerge? But why would she do that? And how on earth would I even begin to ask her? And, of course, I don't try, and thank God for that, because she'd probably wrench that passenger door open and plunge out onto the road if I did.

Maybe that's all down to Cara again. The echoes I'm sensing now of those last few trips we took together. That ever present feeling I had each time that there was some conversation we should be having, some exchange that should be taking place, or was that just hindsight? Am I looking back at a child who was soon to become lost to me, trying to reconstruct moments when I might have tried to find out why?

'What does it mean?'

I look at her, her second sudden question ambushing me almost as much as the first. And, for the first time since she got into the car, she looks directly at me.

'Your name. It's unusual.'

But I can't tell her. Not today, not this day of all days. Because if I do, I know that everything will come out in a great big rush, that I'll tell her all about the anniversary, about everything that happened all those years ago, before she was even born, in all probability. It might constitute some sort of cathartic outpouring on my part, but it would definitely add up to serious information overload for her.

But then she leans forward and looks in the passenger door mirror. At the same time, I catch a flash of light in my rear-view mirror from a car behind. And seemingly out of nowhere, in my mind's eye I'm now seeing the man from the train again, the one dressed in what looked to be a security guard's uniform staring at me in the carriage, the same one I saw running for his car as we pulled out of the car park a few minutes ago.

I glance at Penny as she straightens up in her seat, but when I look in the rear-view mirror again there are no lights to be seen, the car that was behind us having presumably turned off somewhere.

I clear my throat.

'Carmel's just coming up, which house do you want?'

But she cuts across as I put on the indicator and make to turn down a small lane ahead.

'You can drop me here.'

For a moment I wonder if it's those lights behind. Is that why she wants to get out? Have they spooked her in some way? But then I realise it's probably another sensible precaution. That lane leads down to a collection of cottages. She's trusted me enough to get into my car, which given everything that happened on the train might be considered a minor miracle, but she clearly doesn't want me to know exactly where she's heading for tonight.

I nod back. 'Of course.'

Her hand depresses the door handle as I pull up. For a moment panic flashes in her eyes as nothing happens.

'Sorry, sorry.'

I snake out a hand and hit a button on the dash, releasing the central locking. The door opens and she swings her rucksack out onto the roadside before exiting herself. Then she nods at me.

'Thanks again.'

I hesitate, then smile.

'Sorry again.'

She smiles back, then hesitates too. For a moment I get the feeling she wants to say something. But then she turns away and walks down the lane, passing under the first of a small line of occasional streetlights picking out the way.

Almost involuntarily I look behind as she keeps on walking, but again I see nothing. No lights and no sound either, certainly not the sound of an approaching car. Just the usual night-time collection of animals going about their business, providing a gentle reminder, perhaps, that I should now be going about mine.

———

It's like coming out of that deep dive again. As if I've been lost in some strange netherworld and have only just made it back to a place I recognise.

I look round. The house is a tip. No, correction, the house is even more of a tip than normal. The remains of a microwaved meal stain the sofa, red wine dregs splatter the floor. Groaning, I struggle to a sitting position, the door to my bedroom across the hallway ajar, a bed that I obviously didn't manage to navigate my way to visible through the door.

I had intended to spend what was left of the evening packaging up the Frame before checking out online a first edition Edgar Allan Poe I'd been offered, *The Gift: A Christmas and New Year's Present for 1845*, published by Carey and Hart of Philadelphia, which contained his masterpiece, *The Purloined Letter*. Losing myself in work, in other words, but instead I lost myself in discarded food and too much drink. Along the way I blundered into so many obstacles in the shape of chairs and tables that the house looked as if it had been the target of a particularly deranged burglar. One who imagined, the Frame volume aside, that I actually had something to steal.

It's not until five minutes later that I remember Penny, that ride home in my car and all that happened on the train.

Maybe it's age or maybe it's something else, but it's happening more and more these days. It started around the time of Cara's disappearance, and while they were mainly momentary lapses back then, now whole periods of my life seem to fade to black, a giant blank eclipsing even the most recent of encounters, until suddenly it all comes flooding back. Or at least it mostly comes back. Sometimes it's as if I know there's something else that should return as well, but it's no good, because no matter how much I worry away at it, it's gone, seemingly for ever. But now I do remember Penny and that ride home in my car, and I sit, slowly, back down again as I also remember that the last time I saw Cara was in a car on a reverse trip to the very station I drove away from yesterday evening.

I slump back on the sofa amongst the discarded food and the remains of the wine, and now I'm wishing, more than anything, that I hadn't done what I did last night. That I hadn't retraced my steps from my car to the station entrance and made that offer of a lift to the young girl standing there. Because all it's done is bring everything back, perhaps even more forcefully than it would have been brought back anyway on the anniversary of my daughter's disappearance. In fact, now, in the cold light of the approaching dawn, it almost feels like some sort of betrayal to have had another young girl in the car beside me. And for a moment, I feel a surge of irrational anger, as if it was her fault, which is unforgivable, I know.

And then they come. The tears that were threatening all yesterday break. And I forget all about young girls on trains and eyes that suddenly seemed to resemble a pair of eyes that I'll think about and search for every day till the day I die.

I just sit on that old and stained sofa and give way.

CHAPTER 8
TWENTY YEARS AGO

I KEEP TELLING myself that it's still early, that this is just an over-reaction, but I nevertheless decide to call over to Jools's house on my way back to the bookshop. Just in case.

She lives in Red Roses, the village across the estuary from my home. As the crow flies it's about half a mile away. When the sporadic ferry service is operating it's a five-to-ten-minute ride on the water. As I'm not a crow – and as the next ferry isn't due to crank into service for another hour at least – I've now got a near twenty-mile detour down winding lanes to the nearby county town and back out again.

Along the way, I scan every car coming towards me, check for any stray walkers on the side of the road or in the surrounding fields, even pull in as a bus lumbers past in the opposite direction and scan the few passengers inside. It's still more than possible that Cara and Jools have both just turned their phones off, and that Cara is struggling her way home by some means or other. But as I pull up outside Jools's small, terraced family home a few doors away from the village's one café, and a short distance from the embarkation point for the ferry, I still haven't seen her.

A cacophony of small yelps begins on the other side of the door the moment I ring the bell. A moment or so later a woman's voice is heard, shushing the dog before shepherding it into a nearby room and slamming the door. This muffles the yelps but doesn't do much to lessen the volume. A second or so later the door opens and a woman of around my age who I vaguely recognise, Jools's mum I assume, looks out at me.

'Yes?'

I struggle an apologetic smile.

'I'm sorry to bother you. I just wondered if Cara was here?'

The woman just stares at me.

'Cara Petersen?' I supply the prompt. 'She's a friend of Jools.'

From behind her, the aroma of bacon wafts along the dark hall. Behind a nearby door the dog's yelps are becoming ever more manic.

'They were at a party last night. I got a text from Cara to say she was staying here. She said she'd call, but I haven't heard from her.'

The woman regards me for a moment longer, then opens the door fully and turns back down the hall, calling out as she does so.

'Jools.'

I step inside and follow her down the small hall. Inside a kitchen at the rear of the hall, a girl of around Cara's age looks up at me from the table, a doorstep bacon sandwich in front of her. I recognise her immediately; she's been to the house many times.

Her mum nods at her. 'Did Cara stay last night?'

I step in again.

'She texted me, said she was coming back here. After the party?'

Jools shrugs as she picks up her sandwich.

'I didn't go to the party.'

I stare at her, helpless, as she takes a bite.

'We went to the pub. Cara went on. I didn't see her after that.'

I keep staring as her mum stays silent at my side, something feeling wrong here, but I can't work out what. From down the hall the dog's yelps are increasing in volume and fury as the world continues to ignore it.

'Why would she say she was staying here if she wasn't?'

Jools's mum breaks in as she moves away.

'Maybe because she didn't want you to know where she was really staying.'

She delivers a smart rap on the door, which silences the dog.

I feel my cheeks begin to mottle.

'If she was going back with some boy, she'd have said. There's no reason not to – she's eighteen, for God's sake.'

Neither speak for a moment. The dog starts barking again. Then Jools looks up from her sandwich once more.

'Ask Mark, maybe he knows.'

'I already have. He didn't even know there was a party last night.'

Jools considers me for a moment.

'Weird.'

Then she bends back to her breakfast again.

A few moments later I'm back outside on the street, the smell of cooked bacon clinging to me as I stand there, irresolute. Then my mobile rings. Snatching it out of my pocket, I see Patrick's name on the display.

'I sent you the Hemingway contract, Axel.'

His voice wafts down the crackly line from a few thousand miles away, his tone gentle, slightly chiding.

'The auction house will want me to OK it before I leave for the airport.'

Swiftly, I tell him where I am and why. Unaccountably, I find myself apologising as I do so.

'I know it's only just gone twelve, and I know that she's not a kid anymore.'

I stop, stare out past the small houses in front of me, down towards another Boat Club, where the ferry is now being prepared for the first of the afternoon's runs across the water.

'But she said she'd text, and she didn't. She said she'd call me but she hasn't done that either, it's just...'

I struggle, unconsciously aping Jools's one word verdict from a few moments ago.

'Weird.'

CHAPTER 9
PRESENT DAY

WALKING out of the cottage a short time later, the first thing I see is the train again, across the estuary. My cottage borders a small green that leads down to the water. The train line is on the opposite beach, actually running on the sands for part of its journey along that stretch of the coast.

When Donna and I first moved here, a local estate agent espoused the convenience of locating to that side of the estuary, preferably the actual village where the train stops. Within minutes of our drive across there, we'd comprehensively ignored his advice and the selection of local properties on his books and put an offer in for the cliffside house that became our home.

Donna still lives there. After Cara – everything in our lives now seems to be before or after Cara – I found a smaller property down by the water's edge. As moves go, it was hardly of Marco Polo proportions, but it still felt as if I was going from one world to another.

I pause, as I always do for some reason, to watch the train disappear round the headland. Out on the beach cockle-gatherers are already at work, along with a few dog walkers exercising their excited pets, including Aidan, my closest neighbour, stretching the legs of what looks to be the latest of a long line of pit bulls.

Neither Aidan nor anyone else takes any notice of me as I stand there looking across the straits. It was one of the attractions of the place originally. While the villagers were – and largely remain – friendly enough, everyone always seems to keep themselves at a cautious distance from each other. Over the last few years, I've come to see that as not only an attraction, but a blessing.

I check my watch and turn on my phone, which I turned off yesterday evening, and decide to take my car down to the large town further along the coast that's home to my bookshop. After yesterday, I really don't want another close encounter with the kindly, indulgent guard who checked my ticket and who looked anything but kind and indulgent those few moments later. Not to mention the equally wary trolley lady, whose eyes I can still feel burning into my back as I escorted Penny across the dimly lit car park to my waiting car.

I'm also running late, but as there's not usually any sort of queue pressing impatiently against the door, that's not too much of a problem. And Mark will probably amble along sometime in the next half hour or so anyway.

Opening my car door, which I forgot to lock, the first thing I see is my bag on the rear seat. I obviously didn't take it in last night. Opening it up, I expel a silent sigh of relief as I see the Frame still inside. This isn't exactly a high crime area, but a bag on clear view in an unlocked car might still have provoked curiosity, if not any actual ill-intent. Then my mobile rings. As I look at the display, I see that I've had two missed calls already.

'Axel?'

Patrick's concerned voice wafts down the line.

'Have you had a problem? I've been leaving you messages.'

'Not with the phone, just the owner. I turned it off.'

Sympathy mixes in with the concern, and for a moment I'm back there again, to the morning after Cara's disappearance, the same voice wafting down the line, both of us totally unaware of all that was about to unfold.

'That kind of night?'

I don't answer and he doesn't elaborate. There's no need on either count. Anniversaries may not be the near-unendurable occasions for him that they are for us, but he's still journeyed with us through every one of them. He was always going to touch base on this one.

'There's not much to report. A couple of comments have been posted, but nothing to get too alarmed about.'

He does this every year as well – monitors my social media feed, both personal and the one I set up for my business. There was the occasional hate campaign in the past, which he usually managed to head off by threatening legal action. It was a pretty empty threat in truth, given that the posts were anonymous, but it seemed to work.

Then he pauses. 'But someone has posted a picture.'

I still.

'Of Cara?'

'Of you. I can't quite understand. It's from last night, you on a train?'

Briefly, I close my eyes. So, someone did take a photo of the scene I inadvertently engineered. And the fact it has now been posted online means it was taken by someone who either knew me or of me. More grist to the mill, if any more is needed, for the local and not-so-local ill-disposed, and there still seem to be plenty of them around.

Swiftly, I give Patrick the edited lowlights of all that happened on the final leg of the train journey home. I don't mention the lift I offered to Penny a few minutes later. It didn't seem relevant; it was the photo he was interested in.

'You didn't see who took it?'

'To be honest, eye contact was something I was trying to avoid.'

'It's just…'

'What?'

Patrick hesitates, clearly unsure if he should say any more.

'It's another picture of you, Axel.'

We both fall silent for a moment. In the first few years after Cara disappeared, and thanks to the rise of social media, I was plagued by one particularly persistent persecutor. The odd thing was that where other online trolls posted pictures of Cara that they'd found in various places – from school, from social media posts and the like – this troll only posted pictures of me. And obviously he or she had been following me too, because in some of them I could be seen walking into and out of the bookshop, in and out of the old family home, even taking solo walks on the beach. Patrick's legal shots across the bows didn't seem to have any effect, and the pictures, sometimes with offensive captions, kept being posted. We were thinking of taking them to the police and seeing what they could do about them, but then suddenly they stopped. We both thought whoever was responsible had just moved on to some juicier story elsewhere.

'You think all that might be starting up again?'

A soft, almost resigned sigh reaches me from the other end of the line.

'Maybe I'm just being paranoid.' Patrick struggles. 'But twenty years. It's strange – it shouldn't make any difference; it's just a number, like nineteen or twenty-one, but maybe this has kicked it all off again.'

I don't reply. And a few minutes later, and with Patrick promising to keep monitoring the social media feeds and to update Donna when she emerges from her usual self-imposed exile, I climb into my car.

But then I stop again as I see the Frame, which has fallen open on the page with the pencilled annotation, the inscription I seem to have missed until last night as I was preparing to leave the train.

Can I Trust You?

CHAPTER 10
TWENTY YEARS AGO

IT'S early afternoon when I get back to the bookshop. Mark, currently with another customer, looks up enquiringly as I walk in, and I give a slight shake of the head. Still no contact from Cara.

I bring up the Hemingway paperwork on my laptop and try and lose myself in work, but the words on the contract just swim before my eyes. Half of me still knows I'm probably panicking unnecessarily. So far as the other half's concerned, it feels like a giant vortex is taking up residence inside me with one over-whelming question at its core. What if I'm not?

'Why didn't you know about it?'

Mark appears at my side, the customer exiting, having put the volume he was looking at back on the shelf. He's probably about to check it out on Amazon. It's a trend that's been gathering pace lately.

'The party?' Mark hesitates. 'We haven't talked much lately. Not since—'

He doesn't elaborate. He doesn't need to. But all that's in the past; it's the present, the here and now, that's much more on my mind. And now Jools's mum and her parting shot are sounding again in my ears.

I hesitate, but then plunge in.

'Has Cara been seeing anyone lately?'

Mark stills, all this quite clearly still raw; then he hesitates a moment before bringing out his phone.

'There's one boy, Cai. She's been hanging out with him the last couple of weeks, from what I've been hearing. I don't know how serious it is – I don't even know if she's been really seeing him, not like that anyway.'

Mark struggles again, and I feel a pang of sympathy as he scrolls through some images on his screen. The torch my hapless assistant still quite clearly carries for Cara could illuminate the darkest of depths.

Then he shows me a picture, one I recognise instantly. It's a photo the school sent round last year, an end of term barbecue in the grounds that virtually her whole year attended. Mark was there, a smiling Cara at his side, and I see Jools there too. Mark taps the screen, indicating another boy immediately behind them all.

'That's Cai.'

And I stop as I stare at it. Because it's the boy from the beach, the teenage boy I saw a few hours ago struggling to his feet on the sand as he became aware of the lapping water, the one who just stared back at me, blank, as I asked about Cara.

The boy who'd been sleeping, till just a moment before, at the very edge of the sea.

CHAPTER 11
PRESENT DAY

THE JOURNEY down to the bookshop retraces the route I took last night. And as I drive, my mind drifts.

That inscription could be some sort of sick joke. My story's well known in the antiquarian book business. Someone could have scrawled those words as a malicious barb, one of the sellers working in the auction house from where I sourced the collection, perhaps. Or maybe I'm just seeing malevolence where none exists. I'm certainly now discounting Penny as a possible perpetrator and am feeling embarrassed for having even entertained the thought. She'd already suffered enough, having a middle-aged man reach out and paw her on a train, without being labelled a defacer of first editions too.

But maybe the truth here lies with the actual author, who had a chaotic upbringing in a dysfunctional and violent household. Janet Frame suffered the deaths by drowning of two of her adolescent sisters and attempted suicide herself before she was twenty. Spells in psychiatric hospitals followed, as did an intense relationship with her therapist, a sexologist whose specialism of gender reassignment remains controversial to this day. It meant that all through her turbulent life, Frame had trust issues. Time and again, sure foundations ebbed away as she journeyed to find a place in the world. So maybe that inscription was an annotation after all, a previous reader's response to the passage they were reading. A stray record of a connection that the reader felt impelled to preserve.

In the first few weeks and months after Cara's disappearance, there were plenty of trust issues for myself and Donna to contend with. It wasn't just the disappearance of our daughter that erased from our lives all their previous certainties, although that would have been more than enough by itself. It was everything it brought in its wake. From being the most private of couples in two relatively unremarkable professions, an antiquarian and secondhand bookseller, and a university lecturer, we suddenly found ourselves under the sort of scrutiny usually reserved for TV stars and footballers. Journalists and photographers dogged our every movement. Friends who worked in the media would tell us later that they never knew which case might light a particular fire. But we soon found out for ourselves, as one stray photo of the smiling Cara provoked what could only be called a feeding frenzy.

Maybe it was those eyes. That light that always seemed to illuminate them from within. Perhaps, if she hadn't been so photogenic, we'd have ducked under the radar, but Cara was, and we didn't. For a brief period, it was as if every news outlet wanted the answer to the same question that we wanted. Where was she? Where's Cara? And as the days went by and there were no new developments to report, the press turned its attention from the child to the parents instead.

Our joint pasts were excavated more comprehensively than an archaeological dig, old colleagues and customers were contacted, and their opinions sought on what had fast become the burning matter of the moment and the related, equally burning question. Was it possible this was nothing to do with any person or persons of sinister intent who might have intercepted and abducted Cara? Could her disappearance owe more to the home from which she'd seemingly walked away? Was all this, in other words, down to us, or at least one of us?

Cara's old school friends were hunted down and every minor and not so minor daughter/parent clash we'd had was reported in its every lurid detail. And then there were the photographers, and not the anonymous stalkers who later went on to post social media pics, but the official ones sent along by the so-called gentlemen of the press.

I bore the brunt of their attentions back then, Donna having already retreated from most human contact by that point. Little did we know it at the time, but she was already well into a breakdown that, just a short time later, would lead to the breakdown of our marriage in turn. Some of the photos they snapped were of me coming out of various local bars, drink fast becoming my equivalent of Donna's withdrawal, and on a couple of occasions I lost control, roared and railed, all of which made for even more lurid headlines the following day with even more damning photos accompanying them, of course.

It also didn't help that an unnamed neighbour told a reporter that he or she had seen me striding along one of the local roads on the night Cara disappeared. Perhaps it was Aidan, perhaps someone else, I still don't know. I tried explaining that I'd just concluded a large auction purchase, that I was wired, couldn't settle, that I couldn't even really remember being out there, my head was so much all over the place that night, but I soon learnt my lesson. Testimonies like that just raised a hundred more questions and made things a thousand times worse in turn.

Now, turning onto the steep lane that leads down to the town, I still as another memory returns. A caption swims before my eyes, one I saw under a picture some photographer snapped as I came out from yet another bar back then on yet another extended drinking session. It comprised just four simple words.

Can You Trust Him?

I'd forgotten about it until now. And it's a coincidence, it must be, but suddenly the similarity with the inscription in the Frame collection is all I can see. And I'm so absorbed in that curious similarity and the unwelcome memories that are now flooding back, that as I drive down the lane approaching the small settlement of Carmel, I almost miss the scenes of crime tape and the flashing blue lights that suddenly appear before me.

Almost, but not quite.

CHAPTER 12
TWENTY YEARS AGO

AN HOUR OR SO AGO, I knocked, tentatively, on the door of a small, terraced house in the estuary village across the water from my home. This time, that vortex deepening all the while, there's nothing tentative about the way I hit the door of a run-down links house on one of the county town's sprawling council estates.

A child's bike lies on the weed-encrusted small patch of lawn to my side. Peeling paintwork reveals serious decay in the front fascia and soffits. A small hole in the front door bears testimony to some heavy-duty attention being visited on it at some point in the past. It's about to endure more of the same as I raise my fist again, but then it suddenly swings open and a thin, short male of around my age, dressed only in a white vest and tracksuit bottoms, peers out at me.

'What?'

'I need to see Cai. It's about my daughter.'

If the track-suited male – who I assume is Cai's father – is surprised by my sudden appearance on his doorstep or by my hissed and urgent request, he betrays no sign. Like Jools's mum, he just turns and yells down a dark hallway, off which a small staircase ascends into the gloom.

'Cai.'

A door at the far end of the hallway opens, but it isn't the boy from the beach who now hoves into view. A small girl, around six years old, appears instead, sucking on a lolly in one hand, clutching a soft toy in the other.

From the first floor, another male voice sounds.

'What?'

His father calls back.

'Down here. Now.'

Then he turns and bangs into a front room, slamming the door behind him, his part – and presumably any interest – in the day's proceedings over. Down the hall the small girl continues to suck on her lolly and stare at me. A few moments later, a heavy tread on the stairs reveals the boy I saw a couple of hours ago. He hadn't looked his best then, and with his sleep disturbed for the second time in just over as many hours, he looks even worse.

'Cara's still not been in touch. When was the last time you saw her?'

For a moment he just blinks at me, struggling to focus. Down the hallway his small sister maintains her unblinking stare.

'Did she leave the party? Did you see where she went? Did she say anything?'

Then, finally, and for the first time in the two encounters, he speaks.

'She wasn't there.'

Now it's my turn to stare at him.

'She was supposed to be. But she never showed.'

Suddenly, my phone pulses again in my pocket and I snatch it up. Donna's name comes up on the display, and this time it's her turn to plunge straight in.

'Is there still nothing from Cara?'

'I'm with one of her friends now.'

I look at the now-yawning Cai, who's slumped down on the stairs.

'He's saying he didn't see her, that she didn't show up at the party. But Jools said she left the pub to go to it.'

I glance down the hall at the small girl, still just staring at me. Then I check my watch. It's now gone two p.m. And suddenly I don't care if I'm panicking unnecessarily.

I turn back to my phone. 'I think we should call the police.'

I look up again at the small girl, seeing another small girl now, my own daughter in the hallway of our own home at that age.

'I think we should call them now.'

CHAPTER 13
PRESENT DAY

I SHOULD JUST DRIVE PAST, and I don't know why I don't. A car behind me, a car I didn't even realise was there, beeps, irritated, as I slow in front of it. Maybe in similar circumstances I'd have done the same. Everyone hates rubberneckers.

I pull over, as much to let the car pass as anything else, but by now a uniformed police officer is looking over at me, probably alerted by that irritated beep of the horn. But I'm not looking at him. I'm still looking at the scenes of crime tape, barring access to the small lane. The lane where I stopped last night and dropped off Penny.

A pricking begins at the back of my neck as I feel my temperature begin to rise. At the same time a leaden feeling starts to spread, deep in the pit of my stomach, as I see the officer duck under the tape and begin to make his way over. For a moment I contemplate just putting the car back into gear and driving on, but it's already too late. His hand is now raised, a clear signal I should stay where I am. He pauses as another car passes, that driver slowing too as he also sees the blue lights and the tape, but the officer doesn't even look at him, just keeps looking at me. Plenty of cars must have done the same this morning, slowing to take a look. But only one's actually stopped.

I depress the window as he comes up to the car and try to sound normal, natural, praying that he can't hear my heart, which feels as if it's pounding like a jackhammer right now.

'Has something happened?'

He doesn't answer directly for a moment, just looks at my car. Then he looks back at me.

'Do you live around here, sir?'

I nod back along the road.

'A few miles away.'

'So, this would be a regular route for you?'

The officer takes out his phone, stepping back for a moment to photograph my registration plate. I don't know why, and I don't ask.

'Sorry, maybe I shouldn't have stopped. It's just...'

I tail off as he checks his mobile, presumably sending the photo he's just taken, then he turns back to me as I gesture at the crime tape again.

'I just wondered what this was all about?'

'A young girl was attacked here last night.'

I stare at him as he nods across the road.

'Fifty metres or so down that lane.'

I stare behind him now too.

'There're no witnesses to the attack itself, but a neighbour heard some screaming. When he came out of his house, he saw a car driving away at speed, a girl looking very panicked inside. She hasn't been seen since.'

Now my heart's beginning to feel as if it might burst out of my chest, and the officer looks at me, growing more curious as he registers my clear agitation. So, why don't I just tell him? About last night? About the train, about Penny? About the lift I gave her to this very spot? Why don't I just come straight out with it, which will also then explain why I've stopped like this and why I've asked what's happened?

But I know. Of course I know. Because if it is Penny, then I must have been the last person to see her, apart from her attacker, of course. I drove her to this very spot; there was just myself and her in the car, with no other witnesses. Her DNA must still be all over the seat beside me. And what's the first thing I've done the next morning? Returned to the scene of the crime.

Twenty years to the day after my daughter disappeared, a second young girl seems to have vanished too.

All this flashes through my head in what can't be more than a second, but it feels so much longer as all the while the officer keeps looking at me.

'You haven't answered my question, sir.'

I look at him.

'Is this a route you take regularly?'

Feeling as if I'm not inhabiting my own body any longer, as if someone else is now in charge, I nod back, my voice also seeming to come from a long way away.

'I've a business, a bookshop, about twenty miles away.'

For a moment he keeps looking at me, but then two white-suited figures appear from down the lane, returning to a large white Transit van I can now see parked just behind the scenes of crime tape. The officer hesitates for a moment, but then he nods at me.

'On your way then.'

He turns, ducks under the tape and hurries back towards the waiting white-suited figures. Again, almost without realising I'm doing it, I start the engine and put the car into gear.

But even as I'm driving away, reason's finally beginning to take over, all my previous mad panic starting to subside. What the hell am I doing? I've nothing to hide so why am I acting as if I have?

I turn the corner, out of sight of the lane, but now I'm looking for a place to pull in so I can turn round, go back to that police officer and tell him what I should have told him straightaway, But in front of me a man suddenly appears, another man in uniform, also holding up his hand, also signalling me to stop.

I stare at him as I brake. Has that photo of my registration number been picked up already? Have they realised who this car's registered to? Has someone already made an all too obvious connection? I stop the car, my hands shaking again, although in one sense it's a relief because now I don't have to do anything. I don't have to turn back and try and explain that I panicked just then, that it was stupid because I don't have anything to panic about, but I did.

The second officer opens the passenger door and gets in, which is when I realise he's not a police officer at all. He's the man from the train, the young man dressed as some sort of security guard, the man I saw haring for that car last night as I drove away from the station car park with Penny.

And he's got a knife in his hand.

Which he's now pressing into my side.

CHAPTER 14
TWENTY YEARS AGO

THE TOWN POLICE station is housed in a low red brick building, built on a small hill overlooking the river. There have been rumours about its demolition and replacement for years. The paint on the walls is pockmarked and chipped, and cracked tiles cover the concrete floors. I've no idea why I'm noticing all this. Displacement activity, perhaps. For hours I've been worrying about my missing daughter. Now I'm here to translate that impotent worry into, hopefully, constructive action, all I seem to be thinking about is interior decoration.

'Mr Petersen?'

Two officers approach from a corridor leading off from the reception area, one of them a smartly dressed older man in his forties, a Detective Sergeant who introduces himself as John Parry. With him is a much younger man, a Detective Constable who introduces himself as Daniel Adams, and he's anything but smart. He looks as if someone's thrown a whole array of mismatched clothes at him this morning, and he's walked away in the ones that have somehow stuck. Again, why I'm focusing on an officer's dress sense I have no idea. More displacement activity, perhaps.

They lead me into a small office behind the reception desk, where a large jug of water and three glasses are squatting on a table. Donna isn't with me; she's waiting at home in case Cara returns in the meantime. I'm still sensing a slight reserve about all this as far as she's concerned, perhaps because she thinks I really am panicking without cause. I hope she's right.

DS Parry starts straight away; no small talk, no preamble.

'You've filed a report that your daughter failed to come home this morning, Mr Petersen?'

I nod. 'She was out at a party down on the beach last night. It was an end of term thing; she's finishing this year in school. She texted me to say she was staying with a friend and that she'd let me know when she got there.'

DC Adams breaks in.

'How did she say she'd let you know? Did she say she'd text or call?'

'She said she'd text when she got to Jools's house – her friend's house – and that she'd call me this morning. She hasn't done either'

DS Parry glances to his side at a clock on the wall. Five p.m. I can already see the hesitation in his eyes. It still really isn't that late.

'I called at Jools's house earlier on. She wasn't there and her friend didn't know where she was. Jools didn't go to the party; she stayed in one of the local pubs.'

I hesitate again. 'Cara hadn't arranged to stay with her.'

Already, I can hear Jools's mum from earlier, speculating that maybe Cara had gone home with someone else instead. I can almost see the same thought going through both of the officers' minds now too.

'And how old is Cara?'

'Eighteen.'

The quick glance they exchange with each other also makes their thinking only too clear. Maybe I'd have cause to be worried about a thirteen or a fourteen-year-old. But eighteen? An adult?

'She's always told us where she was going, when she'd be back.'

I plough on as they stay silent.

'Something like this just isn't like her, it's not like her at all, and she's still not answering her phone.'

DC Adams clears his throat.

'Have there been any issues lately?'

I hesitate. 'Issues?'

I shift in my seat, uncomfortable. I can't help myself and I see him registering it.

'Disagreements? Clashes at home? Family difficulties? He smiles ruefully. 'I've got a daughter myself. She's six, the apple of my eye. I adore her, she adores me, but older mums and dads tell me to enjoy it while I can, because once a girl reaches her teens...'

He doesn't finish. He doesn't need to.

I hesitate. 'There has been a bit of trouble.'

'Trouble?'

DS Parry's eyes are now boring into mine.

'A boy – there's been some upset.'

'Cara's been upset about a boy?'

'But it's not like they were proper boyfriend and girlfriend or anything like that, and anyway he's not here anymore.' I stop. 'Look, I really don't think any of this is relevant.'

All I'm doing is muddying the waters here and I know it. As well as maybe giving these two clearly reluctant officers even more reason not to act. I take a deep breath.

'But no. Apart from that, everything's been fine. And she was fine last night too. I drove her to the station myself to catch the train; she was looking forward to the party. She was just a normal, happy, excited kid.'

The interview concludes a few moments later. DC Adams takes some more notes. Neither officer says what they'll do next, and I don't ask. Suddenly, I just want to get out of here.

CHAPTER 15
PRESENT DAY

I'LL NEVER FORGET the first time I took Cara into the bookshop. I'd been out all morning, looking at collections for possible purchase. The first was an esoteric selection of sixteenth century theology texts. I knew nothing about sixteenth century theology, but even then, in the early years of my new business, I knew that somewhere in the world someone would, and that same someone would want to know more. It was, and remains, one of the mantras of my line of work. The more specialist the field, the more committed the readership.

The second collection was composed almost exclusively of Book Club reprints, and I quickly decided I wouldn't take any of them. Book Club reprints would soon prove to be virtually unsellable, as they remain today.

The third collection promised as little, initially at least, as the second. The books were housed in a damp flat above an iron-monger and the owner had recently died. The flat and the books stank of mildew and cats. I was about to leave to go home, when I saw the Ralph Austen.

Austen, born 1612, died 1676, was a combination of a self-taught gardener and a religious radical, a visionary whose approach to horticulture was described by contemporaries at the time as innovative, experimental, and sceptical of the authority of theorists. The book in question in that damp and mildewed flat was a fine example of his *Observations upon some part of Sr Francis Bacon's Naturall History as it concernes, Fruit-trees, Fruits, and Flowers*. Not perhaps the snappiest of titles. The volume originated from the Lawes Agricultural Library and was printed by Hen: Hall for Thomas Robinson in 1658. And, on opening it up, I could see the names of nine generations of the same family inscribed on the inside front page, ending with the recently deceased owner, who'd died in a flat that didn't even overlook a single patch of grass.

I looked at that record of a prized book's journey through a family's history, imagining the different hands that had held it, the succession of eyes that must have studied its text, and I bought it on the spot. Then, and still in that same strange mood of nostalgic wonder, I collected Cara from home for her first visit.

I'd been unsure how she'd take to it to begin with. The front of the store comprised then – as now – just a large room with a desk, but a smaller door behind led into a maze of tunnels and passageways, off which were several smaller rooms, all crammed floor to ceiling with books. And at the far end of the furthest passageway down a small incline of stone steps was the rare books room, a specially constructed enclave with no natural light, which was maintained at an even temperature all year round.

It could have seemed forbidding to a small child. But Cara wandered the winding labyrinths in wonder, almost breathing in the old books before her, trailing her hand across what must have looked like acres of exposed spines. Later, when she was able to at least part-understand, I'd try to explain that in their own way each one of the books she was touching possessed what might be called a soul. And not just one soul, that of the person who wrote it, but the souls of all those who'd read it, who'd journeyed amongst its pages and who'd passed it on for more souls to journey with too.

The strange thing was that she already seemed to know all

this. Even at that age, and she couldn't have been more than five or six, she seemed to intuit on some elemental level exactly why I'd taken her there that day, appearing to understand, too, why I'd sold everything I'd owned to begin this business. And why, although I'd never said this to her, I'd always harboured a hope that, one day, she might take it over, before maybe passing it on to her children in turn. And every day since, whenever I walked in through the large front door into that open plan reception room, for a moment I'd live that day again, would see the shop as a small child saw it then.

But not today.

Not with a knife pressing into the small of my back.

———

Twenty minutes ago, I just stared, stupidly, at my unexpected – and very much unwelcome – companion.

'Drive.'

I didn't respond for a moment, just gasping out a panicked question instead.

'What do you want?'

Now he was closer, a lot closer, I could see he looked to be in his early twenties. And he was powerfully built, tendons pulsing in his neck.

'Drive to the shop.'

I kept staring at him. Was he a customer, someone who'd been in before, someone I should know?

'Just drive!'

He positively yelled that last instruction, looking behind him as he did so – checking for the police, perhaps; I don't know. All I did know was that the knife was still pressing into me and the man holding it was getting more and more agitated. Suddenly doing what he said seemed a lot less dangerous than not doing it.

The journey passed in a blur. I remember scanning every passing car, praying someone would look over at us, would realise from the expression in my staring eyes that I was in trouble and needed help. But no one so much as glanced at me. On the few occasions when I slowed at road junctions or stopped at traffic lights, his grip on the knife tightened as he muttered a low warning to me not to do something stupid. And so we pressed on, and if I thought my heart was pounding when that police officer approached, that was nothing compared to the piledriver-like reverberations sounding inside right now.

All the time, the questions that had tormented me as I drove away from the crime scene and the police officer sounded ever more insistently. Why hadn't I just explained everything when I'd had the chance? Yes, I'd probably have been taken into the nearest police station, and yes, I'd have been questioned. For not the first time in my life I'd have endured an awkward, if not excruciating, few hours in a police interview room. But I hadn't done anything. I had nothing to do with what might have happened to Penny. And once the police realised that, I'd have been sent on my way so they could get on with the infinitely more important task of trying to find her. I wouldn't have driven away from the crime scene and those flashing blue lights and I wouldn't now be sitting in this car with an obvious madman beside me holding a knife, with a thin, acrid smell wafting across from him. The stink of desperation mixed in with days-old sweat.

———

'Park round the back.'

Briefly, I wonder how he even knows there's a small parking area there. But I don't ask, because peering in the front window of my still-closed shop is another police officer. The veins in my wrist begin to pulse as I flick the indicator, praying the sudden sound will alert him somehow. But then I feel that knife pressing ever harder into my side. A moment later we turn the corner as the officer keeps looking in through the front window of the shop.

As we pull up in the car park, I stop the engine and turn to the man, but he just gestures at my bag.

'Give me your phone.'

I hesitate a moment. Then I look back at the knife again, and hand it over. Less than thirty seconds later and courtesy of the rear door we're inside. Mark still hasn't arrived and probably won't for another half hour or so. Whether my young abductor realises that or has just been lucky, I don't know. He motions with his free hand the direction we should take, seeming to know to avoid the passageway that leads to the open plan reception room, where we'd be visible to the officer, thanks to its double-fronted windows.

We move along one of the tunnels that lead to the rare books room, the young man with the knife prodding me on all the while, passing a couple of items I picked up from a recent house clearance; an oak Victorian bureau and a Georgian fire screen. Sidelines like that always help when it comes to the shop's finances, but balancing the books is far from my mind right now.

'Look, if this is about Penny, I gave her a lift – you know that, you saw me, but then I dropped her off. That's all I did; I gave her a lift and dropped her off and then I went home.'

But he doesn't reply. We're going deeper and deeper into the tunnels, getting closer to the hermetically sealed rare books room all the time. Once inside, as I'm now only too uncomfortably aware, it would double as a hugely effective cell. But suddenly, he's not looking towards the rare books room, he's looking at something else, and now I see it too, hanging from one of the shelves. It's incongruous, a jarring note in among those walls of old books. A kaleidoscope-coloured scarf, dazzling among the muted browns and greens and greys.

Penny's scarf.

The one she was wearing last night.

The young man spins round, crashing me against a wall, pinning my arms behind my back with one hand, still holding the knife with the other. He keeps me there, and I gasp, winded for a moment, as he hisses at me.

'Where is she?'

I put one hand on the shelf behind to keep my balance and feel my fingers close around another item I picked up in yet another house clearance, one of a pair of Victorian crown green bowling balls I'd intended to put out on display at the front of the shop. The young man leans closer. I can almost touch the menace in his eyes. Then, suddenly, I grab the bowling ball and hurl it at him at the same time as I press down hard on the shelf behind, which instantly gives way, and books start cascading onto us. I'm already shielding my head, so most of them bounce off my neck and shoulders, but some of the ones on the top shelves score a direct hit on his head, which, along with the glancing blow to his shoulder from the bowling ball, gives me the opportunity I need. I've got just a few seconds at most, and I don't waste a single one of them as I hare for a door at the far end of the passage.

CHAPTER 16
TWENTY YEARS AGO

THE PUB'S just a short walk up a steep incline from the station. A footbridge across the tracks connects to another platform, which leads in turn to a path to the wide, sweeping beach a mile or so away. It's a route that's well known to most of the local kids. A few drinks in that nearby pub, an increasingly unsteady stumble across the footbridge, followed by an extended party as night falls on the sands.

I've already been down to the sands, of course. I've searched among the daytime casualties sleeping off the excesses of last night. But what about the pub? Did any of the staff see something, notice Cara when she left at some point in the evening, either alone or in company, pick up snatches of a conversation that might give me some clue as to where she went?

A one-car commuter train keeps pace with me for the last few metres of my journey as I pull up on the road outside the station, which is little more than a halt. It's not manned; there's no ticket office or waiting room, just a machine on both platforms that dispenses tickets, so there's no station staff to grill. Instinctively, I check the footbridge, almost as if I half-expect to see a bleary-eyed daughter treading across from the opposite platform towards me.

Locking my car, I plough up the steep incline, the pub now

visible at the top of the hill, checking my watch as I do so. It's gone six p.m. The staff from last night might not be on again, but at least I'll be able to find out when they'll be working their next shifts.

Only I won't. Because as I come up to the pub itself, the first thing I see is a large piece of plywood hammered across the front door. Similar pieces of plywood bar the windows. A large and peeling 'For Sale' sign is tacked onto the front wall. I stare at the place, rocked for a moment, then dive into a nearby cycle shop where the amused owner tells me the pub has been closed for over six months.

I head back outside, stare down towards the station. I'm sure this is where Cara said she was meeting her friends. I'm sure this is the pub where – only a few hours ago – her friend Jools told me she spent the evening. Only Cara quite clearly didn't meet anyone there, and Jools didn't spend any time here either.

CHAPTER 17
PRESENT DAY

I BURST out of the rear door a moment or so later, checking all the while for the sound of a pursuer behind me, but there's nothing. For a moment I contemplate running round to the front of the shop in the hope the officer I saw earlier is still there, but what if he isn't? And what if the front door opens and that young man appears just as I get there? I might have squirmed away from him once courtesy of a centuries-old bowling ball, a shelf full of books and the element of surprise, but something's telling me my luck isn't going to hold out a second time.

My car's in front of me, and even though he took my phone he didn't take my keys. I flip the key fob, wrench open the door and bolt inside, putting reinforced glass and steel between us if he does suddenly appear. But as I do I spot the Frame volume on the floor of the passenger footwell, and I pause, momentarily puzzled. That wasn't where I left it; I'd put it back in my bag. So, was he looking at it all the time I was driving? I'd hardly dared take my eyes off the road, but did he pick it out from my bag, and if so, why? And why is it open at the page where that person or persons still unknown scrawled that inscription?

Can I Trust You?

And suddenly, almost as I've been transported back in time, I see her again. I see Cara, not as the young woman she was when I last saw her on the day she vanished, but as the young child I'd first taken into the bookshop behind me, pausing momentarily as she stepped over the threshold as if somehow she already knew she was passing from one world to another, from a world that was known and familiar to a world bursting with possibilities and experiences, even if, at her young age, they were impossible to conceive or comprehend. Stray browsers had turned as she stared around, and some had smiled, perhaps recognising in her something they'd once experienced themselves, and were maybe still experiencing each time they stepped over that same threshold. Because who knows what they might find there, what volume might do what so many others had done before, returning them back to that known and familiar world changed somehow?

And it's like a switch has been thrown. Suddenly, all the mad panic of the past few moments, that desperate desire to get out of there, to get away, is replaced by something else. I'm flooded with a new and very different feeling. Flight was the absolute priority just a moment or so ago, but it isn't now.

Now, I have to find out who wrote that inscription in the book and why. I have to find out why that young man kidnapped me at knifepoint and forced me to drive down here. I need to find out what this is all about.

I yank the keys out of the ignition and open the car door. Still, I can hear nothing from inside the shop. Maybe he believes I'm already well away, and the chase isn't worth it. Striding forward, I hit the rear door with my outstretched hand and head back inside.

CHAPTER 18
TWENTY YEARS AGO

MY MOBILE RINGS as I get back into the car, and it's Donna again, but she isn't calling with any sighting of our daughter. In fact, when her voice first wafts down the line I can barely make out what she's saying.

'You sound like you're in a wind tunnel.'

'I'm down on the beach.'

I look up at the footbridge and the path leading away from it as Donna continues.

'There are none of her friends here, not now, but I called into a couple of the cottages on the cliffs.'

Dimly, I remember seeing the cottages as I made for Cai, struggling to rise to his feet at the water's edge, and I curse myself. They directly overlook the sea. Why didn't I think of calling there too?

'They all heard the party going on, but most of them just closed the blinds.'

Donna pauses.

'But one of them, she lives in the cottage at the far end just before the cliff path. She opened the door late last night to call in her cat. The moon was full apparently, and she saw a figure – a girl, she thinks – walking towards the water, but she didn't really think too much about it. Lots of kids go for midnight swims on party nights, it seems.'

I still, those earlier fears claiming me again.

'Did she see her go in?'

'The moon went behind a cloud. But…'

I can feel the hesitation in her voice.

'What?'

'It might be nothing.'

I prompt her again. 'Donna, what?'

She pauses a moment longer, the wind whipping around her more fiercely now, making it even more difficult to make out what she's saying. I lean closer to the phone, but suddenly her voice comes through loud and clear as the wind momentarily dips.

'Before the moon went behind the cloud, she thought she saw someone else, someone behind her.'

She pauses again.

'They seemed to be following her.'

CHAPTER 19
PRESENT DAY

HERE AND THERE MEMORIES RETURN, although sometimes they're more just random images.

I was pretty well out of it back then, a combination of bewilderment, frustration and grief. Bewilderment at the abyss into which we'd suddenly been plunged, frustration at the police for not doing the only thing we were asking them to do – the only thing the whole country indeed seemed to be asking them to do – which was to find one missing young girl.

But it was the grief at Cara's continuing absence that overwhelmed everything. In fact, it was worse than grief in a way, because we hadn't been given permission to grieve. We could observe none of the associated rituals, because no one knew if this was just the sad story of a teenage runaway or something else. And of course, as the weeks went by it was that something else that began to dominate.

More whispers began, more dark mutterings began to circulate. Just when you felt like you needed the support of the whole wide world, that world turned on you. Put your lives under a microscope. And like all lives examined in that way, found you very much wanting.

Indiscretions were unearthed and forgotten misdemeanors

resurrected and they really did have a field day in my case. George Orwell, no less a figure, worked in my trade for a period back in the 1930s, and the constant litany of insane questions from borderline insane customers soon made him realise that, in his own words, *'many of the people who came to us were of the kind who would be a nuisance anywhere but have special opportunities in a bookshop'*.

And I wrote about them. Thinly disguised pen portraits of the human flotsam that washed up sometimes for hours and sometimes for what seemed like days in that open plan reception room and who I'd then find wandering through the tunnels and haunting the rare books room. Sometimes I didn't even bother with any sort of thin disguise. The customer who asked if any of the books were edible deserved no less. Nor did the customer who wanted more books by Jane Eyre or, failing Ms Eyre, then Dracula. By the time those random scribblings in various trade journals had been reported in isolation in the red tops of the day, they took on a much more sinister hue. In truth, the portraits were affectionate for the main part, but they didn't come across that way. Soon, I was an embittered pariah looking out at the world through dangerously deranged eyes.

The colourful warning to prospective thieves I hung behind the desk in the reception room, culled from the monastery of San Pedro in Barcelona, didn't help – *For him that stealeth this book from its owner, let it change into a serpent in his hand, let him be struck with palsy, let him languish in pain, crying aloud for mercy and let there be no surcease to this agony till he sing in dissolution. And when at last he goeth to his final punishment, let the flames of Hell consume him forever.*

Maybe that was why, when I was opening the bookshop one morning a full two years after Cara went missing, a passing woman pushing a child in a buggy spat full in my face before moving on without saying a single word.

———

I move down the passage back towards the rare books room, but suddenly I hear a voice, distant but still clear.

'Mr Petersen?'

Then I freeze at a loud banging as someone hits the front door.

'Mr Petersen, it's the police.'

I look down at the Victorian crown green bowling ball, now lying on the floor, and just put to a use its maker had never intended. Then I look up at the spot where a few moments earlier I saw that kaleidoscope-coloured scarf, but that's gone now, taken by my abductor, I assume. I press on, ignoring the police officer calling out to me again from outside. Somehow, I just know that my best chance of finding out what's happening is courtesy of a strange young man who may or may not be some sort of security guard and who has just kidnapped me at knifepoint. Whether that's madness of a kind never exhibited by even the most extreme of any of my past customers, or something else – some instinct perhaps – I don't know. I just keep pressing on, pausing again as I see a couple of splatters of freshly spilt blood on the floor.

And suddenly, all my new resolve vanishes. Suddenly, I'm back to what I actually am, not some grimly determined avenger in hot pursuit of a quarry, but a middle-aged antiquarian bookseller at the mercy of forces and circumstances I simply don't understand. From behind, I hear the same voice again.

'Mr Petersen, if you're here we really need a word.'

And now I sink to my knees because it's all too much. Yesterday's anniversary, my reaching out like that on that train, Penny sitting in my car, just like Cara all those years before, and then disappearing, just like Cara again. I close my eyes, which is when I hear a single, soft footfall behind me.

I make to turn round, but I can't. Because a strong hand now snakes out, pinning my neck back against an equally strong arm, clasping my mouth tight shut in turn.

CHAPTER 20
TWENTY YEARS AGO

IT'S WHAT I WANTED, right from the start of all this. From the moment I woke up, checked my phone, realised that Cara hadn't texted or called as she'd promised, I'd been wanting people to start taking this seriously.

But at the same time, it's terrifying.

There are only a few officers – perhaps five at the most – but they're spread out in a line, checking the sands all the way up to the water's edge. Occasionally, one of them will pause and lean down, using a small shovel-type implement to excavate something, the other officers pausing too. Watching from the shore, Donna and I tense. But each time, the officer in question just straightens up, moves on, and the rest of the line moves on too.

That sighting from an independent witness of a lone figure, possibly female, walking towards the sea with someone seemingly following them, has changed things so far as the local police are concerned. After my phone call, DS Parry's inspector authorised a search of the sands before nightfall, and he and his younger sidekick, DC Adams, are part of that line of officers right now.

We're huddled together, watching along with a couple of dog walkers who've also paused to take a look. One of them asked us what was happening, but Donna fobbed him off. If you'd asked me to repeat exactly what she said, I couldn't. All that exists for me in the world right now is that line of steadily advancing officers out on the sands.

As well as, and this is even more chilling, the coastguard's boat we can see tacking up and down out in the bay.

For some reason, as I look at it, a stray image flashes in front of my eyes of a couple of fruit scones I picked up from a stall in the market next to the bookshop, earmarked as a treat for Cara when she came home from the party. As it does so the wind picks up again, whipping sand into my eyes, water trickling down my face a moment later, and for a moment I can't work out if it's a response to that biting sand or a sudden attack of tears.

But then my vision clears. And as it does, I see DS Parry break ranks and walk back along the sand towards us.

And as he gets closer, I can see he's holding something in his hand.

CHAPTER 21
PRESENT DAY

THE CAFÉ WINDOW, as always at this time of day, is misted over with steam, meaning you can't see anyone passing on the street, and they can't see you. It's one of the reasons I started coming here. Stepping inside isn't only like stepping back in time, with the café's trademark plastic tablecloths and laminated menus. It's like stepping into a cocoon.

Across the table, Rory faces me. Rory's the name of the young man who may or may not be a security guard, but who is most certainly my abductor. Why he did that, and what he – and all this – has to do with Penny, I still don't know. Hopefully, in the next few moments, I'll find out.

Back in that passageway in the bookshop, Rory continued to hold me by the neck as the policeman, still stationed outside the front door, called out my name again. How long it would be before he'd actually get inside, I didn't know, but not long, probably. I'd read somewhere that the police have special sets of keys for eventualities like these. But then the combination of a locked front door and no sign of life inside seemed to convince him that wherever I was right now, I wasn't there, because in another couple of moments we heard footsteps moving away. At which point Rory relaxed his grip.

Neither of us spoke for a moment longer. But as we looked at each other, and as crazy as this once again might sound – and it does sound completely crazy, I know, given that this was a young man who'd been brandishing a knife at me a short time before – something was telling me that whatever this was all about, we both wanted the same answers. And that same something was also telling me that the best way to start finding those answers lay with each other. Which is why, a few minutes later, we're sitting at a table in my regular café across the street from the bookshop, having just been handed a copy of one of those laminated menus by the perennially bored-looking waitress, who then returned to the counter to watch the ever-present TV.

I asked Rory his name as we sat down. I volunteered mine at the same time, but he seemed to know that already. Which is one question down, the second of many following hard on its heels.

'Why were you following Penny?'

Rory looks at me.

'You were on the train, I saw you, and you were in the car park. I saw you there too.'

For a moment I don't think he's going to say anything. But then he responds with a question of his own.

'Why didn't you answer?'

I stare at him.

'Back in the shop. When that cop called out like that?'

Suddenly, a dark suspicion begins to form, perhaps prompted by memories of other times when questions were answered with more questions. It became something of the story of my life at one point.

'Please tell me you're not a journalist?'

Rory looks at me, a brief flare of something igniting behind his eyes, which could be surprise, but could be something else. Have I just totally misread all this? And for not the first time in my life, too.

'Is that why you were on that train? Is this some sort of anniversary rehash, a chance to rake everything back up again?'

Behind, I'm dimly aware of the waitress beginning to make her way over to us, then stopping. Maybe she can sense from my body language that I really don't want to be disturbed right now. Rory just stares at me, his eyes wary, assessing, but wary of what, and assessing whom? What's he hoping, or fearing, to see?

But then, suddenly, he stills. At the same time, I become aware of an uncharacteristic hush in the café behind. The place is usually a cacophony of noise: yells from the kitchen as orders are being prepared, yells back from one of the two waitresses. Add to that the constant hubbub from customers, both seated and queuing for takeaways at the counter, and this has never been a place blessed with the sound of silence. But it is now.

'Oh fuck.'

I turn as Rory looks behind me. And in a day and a night marked by more strange and bewildering episodes than I want to experience again in a lifetime, I'm suddenly faced with yet another.

Because now I'm looking straight back at myself.

CHAPTER 22
TWENTY YEARS AGO

IT'S AN EXPLANATION, an answer, of sorts anyway. But all it does is usher in more questions in its wake.

Parry is taking an age to reach us, or it feels like it. The wind's buffeting into us even harder now, the sand swirling around as he picks his way, dodging one of the dogs now off its lead, scenting a new friend perhaps, a new opportunity to play.

'It's an evidence bag.'

Donna's the first to identify what he's holding in his hand. Instinctively, we both move towards him, the three of us meeting just as the grassy slope on which we've been standing gives way to damp sand.

'Still nothing from the coastguard.' He has to raise his voice to make himself heard above the wind, indicating the bag at the same time. 'But we did find this; it was on the rocks just by the cliff face.'

He holds up the bag, a mobile phone clearly visible inside, and I recognise it immediately.

'That's Cara's.'

By my side, Donna stares at it too as he eyes me, quizzical.

'It's a very common model.'

Irritably, I snap. 'OK, it's the same model as Cara's.'

Then I stop as Donna takes out her mobile and hits a speed dial button. For a moment, nothing happens. Then, from inside the bag, the phone begins to illuminate with an incoming call alert, a name clearly visible on the display.

Mum.

Donna cuts the call and Cara's mobile darkens again.

'So, she was here.'

It's not a question, more of a statement, but the officer answers anyway. 'Not necessarily.'

We both look at him.

'Her phone's here. It doesn't necessarily mean Cara was.'

We both keep staring at him as the implications of what he's saying sink in.

'Are you saying someone planted her phone on those rocks?'

He just stares at me.

'Why would they do that?'

He just keeps staring.

CHAPTER 23
PRESENT DAY

'What the...?'

I break off, but Rory holds up his hand, shushing me as he does so, staring along with everyone else in the café at the TV screen above the counter. A reporter faces the camera, a microphone in his hand. Behind, I can see the scenes of crime tape I saw myself just a few hours ago. I can't see the uniformed police officer maintaining his previous vigil; in fact, I can't see any officers at all now. Then the face that stopped me in my tracks, my face, flashes up on the screen again.

I stand – I can't help myself – and move closer to the monitor. Dimly I'm aware of Rory doing the same. People tense as I pass. And with the café as silent as the proverbial grave, every word of that news report can now be heard loud and clear.

'Police are investigating the disappearance of a nineteen year-old woman last night in the Carmel area. Penny James was travelling to meet friends when she went missing.'

Briefly, the picture cuts to the reporter again before the same picture of me replaces him, only this time my face is in close-up.

'Police want to talk to a local man, Axel Petersen, in connection with her disappearance. It's believed that Mr Petersen may have been the last *person to see Penny before her disappearance and police are anxious to eliminate him from their inquiries.'*

The coldest of feelings washes over me as I become aware of everyone in the café staring at me, the exact feeling I used to get all those years ago after Cara went missing, when I'd walk down a street, head into a store, go for a walk along a beach, and all I'd see were the same openly inquisitive eyes framing the same silent questions.

I look across at Rory, but suddenly all he seems to want to do is to get out of here, because he curses again under his breath and makes for the door. Instinctively I follow, even though I don't know why, just catching the last of the news report as the screen cuts back to the reporter at the top of the lane.

'Police are becoming concerned for Penny's safety, and if anyone has any information as to her whereabouts, they're urged to contact either the local police here or any police station in the country.'

'Rory?'

We're both outside now, but an agitated Rory is striding away, clearly intent on putting as much distance between the two of us as possible, almost as if he fears being tainted by association.

I call again. 'Hey!'

But he's now actually running down the street. Briefly, I contemplate chasing after him. But then I see the waitress emerge from the café. She has her mobile in her hand and she's talking into it. I turn away, fumbling with my keys, and open the front door of the bookshop, desperately needing time and space to think. Blood's roaring in my ears and it takes a moment for me to realise that the phone's ringing on the desk in front of me. I pause for a moment longer, reeling even more, then pick it up to hear Mark on the other end of the line.

'Axel?'

Outside the window, I see a police car pulling up outside the café, stopping by the waitress, who's been joined by some of the customers from inside.

'What's happening? I've just had the police call me.'

As I keep looking, I see her lift a finger and point across the street towards me.

'They want me to get down to the bookshop and open up.'

Outside the window, I see the two police officers turn away from the café and begin to head across the road.

'I tried calling you on your mobile, but you weren't answering. What is all this?'

The officers are now at the door. I stay silent, don't reply. Then one of the officers raises his hand and begins banging on the door as Mark's voice sounds again.

'Axel?'

I just catch sight of the second of the officers raising his baton, but by the time I hear the glass in the door smash I'm running down one of the tunnels leading to the rear exit. Bursting out into the light I hare for my car again, and a moment later I'm back inside. I'm just aware of one of the officers emerging from the rear door a couple of seconds later, but I'm already speeding out onto the road. As I pull out, I see that the customers outside the café have now been joined by more onlookers, all engaged in what looks like animated speculation.

A few seconds later I've turned the corner ahead and am retracing the route along the coast road I took this morning, although without a knife pressing into my side this time.

CHAPTER 24
TWENTY YEARS AGO

THE COASTGUARD HAS FOUND nothing out on the water. Cara's phone aside, the police have found nothing back on the beach either.

Her phone was found up on an outcrop of rock, well away from any danger of it being washed away by even the highest of tides, and I can see on their faces that the police find that odd in the extreme. I do too. If someone had followed Cara as she'd walked down to the water's edge, someone intent on doing her harm, then why take her phone from her and hide it up there? And if she'd walked into the water intent on doing harm to herself, why bother protecting it like that?

Donna goes home in case there's some totally innocent explanation for all this and Cara simply walks back in at some point. But I can't go anywhere. This beach, like most, is host to a whole array of regular dog walkers, so I stay here until night finally falls, intercepting each one with the same questions, showing them the same picture of Cara on my phone in case they were here last night and saw her, saw anyone, saw anything that might shed some sort of light on all this.

And I stay for a different reason too. I can't explain it, but I feel as if she's close. I can feel her presence even though I've searched every inch of the shifting sands around me, have visited every outcrop of rock, have even climbed the cliff path to those cottages above the beach and have searched around them too. But I still sense something, even though I find nothing.

I keep moving. Up and down the beach, as darkness falls and the last of the dog walkers leave. Still, I continue, as if this act of perpetual motion might keep at bay the horrors that are now threatening at any moment to overwhelm me.

CHAPTER 25
PRESENT DAY

I HAVE to find the friend that Penny was staying with. She – or he – must be able to provide at least some of the answers here. And they must be as frantic as I am. If I can tell them my story and they can tell me theirs, then maybe, just maybe, we might start to make some sense out of all this.

And right now, this must be the last place the police would expect me to head for, or so I reason. To return – and for a second time – to the scene of what's now quite definitely some kind of crime. Or maybe I've just lost it completely and I'm going to find a whole posse of massed police waiting there for me.

But when I pull up, there's no sign of anyone. And no sirens have suddenly sounded behind me on the way over either, and no police roadblocks have barred my way. Dimly, at one point, I thought I heard the sound of a helicopter overhead, but that could have been one of the utility services carrying out a survey. I've often seen them hovering over the hills around the cottage.

I park the car at the top of the lane, duck under the crime tape and scan the houses I can now see immediately before me, trying to remember. Did Penny pause outside one of those houses in particular as I watched her walk away? Desperately, I try and retrace her steps in my mind, but I wasn't actually paying that much attention, of course.

Then, suddenly, out of the corner of my eye, I see a door open. A woman emerges, stopping as she sees me. Then she retreats inside. I follow but she slams the door shut. So, has she seen that news report too, has she recognised me? Another door opens, further up the lane. This time a man appears, who looks to be about my age. And he has a large stick in his hand.

'What do you want?'

'Penny.' My breathing's laboured, but I just about manage to gasp out the name, a pain in my chest I wasn't aware of till now suddenly constricting my airways.

'We don't know a Penny.'

Behind him, a woman of around the same age appears and I appeal to her, maybe because she, at least, isn't carrying a stick.

'I dropped her off here last night. Around ten o'clock. She said she was staying with friends; I have to speak to them.'

The man cuts across, repeating himself.

'We don't know a Penny.'

I advance, ever more desperate, both of them taking a wary step back as I do so.

'Can you think of anyone living here who might? A family with a twenty-something daughter or son, or a young couple living on their own. She was coming here to stay with someone; she told me.'

The woman cuts in again.

'Why don't you just go home and leave this to the police.'

I stare at her as she appeals to me.

'This really isn't doing any good.'

From the doors of the other houses on the lane I now see more people emerging. Then the man cuts across again, but he's not talking to me this time, he's muttering to his wife instead.

'Bit late for that.'

The woman follows his quick glance up to the top of the lane as I turn too. Just ducked under the tape are three police officers, all now striding down the lane towards me. One of them is bigger than the rest; he seems bulked out somehow, as if he's dressed in some sort of protective outfit. In his hand he's cradling what looks to be a weapon. By the man's side, the woman turns back, urges me again.

'Just talk to them. I'm sure this can all be straightened out in no time.'

I gesture round the small lane again, trying to ignore the advancing officers. I've got seconds now and I know it.

'She was coming here, she told me she was, to one of these houses. She said she was staying with someone. Why would she say that if she wasn't? This doesn't make any sense.'

'Mr Petersen.'

The officers have paused now, no more than three or four metres away, the officer wearing the protective vest slightly in front of the others, giving me a clear view of what definitely looks like a gun of some description in his hand. And giving him, of course, a clear sight of me too.

And suddenly, that anger bubbles inside me again, the same anger I felt yesterday evening. I just want one simple answer to one simple question. Much as I wanted a very simple answer to a very simple question twenty years ago as well. In that case, it was all about my daughter; now it's about another young girl.

I stride towards the officers. Maybe I've spent too long at the mercy of forces outside my control, feeling as if I'm being moved around like a pawn on a chessboard. The lead officer raises his hand, a clear instruction that I stop, but I'm beyond all that now too. I just let rip, everything spilling out of me in one manic and, even to my ears, largely incoherent rant.

'You can't do this – treat me like this – I'm just trying to find out what's happening – someone knows something – someone here knows Penny – someone has to know what's happened to her.'

In truth, I barely know what I'm saying by now. Writers who give occasional talks in the bookshop sometimes tell me that they hit times in their careers when they simply write, searching for the story they're trying to tell. As if the simple act of putting down words on a page might unlock something. Maybe I'm doing the same. Firing out words as if they're ammunition, hoping at least some of them might land.

What happened next happens so quickly. One minute I'm standing there, yelling at officers I can now barely even see through a mist that seems to have descended, dimly aware of more doors opening, of more people coming out of their cottages, attracted by the developing commotion. Then I register a quick glance exchanged between the armed officer and his companions, a signal clearly dispatched and equally clearly understood.

The armed officer brings up his gun, although it's unlike any gun I've ever seen films or on TV.

He takes a couple of swift steps forward and raises it. There's a moment when the world turns white and a near-paralysing pain consumes me, flooding every nerve end in my body. Dimly, I'm conscious that I'm falling backwards, but there's no ground rushing up to meet me as I might also expect; it's as if the ground itself has fallen away somehow.

I look up just as unconsciousness descends, and the last thing I see is the castle in the distance high up on the hill, that ruined collection of half-demolished stone walls and battlements that also towers over my cottage by the beach, then everything turns from white to black and I don't see anything anymore.

CHAPTER 26
TWENTY YEARS AGO

I WAKE UP, lashing out with my feet and arms, flailing ineffectually at what seems to be an unseen assailant. But strong hands are clamped down on my legs and I'm dragged along the ground, helpless.

Only it isn't the ground, but wet sand soaking into me from underneath, and as at least a tenuous grip on reality returns, I hear a voice, close by but distant at the same time.

'Axel, for God's sake!'

I look up as we come to a halt, focusing wildly on what I've assumed has to be an attacker of some kind, but it's Donna's brother, her twin, Harry, hissing down at me.

'What the hell do you think you're doing?'

Dim details swim more into focus. I see moonlight stretching out on all sides, I see – and hear – the sea rushing towards us, then receding. I see pinpricks of light up on the cliffs. And I see Harry, gasping from his exertions, straightening up, the pair of us now on the grassy slope, far away from the incoming tide.

I stare up at him. Harry's in the Army, in some sort of special ops unit. He spends most of his time in far flung war zones, meaning he's just about the last person I'd have expected to see on this deserted beach.

'What are you doing here?' I struggle some more, trying to get back some sort of control. 'When did you get back?'

'Last night. Donna called me an hour or so ago. She told me about Cara.'

I spring on the name, everything else wiped.

'Is there any news?'

He shakes his head.

'Nothing. And then she couldn't reach you either.'

I stare down at my soaked clothes, my phone inside one of my pockets, now clearly ruined.

'I drove down here, saw you just lying out there. What were you thinking of?'

I don't know. I have no recollection of anything between searching around those cottages up on the cliff and being dragged back along the sand to safety by Harry. Another of those blanks again, those missing moments I can't seem to retrieve. But none of that matters now.

'Where is she, Harry?'

He just looks at me, silent, his face my answer.

And then, suddenly, and from nowhere, out it comes. That spectacular piece of recent misfortune I've been trying to put out of my head. That inner voice that's been asking me, ever more insistently as this nightmare day unfolds, whether this has anything to do with that.

'I know he's gone. I know all that's over and done with, but...' I hesitate again, wracked. 'Could this be something to do with Jericho?'

Harry doesn't reply. For a moment, I don't think he's going to. Then he nods at me.

'I told you, Axel.'

He hisses at me again.

'I told you he was trouble.'

CHAPTER 27
PRESENT DAY

FROM UP HERE, she gets a birds-eye view. She sees his car stopping and him ducking under the police tape. She sees a couple coming out to meet him, a conversation taking place that, even at this distance, seems intense. She even sees what he can't see: other people congregating in their back gardens hidden from his view, conferring urgently again, at least one of them taking out a mobile phone.

Then she sees the police arrive, three officers getting out of an unmarked car before hurrying down the lane. She sees him move suddenly towards the officers; one of them raises what looks like a taser and then he crashes to the ground.

And she feels like yelling out loud. She feels like running around that grassy area inside the castle walls like a footballer celebrating a last-minute goal, but she doesn't, of course. Apart from anything else, the sight of a lone female doing that sort of victory dance would very much spook the few holidaymakers up here right now, most of whom are looking out towards the estuary and the spectacular views, not back towards Carmel, and, beyond to the county town in the distance. And it would be the second big mistake she'd made too.

That photo on the train could have proved costly. She really could have shown her hand and way, way too soon. But in the heat of that unexpected moment, she just couldn't resist it, and she knew why. It had been that look on his face. That trapped, hunted, look in his eyes as the guard approached. Because all she could see was what she knew to be there all along. She saw his guilt, pure and naked, and suddenly she just had to capture it. She felt as if that one picture could do what no one and nothing else had managed to do all these years. It was as if, suddenly, he'd been stripped bare.

But then, after taking it and posting it online, the doubts crept in. What if he started digging into who might have taken it and why? All this would then have gone to waste, which was an insupportable thought after everything. No wonder she passed the rest of that night in an agony of fear and trepidation.

But no one did start digging, because something else happened, of course; something much more important than a stray picture on a social media site. Another young girl went missing.

She keeps looking down onto the lane as paramedics arrive and begin to treat him. So, what's that all about? Is it history repeating itself? An itch he just had to scratch? She doesn't know, not yet, but time will tell, and not too much time, hopefully too, once he's in custody.

But the lesson's still clear. From now on she watches from a distance, just as she's watching now as he's loaded into the waiting ambulance. She plays silent witness to whatever's about to unfold, she doesn't blunder in like a bull at a gate. But she still feels like running that victory lap around the castle walls as the ambulance drives away with him inside.

It's been so long, too long, but she always knew that one day it had to happen. That one day, all those chickens would have to come home to roost.

CHAPTER
TWENTY-EIGHT

THE FAMOUS ACTOR *was up there on stage in the middle of one of his trademark monologues.*

Its theme was the past and the thesis was simple: to call it that was a misnomer, because nothing was ever really in the past. Whatever you've done, however you've acted, you have to live with it, and live with it forever. You might hide it from your friends, from family, from your partner, be that wife, husband or lover, and they may never suspect a thing. You might even forget yourself from time to time. But you can't erase who you are. You can't undo what you've done.

And even more importantly, it always catches up with you, usually when you least expect it. And then every one of those friends, every member of that family, every one of those wives, husbands or lovers will look at each other and wonder how they could possibly have missed it all those years.

And I listened and I nodded along with everyone else in that transfixed theatre that day. But inside I was silently screaming up at him, because that was wrong.

Things only catch up with you if you've been stupid. They only come back to haunt you if you've been careless. If you've taken pains to cover your tracks then they won't, and then the past will be what it should be, a separate entity, never to be revisited.

Another country, as the old saying has it, and I know that for a fact.
Because look at me.
Living proof.

PART TWO

CHAPTER 29
PRESENT DAY

THE PAIN when I first come round is excruciating, but a couple of paracetamols administered by a sympathetic paramedic begins to ease it. Now it's more of a dull ache down my chest and across my shoulder blades. I also have a hot scar on my neck covered with a dressing, but that's the least of my problems. More pressing than a single charge from a taser is the interrogation I'm now facing.

The interview room is small, with four chairs grouped around a metal table, which is anchored to the floor with bolts. The place is grimy, the walls pockmarked. There's no two-way mirror of the type I've seen in countless television police dramas, but maybe they're the exception rather than the rule, a way of connecting the hunter and the hunted in one single image.

There wasn't one when I was in a different interview room twenty years ago, but it still has the same institutional feel to it. In front of me is a paper cup filled with strong, black coffee, but my hands are shaking so much right now that I can barely pick it up. All I can think about, and all I've been able to think about from the moment I came round, is Penny.

What's happening? Has there been any news? Have they found her yet? I tried asking the paramedics, but they didn't know. I tried asking the uniformed officers deputed with transferring me from the hospital to the police station, as well as the duty sergeant on the front desk when I arrived, but all I got was the same stonewall. So now I wait in a limbo I know only too well. And, at the heart of it, a second missing girl.

I reach into my jacket pocket for my phone to see if I can contact Donna or Patrick or Mark to see if any of them have heard anything. Donna should have emerged from her self-imposed exile by now and Mark might have seen something on the news. Patrick's on his way in to guide me through the upcoming inter- view, so I could wait till he arrives, but he'll be able to talk more freely without police officers listening in. But as my fingers close on an empty space where I usually keep my phone, I remember it was taken by Rory, yet another puzzle in this ongoing mystery.

At least twenty years ago there was only one. Where's Cara? This one seems to be throwing out new mysteries all the time.

A light blinks high up on a wall opposite as a camera, I assume, stares down at me. I spread my hands out on the table, dizzy all of a sudden, trying to keep my balance. Then the door opens and Patrick looms in the doorway, a uniformed PC by his side.

Five minutes later, the uniformed PC is leaving after taking a saliva sample. I don't know why, maybe I was told, but I'm not listening. I'm just waiting for the PC to finish and go, so I can talk to Patrick alone – but as the PC leaves the room, it's Patrick who speaks first.

'Why didn't you tell me?' He pauses, his eyes growing trou- bled. 'I've seen the statement from the officer who talked to you when you stopped in Carmel. According to him, you didn't say a word about the girl, about meeting her or giving her a lift, you just drove off.'

Patrick pauses again, shaking his head in bewilderment. 'I'd talked to you myself. Not ten minutes before. OK, maybe you didn't want to say anything to the police, but...'

He tails off, lost, but I don't answer. I don't get the chance. Because now the door opens again, and two plainclothes officers walk in. I recognise the older one, the male officer, immediately. He's now in his late forties, but he looks much the same as he did when I first saw him years ago, tousled hair, tousled clothes, tousled everything. I can't remember his name for now, but he was one of the officers involved in the original investigation into Cara's disappearance.

His companion is female, a good twenty years younger, at least, and nothing is out of place so far as she's concerned, be that clothes, hair or make-up. Her eyes study me, cool and appraising, as she approaches the metal table and sits down. Already, I'm catching the unmistakable whiff of a good cop/bad cop act. For some reason – that general and overpowering sense of déjà vu perhaps — I wonder briefly if our paths have crossed before too, before dismissing the thought. She could only have been a small child when Cara disappeared.

The male officer nods at Patrick. They clearly know each other, which isn't surprising. Local police and solicitors often move in much the same circles, I suppose. But the young woman keeps her eyes firmly fixed on me. So far as she's concerned, I seem to be the only person in this room right now.

The male officer clears his throat.

'Mr Petersen, I'm Detective Inspector Daniel Adams.'

I nod back. I now have the name to go with the face.

The DI nods at his young companion, now settled in the seat next to him.

'This is Detective Sergeant Lauren Braith.'

I cut in. 'Is there any news about Penny?'

He pauses as he looks at me. By his side, the young DS's stare is still unblinking.

'Inquiries into Ms James's disappearance are ongoing.'

'So, she's still missing?'

Again, he doesn't answer directly, just nods at the female officer to his side.

'Let's get started, shall we?'

Still without taking her eyes off me, she reads me the standard caution. Then she turns to a black box attached to the table, checks the display, then presses a button. Consulting her watch, she announces the time, date and location of this interview. Then the DI to her side speaks again and his tone is mild, even concerned.

'First of all, Mr Petersen, can I check you've received medical attention for the injuries you suffered as a result of the incident with the police taser?'

I nod. 'Yes.'

'And you're not in need of anymore?' A wry, half-smile briefly plays on his lips. 'A shot from a taser's painful, we know.'

Not the ghost of a smile remotely approaches his companion's lips.

'Most officers in this station have had one at one time. All part of our basic training.'

I shake my head and the female DS speaks to me for the first time since she walked in, gesturing towards the black box.

'For the recording?'

I nod again. 'No.'

DI Adams leans forward and begins.

CHAPTER 30
TWENTY YEARS AGO

I'D FIRST CROSSED paths with Jericho a few months before Cara disappeared.

I'd been away on a work trip with Mark. I'd taken him on a few months before, although Donna had been unsure if I should. Painfully shy, both then and now, he always seemed to be trying to squeeze his body into the smallest possible shape, as if apologising for the simple offence of even existing. But there was a passion in his eyes whenever he talked about books, and I knew my regular clientele would warm to him as I had. But it was still a leap of faith. With brief interludes, business had always been an ongoing struggle. But this trip was to change all that, albeit briefly again, and in more ways than one.

Auctions in the book trade are like auctions in any trade the world over. There are always desperately disappointed losers and elated, if nervous, winners. I'd attended several auctions in the previous six months and had left each and every one firmly in the former category, after being outbid by one or other of the big boys. But today, driving back to catch the cross-channel ferry from an auction house in Bordeaux, I was on something approaching Cloud Nine.

The volume I'd been bidding on was one I'd been tracking for months. *Tamerlane and Other Poems* by Edgar Allan Poe. Written in the early years of his career, the great man had turned the manuscript over to a local printing press for self-publication. Only fifty copies were published, all anonymously, with Poe re-christening himself as 'A Bostonian' even though, puzzlingly, he was from Baltimore. It was mostly ignored on publication, but as Poe's work grew in popularity, collectors soon began to hunt out this early effort. A year before, one of the only eleven copies known to be in existence had sold at Christie's in New York for just under fifty thousand pounds. Six months ago, a twelfth copy had been discovered, the subject of that day's auction, and now I was the proud owner of the rare volume, having taken the deepest of deep breaths and bid a fraction over fifty-five thousand. The book wouldn't physically be with me until all the documentation had been completed and the relevant bank transfers effected, which was a relief in one sense. Let the auction house worry about safe transportation.

We disembarked from the ferry as we arrived back in the UK in the same general state of euphoria, mixed now with a high degree of trepidation on my part. I'd put out feelers among some of my regular customers and there'd been interest already, but what if that didn't translate into actual offers and cold hard cash? I'd spread the risk by purchasing a small collection of much lower-value books – modern classics including a few James Bond early editions – and those would definitely sell and make a decent profit, but it was still a concern.

As we approached the border checkpoint, I stopped the car and headed to the boot to retrieve a few sample volumes, proof of our purpose in visiting the Continent, if any were needed. But I was still musing on likely homes for *Tamerlane* as I reached inside.

Which was when I saw a pair of eyes staring back at me.

CHAPTER 31
PRESENT DAY

THE YOUNGER FEMALE DETECTIVE, Braith, is still just staring at me across the metal table as DS Adams leads the questioning. It's all she's done since I started running through the events of the last twenty-four hours or so. Sitting there. Staring. Which, strangely enough, only reinforces my sense that our paths have already crossed somehow.

'Do you live alone, Mr Petersen?'

I hesitate for a moment, unsure why he's asking, but then I nod.

'My wife and I divorced some years ago.'

'I'm sorry to hear that.'

Adams actually sounds sincere.

'And your cottage? It's in Freshwater, yes?' He checks a note on a pad as I nod. 'You're down on the beach, at the far end? Next to Florries?'

Florries is the local fish and chip shop, only open during the summer months when it does a roaring trade. I nod again.

'The last house before you get to the lane up to the castle.'

By my side, Patrick breaks in.

'I really don't see what this has to do with anything.'

Braith cuts in. 'So, you're not overlooked by any near neighbours?'

I hesitate again, the reason for this line of questioning now all too clear.

'There is a neighbour a few metres away, but his house faces out to sea as well, so no, I'm not overlooked.'

'Meaning no one can confirm the time you arrived home last night?'

I look at Patrick, then shake my head, only for Braith to indicate the black box again.

'No.'

Adams takes it up. 'Did you make or receive any phone calls when you got in?'

'I turned my phone off.'

'Why?'

'I didn't want to be disturbed. It had been a long day.'

'Do you usually turn your phone off when you get home of an evening?'

'No.'

'But you did last night?'

'It wasn't a normal sort of evening.'

I don't expand and they don't push it as I expect. Instead, Adams looks over his notes again.

'Can we go back to the train? It's where you first saw Penny, yes?'

I hunch closer over the table, ignoring that for now, questions that have been racing through my mind for the last few hours spilling out instead.

'I don't understand. That report – on the TV – it said I was the last person to see her. How could you know that, and how did you even know I'd given her a lift last night?'

'We received a phone call earlier this morning.'

I stop, stare at him.

'The caller reported Penny as missing and named you as the driver who'd picked her up from the station last night and then drove away with her in the direction of Carmel. We'd already received the report of a young woman in distress in that area, and then we received a further report from uniform that you'd stopped at the scene.'

By my side, Patrick breaks in.

'Who was this caller?'

Braith took it up.

'He didn't give his name, but I've listened to the recording. He was male and sounded panicked.'

I paused, seeing one face and one face only now.

Rory.

Adams looks down at his notes, picking up his original line of questioning again.

'You hadn't seen Penny on the platform waiting to get on board, on the street outside the station, by one of the ticket machines?'

'The first time I saw her was when she sat down opposite me, I don't even know where she boarded the train.'

Braith cuts in again, still maintaining that same unblinking, unnerving, stare.

'The same stop as you.'

'I didn't know that.'

Adams looks down at his notes once more. 'We've interviewed the guard, who tells us there was an incident involving the pair of you.'

He looks back up at me. 'You touched Penny, yes?'

I shift in my seat, uncomfortable.

'Not like that.'

'Like what?'

'Like you make it sound.'

Now both detectives just look at me.

'I didn't grope her or anything. I was distracted. I had things on my mind, for a moment I mistook her for someone else and, yes, I did reach out and I did touch her, but then I realised my mistake.'

I hesitate again. 'I apologised immediately, of course, and she didn't seem to take offence.'

'We've also interviewed another member of the train staff, the lady in charge of the catering trolley.'

Braith takes it up again, not looking down at any notes. She doesn't seem to need any aids to memory.

'She says you approached Penny again when you got off the train.'

I see her again in my mind's eye, pausing as she smoked a cigarette outside the station, watching us all the while, and for a moment – a strange thought, I know – I wonder what it was exactly I saw in her eyes as she was watching us like that. Concern, as I'd previously imagined? Or something else?

'She says you seemed to be having an intense conversation.'

'It wasn't intense.'

'So, what was it?'

Patrick cuts in.

'You already know this, Mr Petersen was offering her a lift.'

Braith keeps her eyes fixed only on me.

'This girl you didn't know, a girl you'd only just met?'

'Yes.'

'Do you usually offer lifts to complete strangers?'

'No, but in the circumstances—'

She interrupts. 'What circumstances?'

'She was a young girl on her own. It was already dark. The last bus had gone, there were no taxis on the forecourt and there weren't going to be any for the next couple of hours at least.'

Adams takes it up. 'And you know that, how?'

'Because I heard her talking to the taxi company on her phone.'

'You were listening to her conversation?'

'I was only twenty or so metres away and the car park was pretty well deserted. I couldn't help hearing what she was saying.'

'And she said yes?'

I hesitate a moment, much as I remember Penny hesitating last night.

'You said, do you want a lift, and this girl who didn't know you, just said yes?'

'She was unsure at first, I think.'

'But you persuaded her?'

'I left it totally to her, of course, but I was concerned. She was a young girl on her own in a strange place, with no means of getting where she wanted to go.'

I struggle a show of defiance. 'I'm sorry, but in similar circumstances I think most people would have done the same.'

'What did you talk about?'

I look at Braith, momentarily thrown as she suddenly cuts in with another new line of questioning. Maybe it's deliberate, intended to unsettle me, and the same thought clearly occurs to Patrick, who picks up on it straight away.

'I also don't see what a simple conversation between Mr Petersen and a girl you've already acknowledged he hardly knew has to do with anything.'

'Just trying to build a picture.'

And now I'm the one to cut in, because I'm becoming more and more frustrated the longer this continues.

'A picture of what?'

'Penny's state of mind. As we've already established, you're the last person to have seen her before she disappeared.'

Patrick interjects, mirroring what's in my mind now too.

'Aside from her abductor.'

Braith ignores that one.

'She might have said something, something you didn't think was particularly significant at the time, but in the light of what happened to her a short time later, might be.'

I pause, trying to calm myself. Put like that, it does sound eminently reasonable.

'She asked me what my name meant.'

Both detectives just stare at me again.

'I don't think she'd come across it before.'

'And what does it mean?'

Adams eyes me, curious, and now Patrick's looking at me too. In all the years we've known each other I don't think it's ever come up.

I hesitate.

'Father of Peace.'

For a moment no one says a word.

'But aside from that, we didn't really talk. She was on her phone for most of the time, texting I think, or maybe checking messages; she seemed distracted.'

'And then you dropped her off?'

'Yes.'

'Not at an actual house, but at the top of the lane?'

'She asked me to drop her there. I thought she was just being sensible.'

'In what way, sensible?'

I feel a low flush begin in my cheeks, but it's too late to stop now.

'I thought maybe she didn't want me to know exactly where she was staying. As you've already said, I was a stranger.'

'Did you get the impression she felt threatened by you at all?'

'No.'

Adams looks down at his notes again.

'And then you went home?'

'Yes.'

'We visited your house earlier today as part of our efforts to speak to you as a person of interest in connection with Penny's disappearance. We gained entry when we couldn't get a reply.'

Adams looks up at me. 'I'm not exactly house-proud myself, Mr Petersen, but to be frank your place looked like a bomb had hit it.'

Another image suddenly flashes in front of my eyes; waking up this very morning, that empty wine bottle at my side, papers everywhere, food tipped over the sofa and the floor.

'I had a few drinks when I got in.'

'Is drinking your normal routine after getting in from work?'

'Not that much, no.'

Adams consults his notes again.

'And neither's turning your phone off. You've already told us that too.'

And suddenly, I just want it out there. They already know all this anyway, I can see it in their eyes, so why are they spinning it out? Are they trying to catch me out, but why? There's no reason to do that, because I've nothing to hide.

'Last night, yesterday, it was a difficult day.'

Patrick interjects again.

'Axel, there's really no need for you to go into all this.'

But I shake my head, insistent. 'I want to.'

I look at the two detectives. 'Maybe then you'll understand why I offered Penny that lift.'

Adams nods back at me, cautious.

'Go on.'

I nod at Adams in turn.

'You must know this, you have to do. I remember you.'

I take a quick, deep breath.

'Twenty years ago, twenty years ago yesterday in fact, my daughter, Cara, disappeared. That's who I was thinking about on the train. I'd sunk into some sort of trance, I suppose. When I came out of it, we were on the final run into the station and the first person I saw was Penny. For a moment, one mad moment – and I know it was mad now, of course – I thought it was her, I thought it was Cara.'

I pause, struggling now.

'And when I saw her outside that station, when I realised she was a young girl faced with a three mile walk in the dark, then, yes, I thought of Cara then too. I thought of her, alone somewhere as well, maybe on the night she went missing.'

I stop, struggling even more.

'I suppose last night of all nights, I just wanted to make sure one young girl got where she wanted to go in safety.'

Adams looks down at the notes on the table in front of him again.

'Your daughter, Cara, was eighteen when she disappeared.'

I don't know if it's an observation or a question, but I nod anyway.

'Yes.'

He looks back up at me. 'Roughly the same age as Penny in fact.'

I look at him.

'Who's also disappeared.'

A silence descends.

A silence that just grows and grows.

CHAPTER 32
TWENTY YEARS AGO

A CUSTOMS OFFICER WAS APPROACHING, clipboard in hand. I was still standing, frozen by the open boot. Mark, frozen now too, was by my side. That same pair of eyes was staring up at us as the prone figure tried, inexpertly, to conceal himself in the boot.

The customs officer paused at the front of the car to take a note of its details, and the partially hidden figure – who I could now see was a young man perhaps in his late teens – whispered one word.

Please.

And it wasn't the word. It was the eyes. Or, more accurately the look in those eyes. I hesitated a moment longer, but only a moment. Then I nodded at Mark to pick up the books, slamming the boot lid back down as he did so. In that instant, I had no idea what I was doing or what the next few moments might bring.

Then I turned to face the customs officer as he made his approach.

CHAPTER 33
PRESENT DAY

'CAN we go back on another part of your story?'

Briefly, I feel a flare of irritation rise inside as Braith maintains that unblinking stare. Is it deliberate, her choice of words? My *story*? Is it just my imagination, or has she already decided that all I'm telling them is pure fiction?

'You paying that return visit to the spot you dropped Penny off this morning?'

I cut across, can't help myself again.

'I didn't pay a return visit; I was driving that way, that's all.'

'On your way back to the station?'

'What?'

'That's where you were going, on your way back to the station, to catch the train to spend the day in your bookshop?'

I hesitate again.

'No, actually, I'd decided to drive in. After what happened—'

I stop, struggling for a moment.

'I didn't want to run the risk of seeing the same guard on the train, or the woman with the catering trolley. I thought it best if I leave it a few days; it might have been embarrassing.'

Adams nods at me.

'That's not the quickest way to drive to your shop.'

I fall silent for a moment, computing the different routes I could have taken, and he's right. There's a main trunk road just a mile or so in the opposite direction that bypasses the town. That would have shaved a good ten minutes or so off the journey, maybe even more.

By my side I can feel Patrick shifting in his seat, clearly finding this part of the story as curious as the two detectives, and now I'm saying it out loud, I'm finding it curious too. But it's the truth, however inconvenient it might be. And while Adams doesn't push it, I already have the feeling we're not yet done with that particular line of inquiry.

'And you stopped when you saw the police officer, the one standing by the scenes of crime tape?'

'Yes.'

'Why? Plenty of other motorists had passed that same spot before you, but none of them had stopped.'

'I was curious.'

'Because you'd dropped Penny off at the same spot the night before?'

'Yes.'

Braith takes it up.

'The odd thing being that you didn't mention that to the officer. You asked what had happened; he told you a young girl had been attacked and apparently abducted and not once did you tell him that you'd dropped a young girl off at the top of that lane the previous evening.'

She frowns. 'You just drove away.'

'I was going to turn back. I regretted driving off like that the minute I pulled away. I can't explain why I did that – maybe I panicked or something.'

'If you had nothing to do with Penny's disappearance, why would you panic?'

'Because of Cara, I suppose.'

I pause, struggling again. 'It felt a bit like history repeating itself. It just felt odd. Sinister, I suppose. I can't really explain.'

'But you didn't turn back?'

'No.'

'Because you were then stopped by a man with a knife, and you were abducted yourself?'

Another one of those silences develops for a few moments. Then Adams leans forward, checking his notes once more.

'Run me through that bit one more time, will you, Mr Petersen?'

I take a deep breath, then relate again all that happened with Rory – his stopping the car, getting in, making me drive to the bookshop before taking my phone, at which point Braith cuts in again.

'We checked before we came in. Your phone hasn't been turned on in the last few hours. So why would this character take your phone if he didn't intend to use it?'

'I don't know. Maybe he thought there was some information on it or something.'

'He'd still have to turn it on to find out.'

I fall silent; no answer to that. And now Adams takes it up.

'But you got away?'

'Yes.'

'Because you managed to overpower him?'

'Yes.'

'In your bookshop?'

'Yes.'

'He forced you to go inside, you overpowered him and then you made your escape.'

Suddenly, I feel a flush begin to spread across my cheeks, and once again I'm sure they're picking up on it. Because the one thing I haven't told them about yet – and again I don't know why – is that scarf, Penny's scarf, hanging up like that in a place it had no right to be, in that passageway. I still don't know how it got there. The only thing I do know is that I've done plenty to incriminate myself in the past few hours anyway. I don't want to add yet another twist to what has to be a very strange-sounding tale.

'And then you ran out of your shop.'

Adams looks down at his notes, then up to me again.

'And then you went back again?'

I take another quick, deep breath.

'I wanted answers. He obviously knew Penny. He seemed to know why she'd come here, even if he obviously didn't know where she was right now. All I could think of at the start was getting away. He had a knife, for God's sake. But when I got outside, suddenly, I had to know what was going on.'

'Which is how the two of you ended up in a café across the street from your shop?'

'Yes.'

Braith's eyes don't leave my face.

'If I'd just been kidnapped and held at knifepoint, I think I'd have run a mile the first chance I got, not bought my abductor a latte.'

I don't answer. Because I don't have anything to add to what I've already said. That was what happened. Chapter and verse, aside from the omission of the scarf. There's simply nothing else I can tell them.

'There's no one down that lane who knows her.'

I tense again as I stare at Adams.

'She wasn't staying at any of those cottages. We've talked to all the householders.'

Braith takes it up.

'We managed to find images of Penny from one of the CCTV cameras covering the station concourse. We showed those images to each and every one of them. No one knew her. And none of them was expecting a visitor last night either.'

'I don't understand.'

'Don't you?'

And even though it's Braith who's speaking, Adams's eyes are now not leaving my face either.

'You just told us yourself it was the anniversary, the twentieth anniversary of your daughter's disappearance. It was an emotional day – it had to have been, anyone could understand that – and it made you do things you'd never have dreamt of doing normally, like reaching out and touching a young girl on a train, a girl who was around the same age as your daughter when she went missing.'

Adams cuts in.

'And you were still acting oddly today; you told us that too. You stopped by that lane, even though you're not sure why, and then you drove off without telling the police officer that you'd dropped Penny off at the exact same spot the night before.'

Braith taps her notes with a ball point pen.

'You've also told us that for a moment you thought it was her.'

I stare at her pen, at her tapping a strangely rhythmic underscore.

'So, what happened when the two of you were alone in the car? Did you go into some weird sort of trance again, much like the one you said you'd gone into on the train? For a moment did you imagine your own daughter was sitting there beside you in your car?'

She hunches forward over the table, her pen still tapping the table.'Did you reach out to her again, Mr Petersen?'

'No.'

'Are you sure?'

Patrick interjects. 'Mr Petersen's just answered that question.'

She doesn't even seem to hear him. It's as if he isn't there, as if her older companion sitting at her side isn't there either. It's as if there are only two people in that room right now. Her, and me.

'Did you reach out to her again only to realise that of course it wasn't your daughter, how could it be? So, what happened then, Mr Petersen, what happened when you realised it wasn't Cara sitting beside you last night?'

Braith nods at me again, her pen not tapping anymore, now poised above the table instead, hovering, like the tail of a scorpion readying itself for a sting.

'Or was it already too late by then?'

CHAPTER 34
TWENTY YEARS AGO

'I'VE ALWAYS THOUGHT Connery was the best.'

I nodded back, trying to control my breathing as the customs official sifted through the early editions of the Bond novels, now in his hand. He was standing by the boot. At any moment I was expecting him to ask me to open it.

'Well, it stands to reason doesn't it? He was the first, the original – they usually are.'

'Barry Nelson.'

I shot a long-suffering glance towards Mark, a stickler for accuracy even now, when we really did not want to prolong this exchange with the man from Border Control any longer than absolutely necessary.

'Who?'

Mark swallowed, now only too aware himself that maybe he really should have just kept his mouth shut.

'Barry Nelson was the first actor to play James Bond.'

The customs official was staring at him.

'In *Casino Royale*.'

The officer kept staring.

'But it was a TV pilot. Not a film.'

The officer looked at Mark for a moment longer, then back at the small collection of volumes he was holding, most of which, it had to be said, looked as if they'd seen better days.

'So, these are – what do they call them – first editions?'

He looked at Mark again, but my recently recruited assistant just nodded this time.

'And that's why people buy them, because they're worth something?'

'Actually, a lot of first editions aren't.'

It must be catching. Now I was taking up the Mark mantle.

'The early Bond novels are valuable because there weren't that many printed at the time, but the later ones were printed in their tens of thousands, so, frankly, you'd have trouble giving them away.'

The officer pursed his lips as he considered a first pressing of *Doctor No.*

'But it's the same book. You're reading the same words whenever it was published.'

And, suddenly, I realised what he was doing. He was trying to get a handle on us – he and his colleagues probably did it with all the drivers they stopped. They'd get them talking, get them to open up, and it was a decent tactic too. I'd read enough crime fiction to know that the guilty usually stay silent for fear of incriminating themselves. If a mark won't engage, what are they hiding?

I took one of the books from the small collection in his hand.

'But you're reading the book in the form in which it was first presented to the world. It's the edition the author themselves would have held for the first time, the one in which they'd have had the most input.'

Mark looked at me as I warmed to my theme.

'And it's the edition that went out to the very first readers, the one that made their reputations, as well as the actual one that broke the laws of the day sometimes, in the case of *Tropic of Cancer* or *Lady Chatterley's Lover* or *Ulysses.*'

Mark, now realising what I was doing, joined in.

'Or destroyed them.'

The officer looked from me, back to him.

'Isn't that what happened to Keats? Don't they say he died in part because of the bad reviews of the very first edition of *Endymion*?'

I stilled the smile that puckered at the edge of my mouth, watching as the officer put the remaining Bond volumes back in their protective bag. He'd got our number now. Two tweedy book nerds.

Then he nodded at us and told us to drive on.

CHAPTER 35
PRESENT DAY

ADAMS RESTS his forearms on the stone parapet and looks down on the rushing water below.

The source of this river is fifty or so miles away high up in the hills, gathering pace and strength as it winds its way down through the valley before broadening out into the estuary, and finally joining the sea not far from the cottage owned by the man they've just interviewed. But Adams isn't thinking about Axel Petersen right now. He's doing what he always does after any interview: clearing his mind, allowing his thoughts to settle. Over the course of a long and occasionally turbulent career, he's come to appreciate the value of these quiet periods of reflection.

Adams eyes a small pool of eddying water close to the bank. Decades ago, a huge sturgeon swam upriver from the estuary and grounded itself in those very shallows. Two passing fishermen believed the long, black shape to just be a log at first, until the long, black shape tried to move upstream. The fishermen in question might not have been the brightest of sparks but even they knew logs don't move upstream. So, they took two large sticks and began prodding away at whatever was down there. Maddened – and frightened now too, in all probability – the sturgeon suddenly burst from the water up at them, revealing itself to be a four-hundred-pound behemoth, eight feet long with a four-foot girth. It was also stuffed full of prime beluga caviar. The fishermen scattered in panic as the sturgeon beached itself on the bank, unable to get back to the relative safety of the shallows. Returning, cautiously, some few moments later, they realised that, unwittingly, they'd just landed the catch of a lifetime.

It would probably have been dismissed as just another angler's tall tale, but some far-sighted soul took a picture, preserving the giant catch along with its two unexpected custodians for posterity. Adams looks downriver, towards the distant estuary and, beyond that, the sea. But no such corroborative evidence is available, as yet at least, for Axel's story. For now, no one has any idea if he is telling the truth, as – and as incredible as it might have sounded at the time – were those fishermen all those decades ago. Or whether he's spinning the tallest of tales.

Adams keeps looking down at the rushing water, a thought now racing through his mind, and it's the same thought he's been trying to banish all day. It's been twenty years. Twenty years, for God's sake. Why does this all have to come back again, and come back like this too?

Then, suddenly, he wheels round as Braith materialises at his side.

'So, what do you think?'

Adams stares at her. The rest of the station would know better than to approach him right now. Everyone else would give him the space and time they all know he demands at times like these. But then his DS has always prided herself on not being, and never intending to be, everyone else.

'I don't buy it for a minute. He all-but assaults her on the train, he pressures her into getting into his car, he takes her to a remote spot where no one knows her. Next thing, she disappears, and the next morning, he can't resist going back to take a look.'

Adams says nothing. He was like her once and it cost him a relationship with his own daughter, Suzy, when she wasn't a great deal younger than the focused and intense young woman now standing at his side. He still sees Suzy most weeks in and around the town, along with two small children he's also had no contact with since his divorce from her mother, and the reason is simple. Suzy hates him and she always will. She hates him for his absorption in his career, for his neglect of her mother, but she hates him above all for the fact that her mum is now dead after a long illness for which she also blames him, and there isn't a single thing he can do about it.

But now and again he does what Axel might have done yesterday. He sees a young girl on a train or in a café or sometimes just passing on the street, a girl who resembles Suzy, and for a few moments he finds himself lost in a similar reverie, staring at a total stranger, remembering events and incidents that are nothing to do with her at all. And in the most extreme of those instances, he, too, can imagine maybe even reaching out a hand.

Braith carries on.

'Maybe he even believes all he's saying. Maybe he's one of those crazies who can separate it all out, who can do something and then convince himself it never happened.

She pauses for a moment and then continues.

'Maybe like he did with his daughter. Maybe that's how he's lived with it all these years. He's just wiped it, like he's wiping all this now.'

Adams finally speaks.

'I was on that case myself back then. We questioned him for days at a time, went over everything, again and again. We never found anything that directly, or even indirectly, implicated him in Cara's disappearance.'

It's as if she simply doesn't hear him.

'Maybe he's like a pressure cooker. He's kept the lid on it all till now. But suddenly, last night, probably because it was an anniversary and a big one too, everything just blew.'

Adams cuts in again, even though he already has a feeling he might as well not be there at all.

'SOCO have taken apart his house. There's no trace of Penny's

DNA there. There's plenty in his car, but we already know he gave her a lift. They've been over that too and there's no sign of any sort of struggle and definitely no blood.'

Braith shrugs.

'Maybe he drugged her. Offered her some water after her trip but put something in it. Then there'd be no need for any sort of struggle at all.'

The same thought has actually occurred to Adams. Braith is good. Very good. She'll probably go far.

'So, what do we do?'

Adams stares at her, his gaze level, taking a moment before replying.

'We watch. And wait.'

Braith's eyes are now flint-like.

'We do nothing? We just let him go?'

Then Braith stares after him, frustrated, as Adams pushes his arms up from the stone parapet, turns and walks away.

CHAPTER 36
TWENTY YEARS AGO

IT TOOK us over five hours to drive home. Partly, that was simple common sense; the last thing I wanted right now was to be stopped for speeding. But mainly it was because Mark and I had always been suckers for a good story.

Jericho – that was the name of the young man who'd stared up at me from inside my boot – was now in the back of the car, hunched on one of the rear seats. I'd stopped on a small country road a few miles out of Dover to make the switch after first calling at a service station to buy some water and sandwiches. He didn't speak for over an hour as he drank and ate and took in his new surroundings. Then, as we joined another in a series of seemingly endless motorways taking us ever further west, he slowly opened up, and his story began to emerge. But when we arrived at the bookshop five hours later, we still felt as if we'd barely scratched the surface.

By the time we settled him inside for the night, a whole array of names and places had already assailed us as Jericho relived the journey he'd endured so far. But it was his re-telling of the events of a few nights earlier that I remembered the best.

'We'd been in the car for what seemed like days, but the Serb border with Hungary was now only twenty or so kilometres away, and from there it was going to be much easier to cross into Austria.'

From the front seat I cut in.

'We?'

I looked at Mark at my side, both of us suddenly panicked, visions of another desperate young soul, still in the boot of my car, flashing in front of our eyes.

'Omar. My brother.'

Jericho, struggling, took another sip of water, the pain of separation clear in his eyes.

'I don't know where he is now.'

He paused a moment, still battling to compose himself, then continued.

'But then there was a problem. The driver took a call and he slammed on the brakes, started arguing with another man in the seat next to him. We couldn't understand what they were saying, but they kept looking back at us, then arguing with each other again. But then the man in the passenger seat turned round and said something to us – it was just the one word, but we understood that at least.'

Jericho paused. 'Policija.'

Slowly, and courtesy of the driver's broken English, Jericho and Omar had begun to piece together the problem.

'They'd had a report of a police checkpoint up ahead. That's what that phone call was all about. They didn't want to risk being stopped with us in the car, so we were told to get out and take our bags with us. The man in the passenger seat – his name was Salar – he was going to wait with us. The driver was going to drive on alone, see if the checkpoint was going to be a problem. If everything was OK, he was going to come back for us. If not, Salar was going to find us a different way across the border.'

By my side, Mark looked at me, tensing. I was tensing now too. In hindsight, it was all too obvious what was about to happen.

'We lifted out our bags and stood outside, waiting. But

suddenly, the driver accelerated, hard, and the car sped off, with both men still inside. Omar chased after it, yelling at it to stop, but I just stood there as it disappeared along with the five thousand dollars, every penny we had in the world, that we'd paid them.'

Jericho was really struggling now, a combination of tiredness and distress threatening to overwhelm him.

'We couldn't stay there. Serbian police are notorious for robbing refugees, even killing them, so we ran into the forest.'

Then Jericho stopped and we didn't get any more out of him for the rest of the journey home, a journey framed by that image of two frightened young men, little more than boys in truth, in a strange country hundreds of miles from home, no idea where to go next, and even less idea how to get there.

We arrived back at one in the morning. The street outside the bookshop was as quiet as the grave. Donna was away at a conference, a Services seminar organised by her brother; Cara was staying with a friend. Ensconced in the rare books room, Jericho should be safe from any prying eyes, but I was still uneasy. There was a chance that someone had seen three men exiting a car at the rear of the shop and heading inside at what was very much a strange time of night, and might have started to wonder why.

And, just as were settling him for the night with more water and food, it seemed those fears might not be unfounded.

'Ssh.' I held up a hand. Mark looked towards the door at the same time. From out in the street there was the sound of someone passing. Jericho half-stood, tensing too, but then I relaxed as a discordant singing started. Just a late-night reveller on his drunken way home.

A short time later, a makeshift bed had been made up and we were heading out of the rear door back to my car again. We were about to separate; Mark lived only a short walk away. But as I opened the door out onto the small parking area at the rear of the shop, he turned towards me, troubled.

'Do you know the penalty for people smuggling, Axel?'

I looked at him.

'We haven't smuggled anyone.'
'He was in the boot of your car.'
'But I had no idea he was there.'
'And now he's in your bookshop.'
I paused for a moment; no answer to that.

And no idea, at that time anyway, that from the other side of the door to the rare books room, a fearful Jericho had heard every word.

CHAPTER 37
PRESENT DAY

THE PILLS WERE A MISTAKE, she knew they would be. She knew it last year and the year before, and every other year stretching back twenty years. But it made no difference; she still took them, and she'll continue to take them until some celestial being, if such a figure actually exists, takes pity on her and ends this annual reunion with the most acute and agonising of torments.

Time heals, they say, and maybe it does in every other case. But in the case of a missing child, it's an open wound that never heals. And every year as the anniversary approaches, it's as if a fresh infection assails it. So, while the pills might be a mistake, they're also a necessity, effectively knocking Donna out and blocking everything else out too. The downside is waking into the fog that now envelops her. Moving, or trying to move, as if her limbs have turned to lead. Lifting, or trying to lift, her head from the pillow, to only actually manage it on the third or fourth attempt.

Struggling to a seated position, Donna checks the clock on the bedside table. The time and date tell her she's lost a complete day and night. Hesitating, she turns on her phone. No messages flash up on the display, but that isn't entirely unexpected. Her number is only known to a small handful of people: Axel, Patrick, her brother, Harry, who now lives some thirty miles down the coast after his retirement from the Army, and a sister she rarely sees these days. And they all know better than to disturb her at this time of year.

Donna looks across at her laptop, but logging on to the net is very definitely a step too far. She's long ago removed herself from most social media sites, but the anniversary always brings trolls crawling out of the woodwork, and a few still manage to find her. How Axel continues with his day-to-day work, how he mans his bookshop, maintains the hundred and one simple interactions that punctuate every one of those same working days, she'll never understand. But he can and she can't, so that's that.

But Donna knows she'll log on before long, even though she knows what she'll find. Always the same lurid speculation as to what might have happened to Cara and who might be responsible. She just can't seem to help herself. Maybe it's because these exact same questions torment her too, and so, moth to a flame, she'll be drawn back to it all, but not right now. Right now, she needs coffee. Strong, black, and lots of it.

Donna swings herself off the bed and opens the door that leads to the central passageway along to the kitchen. Then she stops as, through the partly open door, she sees a large scattering of dried pasta littering the floor. Puzzled, she treads her way along the carpeted passageway. Did she try to cook herself something before she took those pills? Or did she have some sort of episode after she'd taken them? It's happened before.

Momentarily, as she moves into the kitchen itself, all her worst fears seem to be confirmed. It isn't just pasta on the floor in there; it's the contents of most of the other drawers too. Books are scattered around the room as well, and through the open door to the living room, Donna can see what looks to be the same sort of devastation in there.

But this is nothing to do with any pill-induced episode. This is all to do to with the man standing by that same open door, wearing a balaclava.

A man who is staring at her.

CHAPTER 38
TWENTY YEARS AGO

CHAPTER 38
PRESENT DAY

AN HOUR AFTER HIS UNEXPECTED – and perhaps unlikely – saviours had taken pity on him and delivered him to this latest place of refuge, Jericho suddenly jerked awake from a sleep that had already been fitful and was now well and truly over.

He stared towards the door. And as he kept staring and listening, he heard it again, coming from what he assumed was the reception area of the bookshop. Someone was in there.

He rose to his feet, panicked all over again. This had to mean one thing and one thing only. All his worst fears as he listened in to that snatched, hissed conversation between those two men from the other side of that door had just come true. They'd had a change of heart. He'd been reported.

Jericho stared in an agony of expectation as he heard footsteps approaching, looking round wildly for an alternative route out of a room that had been a place of refuge, even a few seconds before, but which now more resembled a prison.

Outside, the footsteps grew closer all the while.

CHAPTER 39
PRESENT DAY

ALL DONNA CAN HEAR IS blood roaring in her ears. All she can see are tiny pinpricks of light inside the balaclava covering the face of the figure in front of her. Her stomach feels as if there's nothing inside but liquid.

In a life filled with more than its fair share of terrible events and their endless aftermath, she's never had this one before. An intruder, a masked stranger no less, in her house and facing her, from no more than a few metres away. And he's standing directly in front of the nearest door leading to the outside, too. Behind her, there are just two bedrooms and a bathroom. The only realistic escape route is past the intruder, which means she currently has no way out of her house.

Donna looks round wildly, searching for anything that might double as some sort of weapon, but this is her home; stocking it with offensive weapons was never exactly high on the list of priorities.

'Whatever you want, just take it.' Donna forces out the words. 'Just take it and go.'

The man in the mask doesn't reply. And he doesn't move. He just keeps staring at her, assessing, appraising. A predator sizing up its prey.

'You can just walk out. I won't do anything, I won't even call the police.'

Inspiration strikes as she spots something left open on one of the work units.

'Look.' She gestures across at a nearly new iPad. 'I only got that a couple of months ago – the password's 'Julia', capital 'J', the rest lower case. It was my mother's name. Keep it or sell it, whatever you want.'

Donna reaches into her pocket, brings it out. 'And I've got a phone.'

Then she stops as he cuts across, speaking for the first time, his voice low, controlled.

'I'm not a thief.'

She stares at him as she takes in again, the balaclava, and – for the first time – registers that he's wearing gloves as well. Almost involuntarily, she looks across at the open drawers, at her belongings strewn across the kitchen and the living room floor. Not a thief? What the hell is he then?

But she doesn't challenge him, some instinct telling her not to confront him directly, to just keep talking, try and open up some sort of exchange; hasn't she read that somewhere? In truth, she doesn't know. All she does know is that right now it seems the safest course of action.

'Maybe you didn't think anyone was home.'

Donna falters, momentarily.

'I'd taken some pills – they'd knocked me out and I've only just woken up, so I can't blame you if you thought the place was empty.'

But then, deep down, a horrible suspicion begins. Is he one of the trolls? She's had them before and so has Axel, the ones not content with posting images online accompanied by all sorts of accusations. Some of them have also come to the house, have photographed themselves by the front door; one even delivered a running commentary as he stood there, detailing every twist and turn in the Cara case. So, is he some sort of weird souvenir hunter? Is that what he meant when he said he wasn't a thief, because in his mind he wasn't? Has he been rifling through her possessions all this time, looking for some memento of her precious daughter to take away with him?

And suddenly all her previous resolve to keep calm, to remain cool, to try and open up a dialogue, vanishes. Her hand grips tighter on the phone still in her hand, a sacrificial offering a moment before, now something very different.

Donna hurls the thin metal device towards his head as hard as she can, praying that the combination of the blow and the element of surprise will do the trick.

Then everything goes black.

CHAPTER 40
TWENTY YEARS AGO

JERICHO FELT a sudden surge of anger build inside as the footsteps drew closer. It was the same fury he'd felt as he watched his brother embark on his impotent dash after that car those few days before, fuelled by the lacerating sting of a betrayal he could do nothing about.

But if he had been betrayed again now, if his two rescuers really had turned into something very different, then he wasn't going to go down without a fight. He'd had no choice as he stared after the car that had taken not only their money but all their hopes as well. But he had a choice now.

The footsteps outside suddenly sounded more hesitant, more uncertain. But then there was a blinding light as the door was flung open in front of him, and for a moment Jericho wheeled, disorientated. At any moment he expected strong arms to grip him, maybe even to hear a gun being cocked and held against his head.

But what he heard instead was a voice. A female voice. Struggling to focus in the still-blinding overhead light, the dim shape of a girl around his own age began to materialise, but what she was saying was clear enough.

'Who the fuck are you?'

CHAPTER 41
PRESENT DAY

CHAPTER 40
TWENTY YEARS AGO

AN HOUR LATER, and with the interview concluded for now, the duty sergeant tells me I can go. For the time being anyway. What happens next is going to be down to the officers in charge of the ongoing inquiry into Penny's disappearance. I can go home but I'm not to leave the county, let alone the country, as I must make myself available for any further questioning.

I sign some forms without registering what they are, but Patrick seems fine about them. Thank God he's here. Twenty years ago, when Cara disappeared, he was five thousand miles away, bidding for me in the Hemingway auction. I just thank my lucky stars he's close to hand this time.

A few moments later we're sitting in his car in the large car park outside the new-look, purpose-built police station that replaced the crumbling old one a few years ago.

Patrick turns towards me. 'Come back to mine.'

I hesitate, briefly tempted, the thought of returning to my empty cottage, perhaps already besieged by the press, not exactly an appealing prospect. But I shake my head. Something else is rather more on my mind right now than sleeping arrangements.

'Does Donna know about all this?'

'Not yet. She's done her usual at this time of year – turned off the phone, locked the door.'

Patrick looks back at the police station.

'If she does what she does most years then she'll probably call me later on or tomorrow to see if anyone's come forward or if there are any new leads. I was going to leave it till then. But I can drive you round there if you like.'

I shake my head again.

'Just take me home.'

He keeps looking at me. 'There's a spare room with your name on it for as long as you want, you know that.'

And I do. But right now, I just want normality. I want to be surrounded by four familiar walls and all my old familiar things, even if they have been manhandled by a team of police officers. And maybe I just want to do what my ex-wife is doing right now too. Close the door, shut out everything and everyone. Sink down into hermit-mode. And so, Patrick, albeit reluctantly, drops me off outside the cottage a short time later. Thankfully there's no press outside.

For the next hour I tick off the various tasks I allotted myself on the drive home. I take a shower, dig out an old phone that I stashed in a drawer one upgrade ago and drive down to a phone shop in the town where a new SIM card's inserted and, courtesy of a call to my mobile provider, all my old contacts appear on the screen once more as if by magic. Practical, everyday stuff that deadens everything. Therapy, in other words, and for now, at least, it's working.

In the same spirit, I package up the Frame volume, complete with that curious inscription. I fire off a series of emails to a collector who wants to know the provenance of a volume I'm advertising that was once owned by Samuel Pepys, complete with the great diarist's distinctive bookplate showing his motto above a pair of crossed anchors. He wants to know how this might have surfaced and why. I explain that Pepys, in strict contrast to many collectors both then and now, rationed the number of books in his collection to a strict three thousand in total, not a volume more or less, because that was the number he deemed correct for a gentleman's library. So, over the years, books would be discarded to make way for new additions, although all would still be decorated with the Pepys bookplate. In my time in the antiquarian book trade, I must have handled at least a dozen such volumes, while other dealers I knew have handled considerably more.

And slowly, I feel calm returning, and it's not just due to getting back into some sort of work routine. It's the nature of that work. It's the books.

When Donna's and my marriage collapsed, I selected a whole pile from the shop and stacked them high on a desk in front of me, escaping from the world for weeks on end. I lost myself in a whole variety of different voices, from Fazil Iskander to Norman Mailer, from Jose Saramango to Marshall Browne. I journeyed thorough dozens of different landscapes, from Hemingway's Spain to David Grossman's Israel and Simin Daneshaver's Iran. I travelled to Mexico in the company of Malcolm Lowry and to Turkey with Orhan Pamuk. By the time I'd worked my way through that small wall of books, it was as if the wall I'd erected inside had somehow been taken down too, and I was ready to go back out into the world again.

And with this new calm comes something else now, and it's so strange and inappropriate in a sense that I have difficulty identifying what it is at first. But it's a feeling of peace. It was the same feeling I had driving along with Penny by my side. I just felt connected. An invisible thread running back to a thousand other similar journeys taken at different times when there was just myself and Cara.

So, in the end, I don't regret it. Despite all the mayhem that's happened since, all the chaos into which I've suddenly been plunged, if I was given a choice, I'd do exactly the same again. I'd approach her, like I approached her last night, and offer her that same lift. Because for those few moments, life was just like it used to be and I wanted her to stay there, sitting next to me, forever.

I didn't want it to end. And I don't understand how or why, but it almost feels like it hasn't. As if she's still with me somehow.

CHAPTER 42
PRESENT DAY

SHE CAN'T BELIEVE her eyes.

He's just walked out. The door opened, she glanced up from the vantage point she'd commandeered in a bus shelter opposite the entrance to the police station, and there he was. Walking – no, correction – strolling, from the police station door to the car park opposite as if he hadn't a care in the world.

Are they just letting him go? She keeps looking across at him, wildly. She's been sitting here for the last few hours, visualising the interview room, savouring the barrage of increasingly hostile questions that must now be being fired his way, imagining a cell door banging shut behind him. And then there'd just be him, alone with his thoughts and memories; nothing between him and the knowledge of all he's done.

But now he's outside, pausing by a car, talking to another man who looks to be around the same age, but at this distance she can't make out who he is. But she isn't interested in him anyway. The only person she's interested in should still be in the interview room facing that barrage of questions, or in the stinking cell, but he's not, he's there, out in the open air, quite clearly free to go.

Which is when a voice breaks in on her.

'Is everything all right?'

She jerks her head round to see a uniformed support officer eyeing her, curious. Flushing, she realises too late what a strange figure she must be cutting right now, standing outside the bus shelter, staring across the road towards the police station. She's been so careful up to now, concealing herself on the bench, as if she's just waiting for a bus, but she couldn't help it – the moment she saw Axel walking out like that she moved from the shelter and out onto the road and has been staring across at him ever since. No wonder she's attracted the wrong sort of attention.

'Yeah – sorry...'

The officer eyes her, growing more curious as she stammers to a halt, a uniformed companion some short distance away eyeing her now too.

'Can we help you at all?'

She pauses a moment longer, then looks back at him.

'Yeah. Yeah, maybe you can.'

And from nowhere, out it comes. She's been told the story herself by someone, or maybe she's read it somewhere, but she starts telling him all about this car crash she's seen. It wasn't anything too serious, but the police were still there in what seemed like seconds, and she watched as they took instant charge, moving from car to car, checking the occupants, making the vehicles safe, liaising with the paramedics who arrived a few moments later too. And it sounds crazy, she knows it does and she knows she's probably way past the age at which she could even be considered for something like this, but do the police ever have openings for someone like her? She's been dithering for the last few minutes over actually going in and making what she knows must sound like a mad request.

Meanwhile, over in the car park behind the two officers, she can see Axel getting into the car, preparing to drive away.

By her side the first uniformed support officer is smiling now as he tells her that it isn't crazy at all. A lot of officers have some similar story to tell, some moment they witnessed, or an incident they became involved in that kick-started their careers too. And now he takes out his phone to show her a website she can visit to find out more about becoming a support officer in the first instance, which could then lead to a full-time post if she wants to take it further. But by now, and even though she's careful to nod in all the right places, she's barely listening. All her attention is on the car approaching from the car park, watching as it pauses at a small junction before turning out onto the road. And as it does so, he looks across from the passenger seat and it's like a charge going through her as for a moment their eyes actually meet.

Does he recognise her? It's been so long, and she's changed, she knows she has, but at this moment, as they look at each other, does he feel that same charge too? Briefly, she half-expects him to reach out to the driver beside him, to stop the car, to get out and march back down the road towards her. But he doesn't. He just looks ahead as the car drives away, and she watches it until it turns a corner at the bottom of the hill with Axel still inside, still looking, so far as she can see, as if he hasn't a care in the world.

CHAPTER 43
TWENTY YEARS AGO

Sleep was always destined to be in short supply that night. But as my head finally hit the pillow after that hours-long drive from France, I had no idea how short it was to prove.

A loud banging on the door woke me from a slumber that felt like it had lasted just minutes. A bleary check on the alarm clock at the side of the bed confirmed that indeed it had. I went to the door and stared at two police officers standing outside. Within another half hour I was back in the bookshop, where all hell had broken loose.

Cara was tearful and Jericho just looked cowed, which only made her even more tearful as she gasped out a halting explanation.

'An alert came through on the house phone. Mum had diverted it to my mobile while she was away. It said, 'Unauthorised Entry'.'

I closed my eyes as I realised. It was the new alarm procedure. Any entry into or exit from the bookshop outside normal trading hours triggered an alert, which could be countermanded only by the keyholders – myself or Mark – cancelling the alarm. With all that happened after we returned from the Continent it was a procedure that had well and truly gone out of my mind.

'I called the police, then came down here to let them in, and then I heard a noise. I knew there were valuable books in here, and I just saw red.'

Cara, ever more wracked, looked across at Jericho, who just smiled reassuringly at her.

And all I could think was, he smiled. He actually smiled. If that had been me right now, and after everything he'd been through, I think I'd have given way completely.

———

Later that day, Jericho was still in custody. Paperwork applying to have him transferred into our temporary protective charge was being prepared to go before the court. News of the refugee in the bookshop had become a big local story, and now she knew more of that story, Cara was even more distraught at the official action she'd inadvertently provoked. Donna had returned from her trip with Harry, and a harassed Patrick, playing catch-up all the while, was telling us all he'd managed to find out so far.

'The Government's official policy regarding refugees is to encourage legal migration to the UK.'

I cut in. 'So that's good?'

He checked more print-outs in his hand.

'At the same time, the Home Secretary has just announced his commitment to reducing the number of asylum claims to fifty per cent of their previous level.'

I kept looking at him. 'In other words?'

'In other words, we're at the start of a difficult process here, Axel.'

Harry broke in.

'Not helped by the fact you effectively smuggled him illegally into the country.'

All I could see, once again, were Jericho's eyes and that one word whispered plea.

Please.

Donna raised an admonishing hand as Harry made to roll on. I had a feeling this was a conversation they'd had a number of times in the last few hours as they drove back from their seminar, a suspicion confirmed by my brother-in-law's body language making it only too clear that he wanted no part of this.

'Be careful, Axel. I've done two tours out in Iraq, and I've met a lot of young men like Jericho, and they all told stories.'

He headed for the door, a parting shot at me fired over his shoulder.

'Not all of them were true.'

CHAPTER 44
PRESENT DAY

CARA REACHES OUT TO ME, her fingers scrabbling for mine, but something's taking her away. I try to move closer, but it's as if some invisible weight is on my chest, and no matter how hard I try, I can't reach her. Her mouth opens into a silent scream as I yell her name, which is when I wake up, the echo of that one-word cry still sounding as I stare around at the four walls of the cottage's living room, coming up out of a sleep I thought was going to be impossible just a short time ago.

I heave myself to a sitting position and put my head in my hands. I've had similar nightmares before. They were a regular occurrence after Cara disappeared. Then I told Donna about them, and it was like igniting a flame. She became convinced those night-time visitations were actually from Cara herself, that she was trying to tell us something. Or that it was my subconscious trying to force out into the open something we'd missed. And from that moment on she tried to get me to reconstruct every detail of nightmares I just wanted to forget.

It was madness, of course. The same kind of madness to which we both succumbed back then. And now it's back, and it always ends the same way too, with that single cry waking me as it previously woke Donna, that same echo sounding around an otherwise empty room.

Suddenly I hear another sound too. A small click from the kitchen at the back of the cottage, as if someone's just opened the rear door. I stand, listening, but I can't hear anything else. Just the sound of waves rolling up the nearby beach, so I start to relax. Which is when I hear it again.

'Hello?' I call out instinctively, but there's no reply, of course. I've always watched, amused, whenever I see that happen in a film. If there is an intruder in the house, they're hardly like to call back with a cheery sounding greeting in turn. Just like I've always watched, equally amused, when I see the frightened householder pad around the property as they always seem to do, looking for whoever might have broken in. Why the hell don't they just get out of there or call the police?

But I do that now too. Maybe it's the same impulse that propelled me back into the shop in pursuit of Rory. I head into the small kitchen that leads off the living room and stare at the rear door, which is closed. There's no one standing by it either and the key's still on the inside. Then, suddenly, I turn back, hitting all the light switches as I go. I head out into the hall and pound up the stairs onto the now illuminated landing. I hare into the cottage's two bedrooms and the bathroom, but it's the same story every-where – no sign of anyone, and no evidence of anyone either, with nothing out of place and nothing disturbed.

Slowly, a lot more slowly now, I return downstairs, head back into the kitchen and fill a glass with water from the tap. Then I pause as I look again at the rear door, something about the angle of the key in the lock beginning to ring alarm bells. I cross over to it and press down on the handle and it gives way instantly, a cold blast of air assaulting me as I stand there, exposed in the open doorway.

Which is when, just for a second out in the darkness, I see what I think is a figure, looking back at me.

Then, the faint sound of someone running away.

CHAPTER 45
PRESENT DAY

'I WANT to see Detective Inspector Adams.'

The duty sergeant, a different duty sergeant from the one manning the front desk yesterday, takes my name and asks the nature of my business, then disappears into the bowels of a police station I was only too eager to escape from less than twenty-four hours ago.

And I haven't even told Patrick about this return visit, which is definitely going to earn me one of his trademark lectures about good practice and protocol. But the truth is I didn't know I was going to do this myself, until I got in my car some twenty minutes ago and acted on a decision I didn't even know I'd made.

An extract from a speech by Cicero, the famed Roman orator, swam through my mind on the drive over. Sometimes, Cicero said, if you find yourself with no way forward and no way back, then start a fight. Because it's only when the fight's underway and everything's in motion that you can even hope to see a way through it all.

'Something to say?'

A voice breaks in behind me, but it's not Adams, it's Braith, fixing me with her usual appraising stare. I shake my head, ignoring the loaded tone.

'Something to report.'

Then the door opens behind her, and Adams appears in turn.

———

Five minutes later we're back in the same interview room as before, and I'm telling them all about last night, that strange clicking sound I heard as if someone had forced a lock, my checking the house but finding nothing, but then realising the rear door wasn't secured and opening it.

'And you saw someone?'

'I think so.'

Both officers remain silent.

'I saw what looked like a figure at the bottom of the garden, watching me for a moment before running away.'

'Running in which direction?'

'Back towards the village.'

Suddenly, something strikes me. If that had been an intruder, that route would have taken them directly past Aidan's house, home not only to my closest neighbour but to his latest pit bull. Normally, anyone passing would provoke a cacophony of furious barks of protest from inside, but last night there was nothing.

'And was anything taken from your house?'

I wrench my attention back to the two officers.

'Not that I can see so far.'

'And do you have CCTV either at the front or the back of your house?'

'It's a quiet area, so I've never seen the need.'

Before Adams can say anything else, Braith takes over.

'But you felt the need to report this, even though nothing was taken, and you can't even be sure you saw someone?'

'Maybe after yesterday I thought I should play this by the book.'

'Meaning you didn't before?'

I take a quick, deep breath.

'I made a mistake before; I should have told that other officer that I'd seen Penny straightaway, not driven off like that. So, when this happened, I thought you should know about it as soon as possible.'

Adams cuts across, nodding at his still-clearly sceptical companion.

'Braith, could you raise a report? And give the nod to Barrett that we may have a potential burglary here. Get a couple of officers along to Mr Petersen's house to take a look round.'

Braith hesitates for a moment, aware she's being dismissed and clearly not liking it. But there's not much she can do about it, so she stands and exits, the door closing just that fraction too firmly behind her, leaving myself and Adams alone.

I look at him.

'She thinks I'm involved, doesn't she?'

He stares back at me. 'Involved?'

'Responsible? For whatever's happened to Penny?'

He hesitates a moment. 'She's young. Committed. Keen to clear up cases as quickly as possible.'

I keep staring at him, well aware he's just swerved that one.

'Do you think I'm responsible?'

But again, he doesn't answer directly. 'Braith doesn't like loose ends.'

'But they don't bother you?'

'Maybe I just don't show it as much.'

And suddenly, I come out with it, can't stop myself.

'Who is she? Penny? Where did she come from? Where does she live? You must have found out something about her by now.'

I don't even know I'm going to ask that until I do. Maybe Cicero knew something after all. Maybe it really is only when you're in the middle of something you can start to see some sort of way through.

'I can't tell you anything, I'm sorry.'

'Why not?'

'Because right now she's a missing person, making Penny

James and anything to do with her police business, and not yours.'

'Am I being set up here?'

Adams doesn't answer, so I carry on.

'I don't know what you think. About Cara. Whether I was involved in all that or not too.'

Adams just keeps his face poker still.

'But if anything has happened to Penny, then everyone's going to think it's finally happened, aren't they? Everything they believed about me will have just been confirmed. I was responsible for the disappearance of one young girl twenty years before, and now I'm responsible for another.'

I nod at him.

'And that'd be that. That oldest unsolved case of yours would be filed away with a great big tick on the front. I'd be locked away and they'd throw away the key. Two cases put to bed. And the truth, the real reason for my daughter's disappearance, would never come to light.'

Behind, the door opens and Braith returns, nods at me.

'An officer will be calling with you around eleven this morning.'

I don't reply. Adams doesn't even look at her. Once again, a silence develops. A silence that just grows and grows once more.

CHAPTER 46
PRESENT DAY

Mistakes and missteps.

Rory has made plenty of those over the previous twenty-four hours.

Yesterday, with the hood of his sweatshirt pulled low over his head to hide his face, Rory moved past an outsize sign showing a family splashing in a large pool filled with clear blue water, the sun shining brightly overhead. Moving further inside the run-down caravan park he passed the real-life pool, now emptied and choked with weeds, the tiles cracked and stained, while overhead the grey sky soaked him in a steady drizzle.

Rory fumbled in his pocket, touching Axel's phone as he did so, but he took out a key instead and attempted to fit it in the lock of the run-down caravan in front of him, surrounded by what seemed to be hundreds of similar sorts of units, most in the same state of sorry-looking disrepair. As he did so, he took a moment to look around. Maybe at some point in the year this place would be filled with happy families, but for now it just seemed to be occupied by people like himself. Shambling figures who snuck in and out, avoiding eye contact for the most part, determinedly uncurious as to who might be staying next door in case those neighbours became curious themselves. The perfect place to hide out, in other words. But it was the only part of this whole thing that was in any way perfect right now.

Briefly, the key failed to turn in the lock, and Rory felt a sudden frustration begin to build inside. For a moment he was tempted to dispense with the key altogether; the door was just flimsy plywood, he could drive his fist straight through it, but then he remembered what she said, that there was a technique to it, that he just had to jiggle the key in the lock a couple of times. He did, and the door swung open before him.

Rory moved inside and sat on the bed, which smelt damp, but he didn't even notice. He didn't see the thin skim of cracked plaster hanging from the ceiling or the mildew creeping up the walls either.

He was slipping back, and he knew it. Back into the darkness. He'd become almost adept lately at not staring down into the abyss that had claimed him so often before. Instead, he'd looked away from it, just like she told him to, because she'd been there too, she'd stared down into that same abyss, so she knew how it can reach out and drag you deep inside if you let it. But he hadn't let it, and it was down to her. To Penny. But she wasn't here now, and he could feel the darkness gathering again on all sides.

He stood suddenly, pacing. Why did he listen to her? Everything was wrong; that weird bookseller, the way he came back for him like that in that shop of his – and that scarf, just hanging there. Penny's scarf. What the hell was that all about? Was it some sort of sign? A signal? Was it supposed to tell him something? But if so, what?

Rory looked out of the grimy window as a dim illumination suddenly appeared. Floodlights, recently installed at the foot of the ruined castle across the estuary, had just been turned on, making the ancient ruin visible for miles around, but once again Rory hardly even registered it. He just reached into his pocket instead and brought out his own mobile – the second of the two burner phones they'd bought before Penny boarded that train –

made sure the battery was fully charged, then checked the time on the display.

One hour to go. One hour to the first contact, as they'd agreed. He just had to wait one more hour, ignore the gathering blackness, refuse to stare down into that abyss.

One more hour, then he would hear her voice and then everything would be fine.

CHAPTER 47
PRESENT DAY

A SHORT TIME LATER, and a few minutes before the officer is due to arrive, I'm home. I stopped off at a DIY store on the way back to pick up some deadbolts for the front and back doors, but they're still in their packaging and destined to remain there for now at least. I'm on my laptop instead.

I'm trying every combination I can think of. The name Penny James throws up a bewildering multitude of options, but even narrowing it down doesn't help much. I try restricting it by geography, try yoking that name with the name of all the nearest towns, then schools in those towns. I even type in the train service we both caught a couple of nights ago in case she booked a ticket online and some record of her might be traced that way, but there's nothing. All the social media sites offer myriad options, most with photographs, and I scrawl through them all, but none of the faces that stare back at me look remotely like the girl I'm seeking.

I'm about to close the laptop and unpack those deadbolts after all, when a sudden thought strikes me. Quickly, I access the photograph that was posted on social media of myself in that train carriage with the female guard standing over me and Penny sitting opposite, although you can only see the top of Penny's head and part of the side of her face. Clearly the only person that photographer was interested in was me. But some of Penny's things are on the table in front of her; a bottle of water, a magazine.

I freeze the image, then zoom in, spotting a pen and a notepad. Then I see a piece of paper next to the notepad, a single sheet torn from a jotting pad, a random selection of times, possibly train times, covering the page in a spidery scrawl.

But I'm not looking at that. I'm looking at the header on the notepad, which looks like the business name of a company, along with a phone number and address.

CHAPTER 48
PRESENT DAY

FOR THE WHOLE of the next hour, Rory paced the thin strip of beach outside the caravan park, each minute dragging by at what seemed a funereal pace. And at the end of it all he was no further on than he had been one hour previously, because there'd been no call. No contact at all.

Turning out onto the main road, he met a bus that slowed as he appeared from the holiday park. Later, he'd find out there were no stops on that out-of-the-way route. Passengers hailed the service as it passed by, boarding and disembarking where they pleased. The driver saw him, the doors opened, and almost on impulse he climbed on and took a seat.

A few moments later, he wished he'd just waved the bus on its way.

'Could you turn it down?'

Two young kids were behind him, no more than fifteen or so, music blaring from an iPhone held by one of them, neither wearing earphones. An old man across the aisle, dressed in a blazer and neatly pressed trousers, was looking at them, speaking for the whole bus from the expressions on the faces Rory could see all around.

'It is a little loud.'

Emboldened by his grinning friend beside him, the boy holding the phone just stared at the old man.

'Fuck off.'

Two girls, whom Rory hadn't registered up to then, started laughing from the seats opposite as the old man hesitated, then turned back to the window. Rory looked at the grinning boy, not seeing the two girls, not seeing the other boy now grinning even wider. All Rory could see was the abyss again, and the next second the two girls started screaming as Rory suddenly put the boy in a headlock.

'What the fuck?'

His companion stared open-mouthed as Rory used his free hand to grab the offending iPhone and fling it out of an open window to their side. All the time he maintained his iron grip on the boy's windpipe. The choking and now-terrified boy began to piss himself at the same time as the alarmed driver slammed on the brakes, the bus juddering to a protesting halt.

'What's going on back there?'

Rory looked at the frightened girls, at the staring bus driver now standing in his seat, at the cowed boy sitting next to his still-choking friend.

What was he doing?

What the fuck was he doing?

Rory rose, stumbled down the aisle, exiting the stalled bus via the opened door a moment later. Immediately, he struck out across a neighbouring field, and within moments the bus, the driver, the girls, the boy he attacked and his friend were lost from view. He stayed where he was, hidden for a few moments longer, trying to control his breathing.

Finally, beginning to calm a little at least, Rory took out Axel's phone and opened Google Maps. He typed in an address and a route appeared from Rory's present location to Axel's home. He tried accessing some 3D shots of the same destination using Google Maps, but nothing was available. Maybe the house didn't border any sort of road and the car with the roof-mounted camera couldn't get close enough, but he could, and he did, later that night – which turned out to be another mistake. Another misstep.

Rory had no idea if Axel had caught sight of him as he'd turned and exited back along the small path that skirted the beach, which was thankfully deserted at that time of night. But if he had then it would be doubly galling, as the whole visit had proved a complete waste of time. He'd managed to hide inside the cottage on hearing Axel return home, but by then he'd already established all he needed to know. Wherever Penny was right now, she wasn't there, and there was no trace of her there either. He still had no idea why her scarf would be hanging up in one of those tunnels in Axel's shop. But it was the only connection to Penny he had actually spotted since she embarked on what he was increasingly convinced was this fool's mission. Thankfully it wasn't that difficult getting out, as Axel had fallen asleep within moments of his return.

Thankfully too, his cottage wasn't the end of Rory's search, more like the beginning, and in that respect the phone he'd stolen was proving a virtual treasure trove, giving him access to all Axel's friends, business acquaintances and remaining family members, including his ex-wife. And the more Rory looked at the entry for Donna, the more he wondered.

Maybe it was because he was on the trail of a bookseller. Even though he wasn't much of a reader himself, a long-forgotten story floated through his mind, a hard-boiled detective tale from the 1940s, which had then been turned into a Hollywood movie. In the edition of the book he'd read years before, the author had written an introduction in the form of a letter to a friend. He'd wanted to write a story, he'd said, in which a couple plan and commit the perfect murder. But then what? They'd find that the world wasn't big enough for two people who share such a secret and would turn on each other.

Which was when Rory had done some long, hard thinking. Axel's marriage had fallen apart within a couple of years of their daughter's disappearance. So, was that what happened to them?

Had they found that the world simply wasn't big enough for the secret they shared, and had they fallen on each other too? If that was right, then he really was about to walk into a lion's den, but he had no choice. He now had to try and find out the truth behind that disappearance, to discover the truth about another.

Rory closed down Axel's phone. Only one thing mattered now and that was moving on, and so he did, to Axel's former wife.

Which turned out to be yet another misstep.

Another mistake.

CHAPTER 49
TWENTY YEARS AGO

JERICHO SPENT JUST over a week in custody. Following his release, practical matters prevailed. Most immediately, while the asylum process ground into what passed for action, the question of where he would actually live had to be sorted out, although the answer was clear from the start.

From the moment he was released, Jericho had patrolled the tunnels leading off from the main reception area of the bookshop with much the same look on his face as Cara all those years before. He might have mumbled something about being able to clean and look after the place – and how being surrounded by all these books would help his English too – but the real reason he wanted to be there was obvious. As well as finding a form of personal salvation, courtesy of his ride in the boot of an antiquarian and secondhand bookseller's car, he clearly felt as if he'd also landed in Neverland when he arrived in my bookshop. So, a travel bed was brought in from our house, which could be unfolded at night and packed away in the morning, and – shades of tumbleweeds shaking down at the rather more famous Shakespeare and Company in Paris – the bookshop acquired an unlikely lodger.

But there was a curious cloud hanging over Jericho from the

moment he arrived in what became his adopted home, and it wasn't the upcoming asylum process, his ongoing separation from a family he clearly missed acutely, or a brother whose whereabouts remained unknown. There was something else and as the days ticked by that cloud only seemed to darken. Donna and I were careful not to intrude too much, but after another few days Cara ploughed in, and within an hour or so she'd uncovered the problem.

It was all to do, so it seemed, with a leaf.

CHAPTER 50
PRESENT DAY

FOUR HOURS LATER, and having endured the cursory attention of the officer from the burglary team, who clearly regarded this house call as a complete waste of time, I've just arrived in a small market town some hundred or so miles to the east.

Sitting on the car seat next to me is a slim volume I picked up some few weeks ago. I selected it partly because of the title, which seemed curiously appropriate given all I now have in mind. It is a copy of Rainer Maria Rilke's *Letters to a Young Woman*, translated by K.W. Maurer, a first edition, first impression. The collection is arranged in much the same way as Maurer's earlier translation, *Letters to a Young Poet*, drawing a few choice letters from Rilke's plenitude of correspondence, in this case written between August 1919 and February 1924.

But it wasn't just the title that guided my hand. A manuscript note, laid in loose, stated that this volume was 'Sent by K. Maurer with his good wishes. Evelyn Cottage, Lakes Lane, Beaconsfield'. Alongside that, I've slid in another insert that was not added by the redoubtable translator, a printout of the headed notepaper, cropped and culled from the image snapped, perhaps unwittingly, by that still-unknown photographer on the train.

The market town in question is one I know well. It's a genteel enclave set amongst rolling hills, home to a largely ageing and affluent population. Before we settled in the far west of the country, I briefly considered it as a home for my bookshop. Footfall is always going to be greater in a town closer to the English border, but I knew even then that any bibliophiles among that ageing and affluent population wouldn't let even a hundred-mile journey dissuade them from making the trip over to my shop if they wished, and so it's proved. I've greeted many visitors from this part of the world over the years.

This town is also home to an animal rescue charity called, perhaps hopefully, *No Tears*. And it's their name and their address on that torn off sheet of paper. I have no idea if Penny just picked up that stray jotter from somewhere, or if she has any connection to them. I have no idea, in short, whether this is going to be a monumental waste of time, but the lead, such as it is, is all I have, so I have no choice.

As I walk in, a young man behind a counter looks up from a laptop with a practised smile, that practised smile fading a little as I open my bag and bring out the Rilke volume. I can't blame him. A small cat, dog or hamster would probably be the exhibit most callers produce when walking in. I can see him already wondering if one of the surrounding local villages has just delivered to his door one of their resident idiots.

I smile, apologetic.

'This is going to sound strange, I know, but I own a bookshop.'

I lay the Rilke volume down on the counter.

'A young woman came in a day or so ago and picked this up along with a couple of other titles. I don't know how it happened, but she left this one behind. I don't have any details for her, not even her name – she paid in cash – but when I looked, she'd left this inside.'

I show him the name of the charity on the scrap of paper annotated with the train times.

'I was passing through so I thought I'd check if she might work here, and I could let her have it back? Or if she doesn't work here, then maybe she brought an animal in or something and you might still know her?'

The young man nods, seemingly eager now to help.

'What did she look like?'

I hesitate.

'Actually, I have a picture. We have CCTV in the shop.

I show him that cropped photo of Penny from the train, still little more than a close-up of her bent head and the side of her face, but the young man recognises her immediately.

'That's one of our volunteers.'

I feel a charge of excitement course through me.

'But she's not here now. I don't know when she'll be back either. She told us a couple of weeks ago she'd had a bereavement in the family. We haven't seen her since.'

'Could you contact her for me? Call her maybe, tell her I've got her book?'

'I wouldn't know how.'

I stare at the now-apologetic young man.

'She turned up here about a month ago, asking if she could help out. I don't think she ever told us where she lived.'

He smiles, helpless.

'To be honest, we were just glad of the help.'

———

Ten minutes later I'm outside a local Chapel of Rest, the nearest one to the rescue centre. It's a long shot, again, but – and again – it's all I have. If Penny's family have suffered a bereavement, then maybe this funeral director is handling the arrangements and maybe they can tell me more about her.

A hearse stands outside, a few mourners milling around. Four pallbearers are carrying a coffin from a side door and are placing it carefully inside, the side door to the Chapel open behind them. I slip inside, unnoticed, and look round. Then I still as I see a photograph on top of another coffin. The photo is of a girl smiling out at the camera. An inscription underneath gives the date of her death, which is two weeks ago.

And it's her.

It's the girl I saw on the train two nights ago.

It's Penny.

CHAPTER 51
TWENTY YEARS AGO

DESIGNED by the renowned architect Norman Foster, the largest single span glasshouse in the world squats on the West Walian landscape like a giant spaceship dropped down from the skies.

The Great Glasshouse, as it's called, houses some of the most endangered plants on the planet – refugees, in a sense, from California, Australia, the Canary Islands, Chile, South Africa and the Mediterranean Basin. And now the Great Glasshouse was playing host to a human refugee too.

Back in the bookshop, the relationship between them clearly building all the while, Jericho had been telling Cara more of his story.

'After getting out of the forest we managed to find our way to a basement in Subotica. Over forty other refugees were already there.'

He paused, images clearly flooding back.

'It was dark – there was a lightbulb, but it was broken. And there was a portable toilet in the corner, but it was already overflowing.'

Jericho paused again, then rolled on.

'But then, after about a day and a half, the door opened, and this man came in with bread and cans of chickpeas. He told us dinghies were being prepared. A few hours later, we joined around two hundred others on the bank of a nearby river. The weather was bad and the river was in full flood, but we still had to cross – it was then or never. The first dinghy was packed with women and children, and it put into the water. We heard a cry from the other side of the darkness as it disappeared. Then nothing.'

Sitting opposite him in the rare books room, Cara just stared at the young boy as he re-lived every moment of an experience he'd never wanted to live in the first place.

'Then, finally, it was our turn. We had no idea if any of the other dinghies had made it across, but we set off anyway. Then something hit us. I didn't know what it was, but Omar was knocked into the water. I managed to grab his arm and he held onto me as I held onto the dinghy, but a few minutes later the whole thing capsized. I don't know how, maybe we were closer than we thought, but we hung onto each other and managed to wade ashore.'

Jericho took a deep, steadying breath.

'We walked for twenty-four hours through more woods, then we reached a checkpoint where soldiers with shields and truncheons were beating people back behind barbed wire. We waited till nightfall, then cut through the wire and we were in Hungary. From there we walked to Austria and hid on a Germany-bound train. Everything was fine for a while until, on one of the stops, we got off to exercise for a few minutes.'

Jericho paused again, really struggling now.

'That's where we found the leaf.'

He took another deep breath.

'A few minutes later the police arrived. We got back on the train the minute we saw them, but they did a search of the carriages and found us. They ordered us to go with them. As we got off, Omar suddenly began to run. I followed. We lost the police, but I lost him.'

Then he fell silent.

The leaf Jericho was talking about was from the Snow Tree. It was pure white and velvety to the touch. It was Jericho and his brother's custom to pick a leaf each from a native tree as a souvenir of the different places they passed through, a way of marking their passage as well as taking something of those different countries with them as they journeyed on to the next. But if they were ever separated, the leaves from those trees would also become a symbol, a promise. One day they'd be together again, and the leaves would be reunited as well.

But during his journey west, Jericho had lost them all, including the last one he and Omar had picked together, and of all the misfortunes and setbacks that had befallen him on his various trips, this one was really playing on his mind.

'Draw it.'

Cara handed him some paper and pencils.

'Close your eyes. Try and remember what it looked like. Then draw it.'

Jericho hesitated a moment, then nodded and bent to his task.

Cara studied the leaf once he'd finished, a dim association stirring. Then, that dim association solidifying all the while, she opened her laptop. A few clicks and she'd found it.

Cara grabbed Jericho's hand and they exited the bookshop. She couldn't return him to that exact same tree. But she could show him something pretty close.

Half an hour later they were walking up the steep slope to the Great Glasshouse, dodging a winding waterway that cascaded down to the entrance. Once inside it was a matter of moments to locate the Pyrus nivalis, more commonly known as the Snow Tree.

Jericho stared at a tree he'd last seen hundreds of miles away in a different country, when he was living a very different life. Cara told him to take a leaf from it to replace the one he'd lost, but he wouldn't even think of it, not without permission. So, Cara called a supervisor and Jericho re-told his story.

Long before he'd finished, the supervisor reached out and

clipped a leaf from the tree herself and presented it to the young man standing by its side. As she told him, smiling all the while, she really didn't think they'd miss just the one.

CHAPTER 52
PRESENT DAY

IT'S GOING to be only his second funeral in the short time he's been working for the company. On the first, three days ago, Luke was told just to stand and watch. Don't talk to anyone, just stay by the coffin with the rest of the pallbearers and try and blend into the background. It's one of the most important qualities in his new line of work, apparently. The ability to become invisible.

When required, he has to help too, of course, but if the mourners leave at the end of the committal and haven't even been aware he's there then that's his job well done. Quiet dignity at all times; allowing the mourners their much-needed moments of reflection and contemplation as well as ushering the dearly departed on their way in the most fitting manner possible. And Luke managed to do both at his first funeral. This second one is proving a little different.

'You've got this wrong.'

Luke stares at the wild-eyed figure who's suddenly dashed into the reception area, following his gesture back towards a coffin, although not today's coffin, in the nearby Chapel of Rest. A photo adorns it, that of a girl not much older than himself. He had quite a shock on seeing her. He still thinks of funerals as the preserve of people like his gran, who they buried last year, taking her place alongside a grandad he'd never known. But that was nothing compared to the shock he's seeing on this man's face.

'There's been a mistake.'

His boss, the actual funeral director, a man he's barely exchanged more than two words with up to now, approaches. They're due to head away in a minute or so; today's coffin is waiting in the hearse.

'Sir, please, can you just calm down?'

The funeral director raises a gentle hand, a pacifying gesture, all part of that quiet dignity again. Luke has been told that an excess of emotion can occasionally boil over, particularly with early deaths. It's another of the lessons that have been drummed into him. Grief is understandable. It would indeed be odd if there wasn't any. But any sort of hysterical outpouring is something very much to be discouraged.

'I'm telling you, you've made a mistake.'

The funeral director is still holding up his palm in the same pacifying gesture.

'This is impossible. I saw her myself, two nights ago.'

Now all eyes, not just Luke's and the funeral director's, but those of the other pallbearers as well, are staring at him in blank bemusement.

'She was on a train. I talked to her, there are witnesses.'

This second funeral of Luke's is fast turning into the exact opposite of a sombre send-off marked with quiet dignity. But still the wild-eyed man just stands there. And if all that has happened up to now really was seriously strange, what happens next takes it into a different league altogether.

'Open the coffin.'

The funeral director is robbed of words, and the man continues.

'This is a trick, some kind of sick trick. Ask the police. They'll tell you themselves, they're looking for her. They took me in, questioned me – they thought I might have done something to her, they thought I might have attacked or abducted her.'

Slowly, perhaps beginning to fear for their own safety now, everyone begins to sidle away. This character is becoming more deranged by the moment. The funeral director, beginning to lose patience, signals to a couple of the pallbearers, who move forward to escort him outside, but the man lashes out with a hand and catches one of them full in the face. As he hits the ground, another pallbearer steps in smartly and before the wild-eyed man can hit him too, he crashes him back against the side of the hearse, the man's head hitting the door, a thin splatter of blood staining one of the recently polished windows.

CHAPTER 53
TWENTY YEARS AGO

JUST OVER A WEEK after his visit to the Great Glasshouse, Jericho was standing in front of a large bowl of tabbouleh stacked at one end of a trestle table. Next to it was a plate piled high with dolma. In between were individual portions of sfiha and another plate of kubba. The sun was high in the sky, the aromas were wafting down the High Street and, just for an hour or so, one small part of the west of Wales had turned into an enclave of Baghdad.

And the expression on Jericho's face said it all. He was loving it. So was Cara, who was helping him. The expressions on the faces of the well-fed passers-by said it all. They were loving it too.

Jericho was splitting the proceeds of his new street food pop-up fifty-fifty with the owner of the café whose premises he was camped outside and whose kitchen he was using, although Cara already had a shrewd suspicion the café owner wasn't actually going to accept a single penny. The whole lot would be going into what he'd already confided in Cara was the Omar fund. A war chest set up by Jericho to find and bring his brother over to the UK to begin his new life here too, although not necessarily in a bookshop.

'A car wash?'

Cara looked at him as Jericho nodded, loading more sfihas

onto yet more plates, hungry customers in a line to her side, all waiting to be served.

'The one at the other end of town. I started last night.'

Cara stared at an energised Jericho.

'I'm doing six shifts a week. Unofficial of course, all cash, no records. But as one of our first customers was one of the police officers who arrested me, and he gave me a tip on top for making such a good job of his wheels, I don't think that's going to be such a problem.'

Cara burst out laughing, she couldn't help herself; Jericho's enthusiasm, his sheer zest for life right now was so infectious. So appealing. So seductive too, in a sense.

But then she paused.

'You can't work all the time though.'

Jericho paused too, perhaps picking up an odd inflection in her voice.

'There's a party on in the school soon. A dance. Come along if you want.'

Jericho stole an uncertain glance across the road towards the bookshop.

'And Mark?'

Cara nodded, bright, maybe too brightly.

'He's coming too.'

Jericho hesitated, then smiled. Cara smiled back. But as he moved on to hand out more plates of sfiha to the people waiting in line, she stilled.

Because she suddenly had the sense that someone was watching her.

CHAPTER 54
PRESENT DAY

FOR A FEW MOMENTS I've no idea where I am or what I'm doing.

Everything fades.

Sight and sound.

Suddenly I'm in the middle of an arid landscape where everything is grey, the earth beneath my feet, the sky above and around me. I can see stray trees in the distance, but their trunks are grey too and there's no contrasting colour from the leaves I can see hanging from their thin branches. It's like a half-way house of a world, just about recognisable as one I once knew, but blasted somehow, as if some massive explosion has taken place and robbed it of all life.

Dim details swim back before my eyes, details that also now seem from another world. That Chapel of Rest, the photo, those bewildered faces staring back at me. But then they fade as if I'm leaving them behind as I travel somewhere, or maybe they've taken some collective decision to leave me. I don't know, and it doesn't matter. Because suddenly, I'm seeing something else.

It's just a shape at first, and for a moment it looks like any of the other dim shapes I can see all around; an entity with no real outline or form. But then the shape comes closer, and an outline does begin to form. Then, suddenly, I can't breathe. And that's not because the air's been sucked from a world that isn't my world anyway, it's because I'm looking once again at my daughter.

Cara stands no more than a few metres away from me once more. If I reach out, I can touch her. But I don't, maybe because I'm afraid to break what has to be some sort of spell. Then she moves closer, and now I see her more clearly; I see that it's not Cara as I last saw her, not the girl in her late teens who walked out of our house one totally ordinary day, turning that totally ordinary day into the nightmare we've been living in ever since. This Cara is older, and her hair is shorter; there are lines on her face that weren't there before. If someone had used one of those artificially ageing computer programs the police sometimes use in their appeals for missing persons, then this is how she might look.

I stand there, staring, a million questions frozen on my tongue, but no words come out of my mouth. I'm a statue staring at a ghost from another world and time, but this is no ghost; this is my daughter returned to me, a vision I've seen in dreams a million times since she vanished, a vision now made flesh.

Then she starts to speak. She opens her mouth, but it's as if the words are too heavy for the air between us to support them. I shake my head, trying to tell her to come closer, but she starts to move away instead, or maybe I'm moving away. Whatever's happening, some invisible barrier's interceding, lengthening the distance between us all the while.

But I can see it in her eyes. There's something she's desperately trying to say to me, and it's something I desperately need to hear. There's a message in those staring eyes that I can't decipher but I have to. I have to know what she's saying, but she's moving further away all the time. Finally, I manage to force out one word, then two, then a few more. But the grey is now enveloping her again; she's returning to the dim shape I saw when I first came round, fading back into nothingness, and even though I keep yelling after her, within another moment she's gone.

And I'm left behind in this world that's no world at all. A world that should never be permitted to exist.

CHAPTER 55
TWENTY YEARS AGO

THE AROMA from the Iraqi delicacies followed Cara all the way across the road to the bookshop. All the time she was looking round. She still had the same sense that someone was watching her, but who? And why?

As she drew closer, she saw the 'Closed' sign on the door. A handwritten note underneath informed any prospective callers that the shop would be open again in ten minutes. Cara turned back, stilling again as she saw Mark now at the makeshift pop-up across the road, laughing and joking with Jericho, so whoever was responsible for this strange, uneasy sensation of hers it wasn't him.

Cara turned back again, which was when she caught – or thought she caught – a glimpse of some sudden movement in the car park at the rear. She hesitated again, then made her way over there. As she did so, she heard an engine suddenly fire into life. Moving quickly, she headed into the car park itself, only to press herself back against the wall as a vehicle roared past at speed. Disorientated, Cara took a moment to regain her breath, then stared after it as the vehicle disappeared around a bend in the road ahead.

She kept staring after the vehicle long after it vanished from view. She didn't catch sight of the driver; it had sped towards her too fast for that, and she'd been more concerned to get out of its way. But as it turned that corner at the end of the street it slowed momentarily, and it looked like it might have been some sort of Jeep.

Cara remained there for a moment longer, no longer feeling as if someone was watching her. That strange sensation vanished the moment that vehicle disappeared.

There was only one person she knew who drove a vehicle like that, but that made no sense. Why would her Uncle Harry have been watching her?

And, if that was him, why would he drive off at high speed like that the moment she made her approach?

CHAPTER 56
PRESENT DAY

SHE DOESN'T HAVE a lot to be thankful for. The last twenty years or so have brought little in the way of conventional blessings to her life. But she's had one stroke of good fortune.

After the perhaps-inevitable break-up of the marriage, the old family home has been retained. It's the one reassuring certainty in what has become a sea of shifting sands. The one place to which she can return, after a fashion anyway, and still feel as if she belongs.

Obviously, she can never visit in any physical sense; that would very much be a step too far. But in this day and age there are all sorts of ways to visit remotely, and every time she does, she feels a peace that otherwise very definitely eludes her. Because when she does watch or listen in from a distance, sometimes a great distance, she can hear and see all the old familiar sights and sounds again.

She listens to the way the wind swirls and eddies around the rear of the house once more, blowing leaves into the alcove that leads to the rear door, ripples layering on ripples.

She listens to the way the wooden floor from the bedroom to the kitchen creaks as it always did when someone walked along it.

She listens to the strange clicks the central heating always used to make when it switched off for the night, as if it was settling to sleep.

And she listens to the distant sound of the sea as it softly permeates from the other side of those thick stone walls.

It's comforting. As if nothing has changed, even though she knows that everything has changed.

But for those few moments, she can pretend at least.

CHAPTER 57
TWENTY YEARS AGO

TAMERLANE ARRIVED ON A THURSDAY. The courier company that delivered it was one that dealt with a whole variety of antiquarian and secondhand booksellers the world over. They were discreet and they were secure, and so they proved again. *Tamerlane* arrived in perfect condition and was then locked in the safe in the house, although not before I permitted myself the liberty of reading it for an hour or so.

Books had never just been commodities so far as I was concerned, something simply to be traded. And I hoped I'd never get used to the thrill of holding one of the earliest editions of a great author's work.

I spent most of the next day, Friday, in the bookshop, fielding enquiries and sifting bids. By the afternoon, I'd agreed a provisional sale to a collector in Madrid, subject to a photographic inspection. I returned to the house to start assembling the necessary images to forward to him online.

It sounds fanciful, I know, but somehow, even just approaching the safe, I knew something was wrong. Everything looked the same. But something was still wrong.

I bent to the safe, took hold of the circular key lock and

inputted the code. The safe door swung open, and I stared inside at a space where *Tamerlane* had once been.

A fifty-five-thousand-pound space where *Tamerlane* had once been.

PART THREE

PART THREE

CHAPTER 58
PRESENT DAY

FROM ACROSS THE FIELDS, Adams watches a school hockey match. Shouts, yells and laughter float across to him, and for a moment he just stands there, rooted, because all he can see is his own daughter on that same patch of grass years ago, playing with friends in a similar match, him cheering her on from the sidelines.

He's become accustomed over the years to steeling himself against moments like these, to choking off associations, but there's always something that manages to ambush him. But maybe it's this case, the disappearance of Penny James. It's definitely bringing back deafening echoes of the Cara case from all those years ago. For another moment, an all too dangerous moment, he feels it start to overwhelm him again, but then he straightens up, banishing memories he doesn't dare re-live. Time to get back to work.

Adams strides down a small track towards Braith, who's been liaising with a couple of uniformed officers.

'Who called it in?'

'A fisherman.' Braith pauses. 'Loose description.'

Adams nods, picking up the qualification immediately. A poacher, in other words.

'There was a storm last night. At the moment they're working on the basis that the extra water flowing into the estuary might have dislodged it.'

Adams stares at her, quizzical.

'It?'

'He couldn't tell us the sex.'

Adams looks out across the fields again. One of the girls from the hockey match has moved closer to retrieve a stray ball and is pausing as she takes in the police activity a few hundred or so metres away. Up on the lane other passers-by have probably also seen the uniformed officers standing by the cordon of police tape. There might be no media interest yet, but it isn't going to stay that way for long with the combination of inquisitive schoolkids, stray walkers and a probably voluble fisherman/poacher, about to give it large in some local pub somewhere about this discovery of inde-terminate sex.

Adams looks towards a crime tent, erected behind different coloured tape, red and black this time. The tent's flap is pinned open, but he can't see inside. A series of metal plates tracks a circuitous route up to the tent itself. No one at this early stage wants to risk spoiling any evidence.

Taking the path marked out by the metal plates, Adams approaches the tent just as Maya Judt emerges, the pathologist and a woman he's worked with before. Maya hasn't been in her new post long enough to develop the world-weary cynicism or heavy-handed humour adopted by her older and almost exclu-sively male companions, for which relief he's always muttered grateful thanks.

Behind her, Adams can now see the largely disarticulated skeleton, and he stills as he always does at the sight. He's seen lots of dead bodies in his time, all in varying states of decomposition, but skeletons always hit him hard. They just feel anonymous somehow, a collection of bones that could belong to anyone. Whoever committed these murders seemed to have robbed their victims not only of their lives, but of all their individuality too.

'Victim has been dead for at least ten years and probably longer.'

Maya plunges in straight away, exhibiting none of the habitual caution adopted by her male colleagues either. She tells people exactly what she knows exactly when she knows it, another refreshing deviation from a well-worn norm.

'We'd have expected total decomposition in that time, and while we have to carry out tests on the soil, my guess is that there's a high concentration of lime around these parts and that's slowed things down in this case.'

But Adams is looking at Braith, who is looking back at him, the same thought in both their minds.

At least ten years and maybe more?

'Male or female?'

'Depends on the age. This victim is of slight build so it's possible we could be looking at a girl, but if we're looking at a very young girl, then the changes to the bone structure that differentiate the sexes wouldn't have taken place.'

Maya pauses.

'But if the victim's in his or her teens, then we may be able to identify the sex based on changes to the pelvis. We'll know more when we get to the lab.'

Braith cuts in.

'There are no clothes. Does that mean the victim was naked when they were buried or have the clothes just decomposed?'

'Depends on the material. Cotton would have perished in that time, but if he or she was wearing wool, for example, there'd still have been traces. But my best guess for now is that this body was stripped bare prior to burial.'

Maya nods through the open flap.

'I can tell you one thing though.'

Adams, reluctantly, looks towards the skeleton again.

'There's a jagged break between the bones in the neck that form the cervical vertebrae. My other best guess for now is that this poor soul suffered a heavy blow to the throat, and a savage blow with a sharp object, to cause that kind of injury.'

Adams nods, more pictures he really does not want to see right now flashing before his eyes, and he steps in, as much to dispel them as anything else.

'If we can provide you with a DNA sample, how quickly could you establish a possible match?'

Maya looks at him, taken aback. Usually, these sorts of cases work the other way round. She provides the DNA and then a trawl begins through various databases.

'Pretty quickly. A day or so, maybe.'

Adams and Braith exchange glances again. At this stage they don't know anything for sure. They don't know if this is the skeleton of a man or a woman or a boy or a girl. They don't know how old it was or exactly how long it has been dead. But this body surfacing, at virtually the same time as another old cold case has resurfaced, albeit in a different way, is already ringing all sorts of bells.

Have they just stumbled across the remains of Cara Petersen?

CHAPTER 59
TWENTY YEARS AGO

THE POLICE WERE CALLED IMMEDIATELY. They quickly established what I knew already because I'd checked all the doors and windows. There was no sign of a forced entry, and no sign of anyone having tampered with the safe either. So, whoever had opened it must have used the code.

Working through the house carefully and methodically, the scenes of crime officers dusted each room for prints, having first taken all our prints for the purpose of elimination. All of us were asked who might have access to the house aside from the three of us and we all gave the same answer. No one. There was absolutely no reason for anyone aside from the immediate family to access the property or to have a key. None of the neighbours had ever been given a spare for any reason, and there was no way in which anyone, immediate family aside, would have been able to even get close to the safe.

But someone had accessed it. At the very moment it was playing host to the most valuable volume I'd ever acquired. It was insured of course, but that wasn't the point. Who could have – would have – done this?

Half an hour later, the chief scenes of crime officer called me into the sitting room. Cara and Donna were out on the beach by then. None of us really wanted to stay in the house while this exhaustive trawl through our home and our belongings was taking place, but the police had asked for one person from the household to be present at all times.

The officer nodded at a book and a framed photo, both on the same side table. They'd found sets of prints on both, prints that didn't belong to me, or to Donna or Cara.

So, who did they belong to?

CHAPTER 60
PRESENT DAY

THE TWO UNIFORMED constables are puzzled, and Donna can't blame them. She's pretty mystified herself.

Donna came round after that encounter with the balaclava-clad man in her house to find two paramedics standing over her. She was still in the sitting room of her home, lying on the floor. For a moment she was about to lash out at them, believing they were intruders – until she remembered the actual intruder. The man in the balaclava. The last person she'd seen before the darkness descended.

Twenty minutes later she was in the local A & E, a young doctor confirming what she already knew, now her wits had slowly begun to return. She hadn't had one for years, but the shock of seeing the intruder, as well as her doomed attempt to force him from her house courtesy of that hurled iPhone, had brought on an asthma attack. She'd had a few in the years since Cara disappeared, although they'd become rarer. But a couple of hours ago she'd had another attack, and it had been a big one too.

It seemed that her intruder had realised that. Because when the paramedics gained entry to her house after an anonymous report of a women in distress, entry they'd gained by a conveniently open door, they'd found her in the recovery position. As intruders go, as the lead paramedic had remarked to his companion, this one had to have been one of the more considerate.

Once they arrived at the hospital, it had been a familiar procedure. Donna was administered Albuterol, the short-acting beta agonist she'd been treated with before. It was the same medication the paramedics had used back in the house with a quick-acting rescue inhaler. The attack wasn't life-threatening, so she didn't need a breathing tube, as she had needed on occasions in the past when help hadn't been summoned quite as promptly and oxygen had to be pumped into her lungs. The attending doctor had simply admitted her to the nearby emergency room to make sure everything was under control. Then the two uniformed police constables called in on her.

One of the constables, a young man with a full beard, perhaps trying to make himself look older than he actually was, tells her that the intruder seems to have caused no damage on his way in or out of the property and that, so far as they could see, nothing appears to have been taken. Her iPhone is still on the sitting room floor. Her computer has been left untouched. The TV and the music system are still there too. Some small amount of cash left lying on the kitchen table – in full view of one of the kitchen windows, the young constable with the full beard gently chides – has also been left untouched. That could be down to the intruder panicking, following her discovery of him, but as he seems to have put her in the recovery position and summoned the emergency services for help, that doesn't exactly add up.

After making her initial statement, Donna falls silent. The truth is she simply doesn't know what to make of all this, and the constables exchange a look as her silence continues, a look that says it all. Has she simply imagined all this in her asthma-induced state of collapse? Has anyone even been in the house at all? Has she hallucinated some intruder in a balaclava who apparently levitated himself inside and then wafted himself out again, leaving not a single trace? By now Donna is almost beginning to wonder herself.

At this point, the two uniformed constables clearly decide they've had enough. They tell her that a detective from CID will be in touch to investigate further and to do a thorough sweep for fingerprints and DNA. A few hours later, the doctor returns to check on her and finally confirms she's ready to go. Donna walks outside to wait in the reception area. Harry has already been in touch and offered to drive her home.

Which is when, for the second time, a figure appears in front of her, but it isn't an intruder this time.

This is someone else.

CHAPTER 61
PRESENT DAY

A TASER WASN'T USED to subdue me on this occasion, making treatment a lot simpler. A dressing to my head wound in the nearest hospital to the Chapel of Rest, a quick check on my blood pressure and I was told I was free to go, albeit with a firm instruction that I have the dressing changed in my local outpatients on my arrival home.

A few hours later I walk away from that second treatment room, another nurse's kindly meant exhortations to take things easy for the next week or so ringing in my ears.

Which is when I stop dead as I see the small, slight figure of my ex-wife waiting in the corridor ahead of me.

———

Half an hour later, we're back home. Or at least, we're back in Donna's home. It wasn't my choice. Harry drove us here. I could have asked to be dropped off at the cottage, I suppose, but we have a lot to talk about.

I look around as we head inside. It must be ten years since I've actually been here. Any meetings since the divorce have taken place on what the lawyers called neutral territory. But that isn't the only reason I've avoided the place.

The simple act of walking back into our old family home proved excruciating in the weeks and months after Cara's disappearance. It was one of the clearest examples of how that terrible event both scarred and differentiated the two of us. I literally couldn't stand to be in the place. All I could see, everywhere I looked, was our daughter. All I heard in the new and strange silence left behind by her absence was the sound of her voice. But Donna was the opposite. She couldn't bear to be away. She took intense comfort in the constant reminders of Cara's presence where I could take none.

We seat ourselves in the small kitchen at the rear of the house, and I try to avoid looking at the different photos of our daughter that still decorate the walls. Taking a deep breath, I plunge straight in, telling them all about the crazy last couple of days, beginning with what I'd believed to be a simple misunderstanding on a homeward bound train, but which had turned into something that was anything but simple. As well as so much more than a misunderstanding.

'The man, the young man who pulled the knife on you, made you drive to the shop...'

I nod as Donna tails off, the same thought in my mind as hers.

'Rory. It had to be him who was here too.'

'But why? What was he looking for? What does he want?'

'He's looking for Penny.'

'And he thought he'd find her here?'

'Or maybe some clue as to where she is.'

Donna just stares at me, as does Harry, both looking every bit as bewildered as I am right now, but what can I say? How to explain what's fast become the totally inexplicable? And then I tell them all about that photo on the coffin in that Chapel of Rest. A photo of Penny, but how could it be? How could she have died two weeks ago and then mysteriously appear before me in a train carriage two nights ago? And then suddenly, unable to help myself, I find myself telling them all about that trance-like dream, about Cara reaching out to me like that, her eyes pleading with me as she tried to tell me something, but with no words coming out of her mouth, as if she was speaking behind some sort of invisible veil.

All the time, Harry barely speaks, but he's always been the strong, silent type. Donna puts it down to his military background, but I've always thought it's more than that. He's always slightly unsettled me, in truth, much as he's doing right now, but maybe I'm being unfair. Maybe all this is raising uncomfortable echoes for him; anything with kids always does. Harry and his wife split up years ago when she refused to have any children, and he sank into a deep depression. The fact that she re-married a couple of years later, and promptly had the children with her new husband she'd always denied to Harry, only added fuel to the flames.

But then my mobile rings. Looking down at it I tense as I see the name on the display.

Adams.

I take a deep breath.

'It's the officer who questioned me about Penny. I'd better take it.'

Donna nods, then stops as her mobile begins to ring too. I stand, intending to go outside and give her space for her own call as well as steel myself to whatever fresh developments Adams has managed, or more likely not managed, to uncover.

But then, as I reach the door, I hear a puzzled Donna as she answers.

'DS who?'

I look back at her as she repeats her caller's name.

'Lauren Braith?'

I glance down at my own phone again, my caller from the same police station still waiting.

CHAPTER 62
TWENTY YEARS AGO

IT WAS JUST one simple word. That was all she had to say, and it was all she desperately wanted to say too. One simple, one-word answer to one very simple question. But a boy's whole future was hanging on it.

The fingerprints found on the book and the framed photo in the sitting room had just been confirmed as Jericho's. Which made no sense. Since he'd arrived in the country, he'd never been near the house. Cara had spent time with him, but that was always down in the bookshop or on trips out somewhere. She'd never brought him home and neither had her mum or dad.

But all she had to do was say that she had done, and then all this would just go away.

Because this theft couldn't be down to him. Cara was surer of that than she'd ever been of anything. So, when the officer, his notepad in hand, asked her whether he had ever been inside her home, all she had to say was, yes. But she didn't. Because in her heart of hearts, she knew it was useless anyway. If she stared the officer full in the face, swore blind he had been there, she knew that Jericho would say no. He wouldn't lie; she knew that already. He wouldn't even take a single leaf from a tree without permission, for God's sake. Which made it even more impossible that this theft had anything to do with him.

But why were his prints in their house? Why – and when – had he touched that framed photo and book? It just didn't make sense.

Cara felt as if time was stretching out before her. The officer stayed silent, his pen poised over his notepad, waiting for her reply. Across the room, Mum and Dad stayed silent too, their own confusion clear on their faces as well. But finally, Cara did it. She gave that simple answer to that very simple question as the police officer put it to her again.

To the best of her knowledge, because she'd invited him in perhaps, had Jericho ever been inside the cottage?

Cara said no.

CHAPTER 63
PRESENT DAY

HE DOESN'T WANT her here, and she knows it. Braith can see it in his eyes. In fact, he doesn't really want her around at all, and she knows why. It's something the young officer has encountered all her life, long before her fateful and – for most of her family – irrevocably damning decision to join the police. Attitudes. Assumptions. Or just pure and simple prejudice.

She first witnessed it back in primary school. The way a teacher's eyes would glaze over as, along with the rest of her class, she repeated what had been drummed into her. Every child, no matter how young, should always know their address. That way, in the event of some catastrophe taking place on some school trip – such as a child wandering off – that child would always be able to tell a police officer or shopkeeper or train guard, or anyone who might come across him or her, just where they lived.

Other catastrophes were possible too of course, some of them a lot more sinister than a child suddenly becoming detached from a peer group while out on a trip. But that realisation would only dawn later, and it was Cara's disappearance, that now-notorious local case, that had made Braith and all the other local kids first fully understand this.

Back in school, she'd begin with the house number, and then

the street. Even by that stage the smile on a teacher's eyes would start to become just that little bit fixed. By the time she reached the postcode there'd be a slight, but definite, tightening of the lips as the teacher nodded, then moved on, just that little bit too briskly, to the next small child on the register.

The simple truth was that few made it out from her home estate, a sprawling complex of council properties that had remained mostly council properties even after the Thatcher-inspired sell-off over twenty years before. Most residents remained there, too, locked in a never-ending cycle of long-term unemployment and crime. The names on the streets might differ, but for most outsiders there was only one name for the whole place. They were all lumped together on Benefit Street.

Her family thought it was a joke when she first said she wanted to join the police. When they realised she was serious, a couple of her older cousins took her for a late-night ride in what was probably one of a whole fleet of stolen cars to put some not-so-subtle pressure on her to change her mind. The subsequent beating she'd endured had also led to another lifestyle choice, as the next day she visited a local gym and enrolled in a class that was to become a passion, which was boxing. But it wasn't just the sudden and unlooked for threat to their precarious livelihoods that was the issue for the clan she was about to leave; there was a wholesale sense of betrayal as well. But she'd stuck to her guns. And one by one every member of her former family had vanished from her life as she'd quickly become what she now always would be so far as they were concerned: the pariah.

In a sense she'd challenged two sets of assumptions with her decision. The assumption on the part of her teachers that a child from that part of town would never – could ever indeed – amount to anything. And the assumption on the part of her family and friends that she'd ever want to. And again, it was the Cara case that had been instrumental in seeing her take her place amongst a hundred other new recruits as she posed for the official photographer capturing her graduation as a fully qualified, fully fledged

PC, soon to become a DC, before becoming one of the youngest Detective Sergeants in her local force's history.

Other kids went missing. She personally knew of at least two – one boy, one girl, both living a couple of streets away from her when she was growing up – who'd walked out of their respective houses one day and never returned. Their shared history of drug abuse made it unlikely in the eyes of the authorities, and most of their family and friends, that they ever would. They were written off, in other words, and little or no effort was taken to ever track down the crack den in which, in all probability again, they'd most likely spent their last miserable days.

But then came Cara. Braith was six, going on seven, when that story broke, but she remembers it as if it was yesterday. She was there right at the start of it, after all. Axel Petersen hasn't put two and two and together yet and he probably never will, but their paths crossed on that never-to-be forgotten day when he all but broke their front door down, demanding to see her older brother Cai. Braith watched the whole exchange from her vantage point in the kitchen doorway. She can still taste the lolly she was eating at the time.

Then came all the reports in the papers, and she can also still see the older girl's face, culled from an old school photo and smiling out at her from the front pages, a story that ran for weeks as different twists and turns unfolded, and like everyone else in the town she followed it avidly. But even then, there was that nagging unease at the back of her mind. Even then she knew that there was no way similar attention would have been paid to the disappearance of a girl from her background. Cara was from a different class, she came from different stock, so her disappearance merited more of everything. More attention, more investigation and more sympathy. Which all went back to those attitudes and assumptions again. As well as that pure and simple prejudice.

And it's why the proverbial and maybe even literal wild horses wouldn't keep her away from this house visit.

It isn't just the fact that to be part of a team that finally cracks a twenty-year old disappearance, at the same time as a modern-day mystery, will do no harm at all to a career that has now become her life. It's the irresistible squaring of a circle as well. A girl like her finally uncovering the truth about a girl like Cara.

The fact that her DI was actually on the original Cara case back then is more grist to the mill. Because he and the rest of her home force failed. Maybe that explains the wariness she always senses whenever she tries to talk to him about it. Maybe it's an unwelcome reminder of past failings, a fear that a younger officer might succeed where the old guard did not. Or maybe it's something else. The longer this investigation has gone on, the more she has begun to wonder.

'The decomposition of the body makes it likely that the killing took place at least a decade ago, if not more.'

Adams pauses, facing both Axel and Donna. There was another man there when they arrived, Donna's brother, but he left almost immediately. It was as if he couldn't get out of here quick enough.

'We'll know more when we've received a detailed report from the forensic pathologist.'

Donna just stares at them, frozen. But Axel seems bewildered, not only by the ostensible reason for their visit, but by all Adams is telling them. Maybe he is, or maybe he's just a good actor. He's had a lot of practice after all, if so. Twenty years' worth, in fact.

'What she can tell us is that the cause of death was a violent blow to the throat.'

Donna's grip on the arm of her chair tightens, perhaps as she imagines, involuntarily, the last few moments of her own child's life.

'We don't know yet whether the victim was killed at the spot they were found, but again we'll know more when the detailed report comes through.'

Braith keeps her eyes firmly fixed on Axel, whose eyes in turn haven't left those of her senior officer. The body isn't Cara. It will probably turn out to be one of the nonentities from her home estate who disappeared all those years ago, at which point the world will very much lose interest. But for the time being, the whole town is buzzing. Everyone knows by now that a decomposed body from years before has been found, so is it her, is it Cara? It's all everyone wants to know, so they've had to make this house call the moment her name was eliminated by the pathologist.

But there's another reason for this visit too. Because if either Donna or Axel did have anything to do with Cara's disappearance, they must have feared this moment on an almost daily basis. The knock on the door. Police officers asking if they can have a word. The actual discovery of their daughter's body aside, something like this must amount to a moment of massive pressure. So, will one, or the other, crack? Let something slip at last?

'We're aware a discovery like this is always going to be massively difficult for you, given everything, which is why we felt it important you both know about it as soon as possible.'

Donna suddenly rises with a near-strangled cry. She turns, and almost runs down a passageway to a room Braith assumes is her bedroom. The door slams shut behind her. In front of them, Axel doesn't move. For a moment Braith doesn't think he's going to, but then he stands too and walks out of the front door, in the opposite direction to his ex-wife. Through a nearby window both officers can see him moving away down the road that leads in turn to the beach, walking as if he is in some sort of daze.

Adams looks at her, exhaling a quick, deep breath as he does so.

'Wait around for a few minutes, see if Mrs Petersen comes back out and whether she wants to say anything.'

Braith nods as he stands and makes for the front door too. For a moment she wonders if he's going to follow Axel, but through the same front window she sees him head into the garden at the side of the house, where he just stands, looking as if he also needs a moment to recover from all this.

But Braith doesn't remain still. Waiting around has never been her strong point. Besides, right now might be just the time to hit Donna and hit her hard. Some might call it insensitive. She calls it smart.

Approaching the closed bedroom door, she's about to tap on it, but then she stops as she hears Donna's voice from inside, obviously talking on her mobile. Keeping as quiet as she can, Braith moves closer, praying no squeaks from the wooden floor under her feet will give her away.

'Is this us?'

Donna sounds agitated, wracked. That much Braith expects.

'Are we being punished, is that it?'

Braith stares at the door. That she didn't expect. What the hell did she mean by that? From the other side of the door, Donna's voice cracks as she stifles another sob.

'What did we do? What the fuck did we do?'

Then there's a sharp crash, perhaps as Donna throws her mobile to the floor or against a wall.

Reeling now, Braith moves quickly back to the sitting room in case Donna comes back out of the bedroom and discovers her. But then she pauses, her mind racing. All her focus up to now has been on Axel. But has she been looking at the wrong parent all along?

But then Braith stops again. Because through the front window she can now see Adams, still out in the side garden and putting away his mobile, having clearly just finished a call.

CHAPTER 64
TWENTY YEARS AGO

JERICHO WAS BACK IN CUSTODY, being questioned. Patrick was frantically trying to source the best criminal solicitor he could find, and there was no time to lose. Everyone was well aware of the stakes here.

The theft itself was serious enough. The value of the item in question took this way out of something that could be dealt with by anything less than a Crown Court, even for a first offence. But Jericho was – and remained – an illegal immigrant. A conviction of this kind would irretrievably damn his chances of any sort of settled status. As well as virtually guaranteeing his repatriation to the country he'd fled and, once there, most likely his death.

Cara could see in Axel and Donna's eyes that the last thing they wanted was to think the worst of a young man they'd taken in at considerable personal risk to themselves, especially to Axel. But how the hell had his prints ended up in their home?

And one of the scenes of crime officers had now found a third item – an old diary that Cara kept in a drawer in a bedroom – that also had Jericho's prints on it. The police were working on the – not entirely unreasonable – assumption that he hadn't been as careful as he'd imagined in eradicating all traces of his unauthorised presence. It was the only logical conclusion in truth, but it was wrong, Cara was still sure of that.

She headed down to the bookshop half an hour later, a sudden thought impelling her flight. Had Mark ever taken him to the house? Jericho had been out with him a couple of times, helping him collect items from a house clearance, checking out a potential sale. So, had they ever detoured?

Mark was alone in the reception area. He looked flustered when he saw her but listened intently as she related all that had happened. He quickly confirmed that he'd never taken Jericho anywhere near the house on any of their outings, and he didn't have a key anyway, but Cara wasn't really listening.

Mark might have thought he'd concealed it, but he hadn't. Because as she walked in, he'd opened a drawer in the reception desk behind which he'd been standing and had slid something inside.

CHAPTER 65
PRESENT DAY

I RETURN to Donna later that night.

She doesn't say anything as she opens the door. She just turns and leads the way to a small room at the rear of the house, looking out onto the garden and beyond that down to the sea. Heading inside, she sits on the single bed. A moment later I join her, and we sit together in a silence that seems to stretch back centuries.

We used to share a lot of silences like these. Companionable. Easy. Years ago, not long after we first met, I took her on a trip I'd long promised myself to the States. I'd just started my new business, as well a new relationship, and I wanted this trip to mark and celebrate both. We were to visit some of the most renowned book collections in the western world, and if that doesn't sound all that sexy for a first trip abroad for two new lovers, it's perhaps worth remembering that a lifetime of legendary sexual adventure finally ended with Casanova finding his true calling as a librarian in the castle of Count Waldstein at Dux in Bohemia.

We began at the holy of holies, the Huntington Library in California, where two floors below ground level we stood in front of five thousand incunabula, the nomenclature used for any books printed before 1501, before handling and opening a large 1472 copy of the first printed edition of Dante's epic poem, *The Divine Comedy*.

In the Houghton Library in Massachusetts we inspected a double elephant folio of Audubon's masterpiece, *Birds of America*, while at the Library Company of Philadelphia we were handed the first copy of Newton's *Principia Mathematica* to be brought to North America. In the rare book stacks at the Lilly Library in Bloomington we also came across Herman Melville's annotated copy of *King Lear*.

More treasures followed at the Folger Shakespeare Library in Washington, where we gazed on seventy-nine First Folios of Shakespeare's plays, one shelf stacked on top of the other, before opening the copy numbered '1' at the title page, which was signed in 1623 by the London printer Isaac Jaggard.

I don't know when my own fascination, some would say obsession, with books began. It's difficult to know now what's original inspiration and what's retrospective justification. All I know is that it's undeniably true, as Carl Sagan once wrote, that even with the treasures on display in all those collections we visited back then, our written records as human beings only carry us about a millionth of the way back to the origins of life. Our beginnings, those crucial, key events in our history, simply aren't available to us anymore, because we can't access any first-hand accounts of any of them. The overwhelming majority of our ancestors are unknown to us, shadows lost forever with no names or faces, and we can't reclaim them.

But then along came language, sometimes described as the miracle of our species. And then came writing, its witness. As Cicero, soon to become one of my all-time heroes, wrote, '*All literature, all philosophy, all history, abounds with incentives which would be buried in black darkness were the light of the written word not flashed upon them.*' Or, as Shakespeare's Prospero had it, '*Words that are spoken dissolve, like an insubstantial pageant faded.*'

When writing originally appeared, first on clay tablets in Mesopotamia some five thousand years ago, it quickly became an object of veneration. A full century before the birth of Christ, a traveller, Didorus Siculus, visited a hall outside the tomb of the Egyptian Pharaoh Ramses 11, where texts had already been kept for more than eleven hundred years. Above the portals were inscribed the words, '*The house of healing for the soul.*'

At that time, I thought books would always lead me through. That whatever happened, they'd become a sort of road map. At the time too, it seemed impossible that Donna and I would ever part. As we gazed on the treasures before us, we seemed to be indivisible parts of the same whole. Then Cara disappeared, and like so many couples before us, that seemingly eternal bond shattered.

But I have wondered from time to time ever since. Was it just Cara? Or were the warning signs there before? Was there something I missed before Cara disappeared that should have alerted me to things already going wrong between us? At different times over the last few years, I've wracked my brains, trying to resurrect moments from those days, searching for clues, but everything from that time is now mixed in with everything that happened with Cara, and I can't separate it out.

Those memory blanks don't help of course. Those moments – sometimes more than moments and multiplying over the years, too – when I simply have no recollection of what's just happened, or what I've done. Or maybe there's nothing and I've done nothing. Maybe I'm just inventing needless torments. Searching for solutions to problems that never existed in the first place.

The two of us still haven't exchanged even a single word. I look around the room at Cara's books, a hotch-potch collection capturing a girl's journey from child to adult, one of the reasons they've stayed there over all the years. But there are other reasons too, of course, prime among them being that sense of betrayal we'd both feel if we cleared that room of our daughter's possessions before we know what's happened to her. I keep looking round, taking in posters still tacked up on the walls, snapshots of old school friends and various trips, clothes still hanging in her wooden wardrobe.

If that body the police found had been Cara, then at some time in the future we would have had to decide what to do with all this, of course, but not now. And maybe not ever, because I'm still haunted by that strange half-dream, half-nightmare. That vision of her reaching out to me, speaking those soundless words, and as I keep resurrecting it there's something else too – something I see in her eyes. It's something I didn't recognise at the time, but the more I worry away at it, the more it almost seems like some kind of accusation. But that makes no sense, I know, because an accusation about what?

I look across at Donna. We've still not spoken, and suddenly there's going to be no opportunity because my mobile rings. Donna doesn't even seem to hear it as I stand and step outside.

It's Detective Inspector Adams again, telling me he wants to see me.

He thinks we should talk.

CHAPTER 66
TWENTY YEARS AGO

'I DON'T KNOW.'

It was all the young man kept saying. It was all he'd said from the moment the interview had begun. And he seemed genuine too. But although Adams was still a rookie cop, he kept asking the same question over and over again, even though the same answer was repeated to him every time.

It was standard police procedure for one thing. If a suspect was going to crack, it would never be in the first few moments of an interview. You had to keep them in the same place and keep hitting them with the same question or the same set of questions, because if there was a weak spot then the continued repetition would often prise open that first tiny chink in the armour, leading, hopefully, to the whole edifice finally collapsing.

But still the same answer kept coming back, albeit with slight variations. Jericho didn't know how his prints had appeared in the Petersen house. He couldn't explain it. He simply had no idea.

Adams eyed him. He'd asked to be in on this interview and his hard-pressed DI had agreed readily enough. An extra pair of hands was always welcome. If the DI stopped to think about it, he'd probably have just assumed the young officer scented a career opportunity. This was a major theft, given the value of the item that had gone missing. A feather in the cap for any ambitious cop who might locate it, but it was more than that, although DS Dan Adams had kept that very much to himself.

They intrigued him, he had to admit. The Petersens. Although maybe the wife more than the husband. She was attractive, of course, and that was part of it. But he sensed something in her too, maybe because he was aware of something similar in himself. A restlessness, a dislocation. He knew his relationship with his wife was going south, and faster each day too. And he sensed the same restlessness, the same dislocation in the bookseller's wife as well. Maybe that was why they'd connected in the way he was beginning to believe they had, courtesy of the half-glances she'd shoot his way in the exchanges they'd shared up to then, the similar half-glances he'd shoot her way before they both looked down at the floor before anyone noticed.

Adams hunched closer to the distraught young man in front of him. It was time to mix it up a little, because they'd already decided what to do if these interviews didn't bear fruit. The evidence might seem strong, but it was still circumstantial, in truth. But if this young man did have that valuable book somewhere, there'd be only one thing on his mind, and that was selling it and fast. Adams himself had suggested the tactic and his DI had agreed. They were simply going to let him go. They'd release him, but then track him. Keep the sort of tabs on him that meant he wouldn't be able to order a coffee without the local police knowing if it was a mocha or a cappuccino. Then, if and when he made his move, they'd pounce.

But first, it was time to unsettle him even more.

'How much would you get?'

The young man stared at him, blank.

'Ten thousand, maybe more?'

He kept staring.

'That book's worth a hell of a lot more than that, but you wouldn't get the full market value of course, not without proper provenance.'

'I don't understand.'

'It'd still easily be enough to get you over to Germany, help you track down your brother, maybe even set yourselves up in a small place somewhere.'

And now Adams could see it in his eyes. The hurt and confusion mixed in with the bewilderment. Because there was only the one person he'd talked to about his hopes and dreams for himself and for Omar.

But of course, that didn't mean Cara hadn't talked to someone else.

CHAPTER 67
PRESENT DAY

ADAMS SHOWS me into his office the next morning. For the first time I notice the dark rings under his eyes, the sure sign of a man under pressure. I've been there myself. The reason's obvious enough in my case. What demons are haunting DI Adams right now I don't know, and frankly I don't care. All I want to know is what this latest summons is all about.

'We've tracked down CCTV from a couple of street cameras outside your shop.'

Adams hits a button on a remote, a grainy image appearing on a monitor on his desk. For a few moments all I see are a couple of pedestrians passing the camera, but then I see a figure I now know well. A couple more images appear, showing him clearly hovering, probably keeping watch.

'That's him. That's Rory.' I turn towards Adams, who's also studying the face on the screen. 'Who is he?'

He hesitates. And is it my imagination – my now ever-present paranoia, maybe – but does he hesitate just a fraction too long?

'We don't know, not yet.'

I keep looking at him.

'We lifted some prints from your car, but he's not on any police database, meaning either he's not been in any trouble, or he just hasn't been caught yet.'

He turns to me, looking almost out on his feet, and now I do feel a small stab of sympathy as an all too obvious reason for those dark rings presents itself. He was involved in the original investigation into Cara's disappearance. Now he's involved in this disappearance too. Cara hasn't been found, and so far, Penny hasn't been found either. And in both cases, no arrests have yet been made. To fail in one case might be put down to bad luck. To fail in two might strike some as downright incompetent.

Adams continues to study me.

'Obviously not a figment of your imagination then.'

Which is a small, if a very small, move towards me from a man who's pretty well kept his distance up to now. He hasn't been as hostile as his younger companion, but at times it's been a close-run thing. But now I'm beginning to sense a shift here, as if he's starting at least to consider the possibility that my story might just be true. Which is maybe why I now try and push this along.

'What about Penny?'

'What about her?'

'You must know more about her by now.'

He doesn't say anything.

'I don't know why any of this is happening. All I do know is that meeting wasn't accidental. She sat down opposite me on that train, my train, for some reason, and no, she didn't expect me to do what I did, to reach out to her like that, but she reached out to me just by being there.'

I break off.

'But that photo of her, the one on that coffin, I don't understand.'

I stare at him, desperate for answers, and he must have some, or why else would he have called me down here?

Adams hesitates a moment longer, then he leans forward on the desk, taking a quick, deep, breath as he does so.

'Penny was one of two sisters; we know that much now. She had a twin.'

'A twin?'

I keep staring, dim comprehension finally beginning.

'So, the girl in the photo?'

Adams nods as I tail off again.

'They weren't identical but there was a very strong physical resemblance. To be honest, when I first saw that photo, I was pretty rocked myself.'

Suddenly I'm back there again, inside that Chapel of Rest, looking at that image of the girl inside the coffin. So young, so wrong.

'So, what happened?'

Adams looks out of the window and doesn't reply for a moment. At first, I think he's trying to collect his thoughts. Then I realise he's actually more than a little upset and, briefly again, I wonder. I know nothing about him, but does he have children? A daughter, maybe? Is he responding to all this now not just as a professional, as a police officer, but as a father as well?

'Her name was Jen, abbreviated from Jennifer much as Penny's name was abbreviated from Penelope. Old-fashioned names in a sense, I suppose. Both girls had lived at home with their mum up to a few years ago. They'd been home schooled largely, so there really isn't much out there on either of them. None of the usual social media triggers, school photos and the like, that you might expect with other teenage girls.'

Which I largely knew already, but I didn't tell him that.

'Health issues on the mum's part meant they had to be taken into care and after that they went into supported accommodation.'

Adams pauses.

'Neither girl exactly settled well, but Jen really seems to have struggled. Two weeks ago, she walked out, dressed only in her pyjamas. She managed to get on a train to Bristol, although God knows how, dressed like that and with no money or ticket. She made her way to the suspension bridge where CCTV captures her on the parapet.'

We both fall silent for a moment, our minds filled with that one dreadful, tragic image.

'And Penny?'

'She disappeared from the same supported accommodation that same night. The next time there's any sighting of her is on your train.'

Adams picks up a couple of printouts from the CCTV footage outside my shop, jabbing his finger at Rory.

'Where she went in the meantime and what this character has to do with her, we have no idea.'

CHAPTER 68
TWENTY YEARS AGO

CARA WATCHED Mark cross the road and head into the café. She'd asked him to collect a couple of takeaway coffees while she put some food and drink supplies in the rare books room for what the police had told them would be Jericho's imminent return. But all she was really thinking about was that now-closed drawer she could see on the other side of the reception desk.

Cara crossed to it. It was an impossible thought – inconceivable even – but had Mark taken the *Tamerlane*? Is that what he was hiding in there when she'd walked in? Keeping an eye on the door and the café beyond it all the while, Cara slid open the drawer. There wasn't a book in there, but a small box instead. Cara hesitated, then opened it to reveal a ring.

Cara stared at it for a moment, then looked back towards the café again. Was this what she thought it was? Was Mark – another impossible, near-inconceivable thought – planning to propose to her? Did he really imagine this relationship of theirs had ever been that serious?

But hard on the heels of that question came another even more unsettling one. Because if he did think their relationship was that serious, what might he do if he felt it to be under threat?

CHAPTER 69
PRESENT DAY

RORY FEELS his stomach lurch even before he sets foot inside, and that isn't down to the occasion, it's the place.

He stares round at the wooden benches lining each side of the central walkway, at the red velvet drapes partitioning off the curtained area at the front – and why are they always red and always velvet? He stares at the pulpit to one side, at a board displaying hymn numbers if hymns have been requested, left blank if not. Then he takes a moment, willing his stomach to settle, his breathing to begin to return to normal.

These places aren't like churches. People gather for celebrations in churches, for weddings and christenings; they come together on Sundays to offer thanks and engage in prayer. But a crematorium is there for one business and one only, the business of death. And it seems to seep somehow into its very walls.

He arrived a full hour beforehand. He won't be there for the actual service itself; he can't risk that. There's too much interest in Penny already, meaning there's bound to be a police presence here, and he can't risk the same interest being taken in himself. He has too much to do right now just trying to find her, and he can't do that if the local police decide he merits some heavy-duty questioning for a couple of days. So, he bows his head in front of the pulpit in the best approximation he can make to a silent tribute, then retreats outside and keeps watch, making sure all the time that he's concealed from view.

The hearse arrives just under an hour later. Mourners, mainly from her previous care home, have been trickling in for the past half an hour. He scans every arriving face before looking away and scanning the next. But he already knows in his heart of hearts that Penny's is the one face he isn't going to see today, and he's right. Nothing would – nothing should – keep her away from her own sister's funeral. But something obviously has.

But when he hears the first of the hymns begin inside and a straggly chorus of subdued voices start to sing, he sees him. Like Rory, he's staying outside, in his case in his car, his eyes fixed on the now-closed door before him.

And like Rory, it appears that Axel has been unable to stay away.

Rory bites down on the sudden bile that rises in his throat. Once again, he feels himself having to almost physically battle the overpowering urge to storm over there and drag him from his car. But he's done that kind of thing too many times in the past and it's cost him nearly everything. If he fails now where he's failed before, gives way now as he's given way before, then he'll be failing not only himself but Penny too.

But hard on the heels of all this comes something else. Because Axel looks wrecked; there's no other word for it. Looking at him is almost like looking into a mirror. Rory sees the same pain and confusion he's feeling etched on the older man's features too, but why? Is it guilt, as Penny always hinted? Or a genuine connection with a girl who remains lost?

Rory doesn't know. So, he stays where he is, concealed and unobserved, watching a man in a place he has no right to be.

CHAPTER 70
TWENTY YEARS AGO

ON JERICHO'S RELEASE, it had been a very different young man who'd returned to the bookshop. He was a lot quieter now. Cowed, almost. There was a different atmosphere among the customers too; everyone seemed more reserved, more guarded around him. Which only depressed Jericho's spirits further.

Oddly enough, it was Mark who came up with a possible way forward.

'The dance?'

Cara stared at him. Little did he know it, but she'd already mentioned that to the young refugee herself. But as Mark expanded on his idea, pointing out that taking Jericho along would be a statement without actually having to make one, a clear demonstration of faith by a member of the very family he was suspected of having wronged, she felt her heart warm towards him.

Then Mark paused.

'We could take Jools too.'

Cara looked at him.

'You must have seen the way she looks at him sometimes.'

And Cara felt her warm smile start to fade.

CHAPTER 71
PRESENT DAY

CHAPTER 70
TWENTY YEARS AGO

FOR NOT THE first time in the last few days, Patrick's looking at me as if I've just landed from Mars.

'You want to do what?'

'I don't want to. I have to.'

He keeps eyeing me, quizzical.

'Have to, as in you're being compelled?'

Sometimes I really hate lawyers.

I pause. No one's making me, of course. Like no one made me go along to that crematorium for the funeral of a girl I'd never met. Like no one made me remain there long after the service had ended, and all the other mourners had gone. But I could no more have not gone and not stayed there than fly.

'I just need to know, Patrick, and if I could find anything out myself I would, but I can't, and that has to be telling us something, doesn't it?'

Patrick looks like he always does at times like these, like a kindly old schoolteacher being pushed to his limit by a wayward child.

'There's plenty on Jen, Penny's twin. Plenty from the last couple of weeks anyway. That jump from the bridge was big local news in Bristol, so that's not surprising, I suppose. But if you try going back any further than that, if you try and find out anything else about her or Penny, you just hit a brick wall.'

I lean closer.

'I don't care what Adams said about the mother and home schooling, it's just not credible that two girls in this day and age would have no digital imprint at all. It's as if Jen suddenly appeared out of nowhere only to jump off that bridge, and Penny came out of nowhere to suddenly appear in that train carriage, and then vanish again.'

Patrick keeps eyeing me.

'So, you're saying?'

'Has some sort of restriction been placed on them or something?'

'Restriction?'

'An injunction of some kind, like a privacy notice maybe, and that's why any information anyone would normally expect to be able to find has just been wiped.'

'And how could I find that out?'

'You're a lawyer.'

'I'm a solicitor, Axel. I sort out boundary disputes, and planning applications.'

He nods at me.

'I occasionally bid in book auctions for friends.'

Then he shakes his head.

'Give me a tricky conveyance or a drunk and disorderly and I'm your man, but this sort of thing…'

Patrick doesn't finish. He doesn't need to. But I push it, nonetheless.

'Film stars get these sort of privacy notices sometimes. Or footballers – I've read about them.'

'And this girl, did she look like a film star or a footballer?'

'The mother then? Can we find out anything about her? Why did those two girls end up being taken from her into care? Who is she, where is she? If I could talk to her, maybe I could start to get some answers at least.'

'Can I give you some advice?'

He doesn't need to. I can see what he's going to say in his eyes. Leave this alone.

I persist. 'Or maybe you could talk to Adams. You've known him for years – don't you two actually live near to each other?'

'I've known a lot of people round here for years. I live near to a lot of people too.'

I make one last attempt.

'Couldn't you just have a word? Strictly off the record?'

Ten minutes later, I'm back out on the street. A reluctant Patrick's told me he'll see what he can do, and I know he will. I also know I'm pushing him way beyond anything that might even remotely resemble his comfort zone. Join the club.

I approach my car, pausing as I do so. On the windscreen, tucked under one of the wipers, is a small white piece of paper inside protective cellophane wrapping, and I raise my eyes to the skies. Insult upon injury; a parking ticket on top of everything else.

But it isn't. As I take it out I still as I see the same words I first saw pencilled in that book on the train, the four words inscribed in the Frame collection of short stories.

Can I Trust You?

I look round, wildly, but there's no one in sight. I stare at those four words again, then turn the single sheet of paper over. On the back there's something else.

The Castle. 2pm

CHAPTER 72
PRESENT DAY

I JUST STARE at the message for a moment, unable to take it in.

Who wrote this? And who left it on the windscreen of my car for me to find? But all the time of course, one name swims before my eyes.

Is this Penny? Has she finally broken cover, decided to come back and finish what she started that night on the train, whatever that might be? Meaning, if this is her, then she has to be OK, of course. She's not been hurt, or worse.

But what if it's some troll? The same one who maybe scrawled that inscription in the Frame book in the first place. What if this is nothing to do with Penny at all? What if it's some lowlife who crawled out of the woodwork on what was always going to be one of the biggest of those macabre anniversaries, intent on playing some twisted game? Or someone with even more evil intent in mind.

I just keep staring at the message, then turn it over and look again at the four words on the other side.

Can I Trust You?

But this has to be Penny; surely, it can't be anyone else. I know that inscription wasn't there before. I simply wouldn't have missed it – this is my job, it's what I do for a living, what I've done for decades now. But then I pause once more. Then again, it was the anniversary. Maybe I could be forgiven if I was just a little bit distracted.

I check my phone but there's nothing, no new messages. I briefly think of returning to Patrick, but I can hear him already. This could be the work of some complete maniac and I'm seriously contemplating going to meet them on the basis of an anonymous note tacked on my car windscreen.

One second later, I'm in my car and driving away, back towards my cottage and the castle that towers above it and the surrounding countryside, checking my watch as I do so.

1pm.

One hour to go.

CHAPTER 73
PRESENT DAY

THE TRAFFIC'S LIGHT, but it still feels like a journey that takes forever and the clock on the dash seems to tick ever faster in front of my eyes.

Pulling up outside my beachside cottage, I hurry up the lane that leads to the castle. It's a cold day so there's no one around to keep me company. That may mean that whoever wrote that note knows it will be quiet, so it could be a local. Or someone who's just done their homework.

The castle's open to the skies, looking out over the estuary to one side, with open fields and a view down towards the county town to another. A large open space dominates as I walk inside, and a quick glance round tells me no one's here. There are a few old, ruined rooms dotted around the edge where people can take shelter or hide, but it takes me roughly two minutes to visit and inspect each one in turn. I check my phone again. Still no message, but then it pulses with a text alert.

I scrabble for it, then almost howl in frustration as I see the message on the screen.

Just been talking to Patrick. What's happening? Are you OK?

It's Harry. He's tried to contact me a couple of times since he drove Donna and me home from the hospital that night, and I struggle to keep my temper. My concerned ex-brother-in-law is only thinking of me, after all. Then again, he hasn't been that concerned up to now. I've hardly heard from him in months. So why this sudden interest?

I look around again. There's still no one in sight and I can't hear any approaching footsteps, but I call out anyway.

'Hello?'

A stern silence is the only reply. I go back to the entrance, look down the path. There's a small car park a hundred metres away for those visitors unable or unwilling to make the climb on foot. I didn't want to drive up as I wanted whoever left that note to see that I'm alone. But the car park is empty too. I turn back and look out over the estuary, and time seems to elongate. The normal sounds of the surrounding fields and the water below fade at the same time. For a moment, there's just me and this ancient, empty ruin.

Suddenly, my phone buzzes again. For a moment I'm tempted to ignore it, really not wanting any more messages from Harry. Then I see the message on the screen.

Go to the estuary wall.

I wheel round. On the other side of that wall is a steep drop. But I take a deep breath and do as I'm told. I cross to the estuary wall and stand there, alone and in full view of anyone from miles around. But nothing happens. No more texts. So, am I being played? Teased and tormented? Were all my dark suspicions outside Patrick's office right? Is this some sicko after all?

Then my phone pulses again as another message appears on the screen.

The police are on the beach.

I look down. Sure enough, a police car has just pulled up. It could just be a routine patrol. Or it could be something else. Another message comes through.

The Old Folly. Come alone.

I hesitate for a moment, danger signals now sounding loud and clear. As a perhaps-belated nod to common sense I copy the message to Patrick, just in case.

Then I turn and hare back down the path towards my car.

CHAPTER 74
PRESENT DAY

SHE ALWAYS KNEW she wouldn't be able to stay away.

She's circled the house several times, biding her time. It helps that while it's away from the beach, it's next to one of Freshwater's small car parks, so there are often people passing. All she has to do is wait for a small group to park up and then follow them down to the sands, looking to any casual eyes as if she's just another tourist.

Actual recognition is unlikely after all these years, and she's always careful to wear one of the large hats she brings along, seemingly as protection against the elements. And she's always made sure she keeps her eyes averted as she passes the actual house in case anyone is looking out from inside. But this is the fourth or fifth time she's enacted the same charade, and she knows she won't be able to resist the next step. Sooner or later, she has to try and get inside.

Her chance comes sooner than she expected. As she approaches on her latest visit, this time in the company of a small coach party of senior citizens, she tenses as she sees a figure move from the rear door of the house and climb into a car before driving, quickly, away. Where Donna is going, and why she seems to be in such a hurry, she doesn't know and frankly doesn't care. All she does know is that the house is now empty.

Getting in is not going to be difficult. The village has always been a low crime area, which strikes her as grimly ironic. Household security is way down the list of priorities for most residents. She doesn't expect to find the door actually unlocked, but she is fairly confident one of the windows won't be secured as firmly as it should be, and she's right.

On gaining entry, she doesn't even look at the kitchen, which is the first room she steps into, or the sitting room beyond. She's interested in one room and one room only, and as she swings open the door she almost cries out in stunned recognition, because it's exactly as she remembers it. The posters on the walls, the photos on the small chest of drawers and desk; there even looks to be the same random collection of books on the bedside table. It isn't just stepping back in time. It's as if everything has been frozen in aspic. A museum-like set-piece right there in front of her eyes.

She moves inside, hesitates for a moment again, but then, and on an impulse, lies down on the bed. The sheets smell freshly washed, and when she lays her head down on the pillows the covers smell freshly washed too. Which all reinforces the feeling that she's simply picked up where she left off all those years ago.

But she has been away of course. And there'll be no picking up where she left off; that option is closed to her.

From now on, there's only one option left.

CHAPTER 75
PRESENT DAY

THE OLD FOLLY is a well-known local landmark, some few miles inland from the castle.

Local legend has it that a nobleman in the eighteenth century had attempted to bribe the newly enfranchised population of the town with copious amounts of ale, as well as the promise of a new bridge across the local river, in exchange for their votes to secure his place in Parliament. The new voters gladly accepted the beverage, but when it came to the actual voting most were in such a stupor they simply didn't show up, and the nobleman lost his seat. He couldn't take back the ale, but he could, and did, promptly abandon all plans to build the bridge.

Instead, he commissioned a folly a mile or so down the valley. A towering structure appeared within a matter of weeks; a structure that served no practical purpose save as a visual reminder to the town of its treachery in not seeing through its side of their deal with the devil that day. Three hundred years later I'm speeding along the lanes that lead up to that same landmark, trying not to reflect on my own potential folly right now and desperately hoping there's no modern-day devil waiting for me.

The lane leading up there is single track, but no approaching car or tractor blocks my path, forcing me to reverse, and I swing into a small car park just a few hundred metres from the summit. I switch off the near-overheated engine, and from the rattle it gives out as I do so, it sounds as if it's not before time. I look out of the window, but again can see no one. I check my phone in case there have been any fresh messages during the short drive over from the estuary but there's nothing. So I send another text myself.

I'm here. Where are you?

Time ticks on. A full two minutes elapses according to the clock on the dashboard. But then, suddenly, my phone pulses once more.

Get out of your car, walk up to the south side of the folly.

And now I don't need the echo of previous dark suspicions to tell me this is potentially a very bad idea. The south side of the folly is another well-known danger spot. A sheer cliff falls away at that point, with signs dotted all around the approach to it, warning sightseers to stay well clear. But I'm here now and I can't just start up my engine and drive away. Whatever this is all about – and I have less and less idea the longer it goes on – I have to at least try and find out.

But I can take some precautions at least. I get out of the car and cross to the boot. Using the raised boot lid to shield myself from the view of anyone watching up at the folly itself, I take the metal handle from the car jack. Slipping the handle inside my coat I begin to make my way up the hill, passing one of the signs that warn against heading over to the south of the summit. The side I'm heading for right now.

The wind's picking up, hammering into me as I climb, almost as if the elements are adding their own voice to the inner voice I can now hear, telling me ever more insistently to stop this and stop this now, to turn around and go home, but I keep walking, the drop over the sheer cliff getting closer all the time. Then I pause, a matter of feet from the drop itself now, but there's still no one in sight.

So, is my mystery texter observing me through a pair of binoculars maybe, making sure I've kept my promise and am here alone? Or is it just one more twist in a cruel deception? Am I destined to stay up here, waiting for a texter who's never going to show?

A soft thud sounds behind me. My neck tingles and the hairs on my neck and arms stand up as I sense movement behind. A second later, I turn and see a figure who's just jumped down from a ledge inside the folly.

I stare as Rory stares back at me.

CHAPTER 76
PRESENT DAY

A FRESH GUST of wind whips into me, the strongest yet, buffeting up from the valley below, making me all too conscious of that sheer drop down to oblivion behind. In front of me, Rory still just stands there. He doesn't have a knife in his hand this time, but he really wouldn't need one. A few steps separate us, a few metres at the most. If he turns violent, this is only going to end one way, and that's badly for me.

And if I'm feeling paranoid right now it's not only down to the fact that I'm inches from a sheer drop, it's also Rory himself. He looks wired, as if he hasn't slept for days. Suddenly my mind flashes back to our first meeting, or at least our first face to face meeting after those two stray sightings on and off that train. He has that look in his eyes again. If I'm a man on a literal edge right now, he looks as if he's on the edge too.

'What's this all about?'

He doesn't reply, just keeps staring at me, his eyes bloodshot, raw. And suddenly, I realise something else. Because if this really is it, if this is the end, if the next few moments see me plunging down that sheer drop behind, how convenient – again – would that be? Courtesy of that re-directed text, the police would have Patrick's testimony that I was going to meet someone, but there'd be no other corroborative evidence. And a river snakes along that valley floor. If I hit that, the chances are they wouldn't be able to retrieve my body either; it would be washed out to sea. Most people would probably write it off as suicide. The last desperate act of a soul tortured by the aftermath of a particularly poignant anniversary. The fates finally catching up with the man responsible. For most in the local area this really would put the whole Cara case to bed.

And as all that races through my mind, I feel any fear ebbing away again. Because that cannot happen. I cannot go to the grave without unlocking the mystery of what happened to my daughter – and what's happened all these years later to Penny. And right now, the man standing before me may be the closest I've got to any sort of key.

My phone pulses again but I knock it onto silent as suddenly, and for the first time, he speaks.

'Why did you go?'

I stare at him, puzzled. What's he talking about?

'The funeral. Jen's funeral. I saw you. You were there. Why? You never even knew her.'

He takes a step towards me, but I hold my ground and he stops, his eyes searching mine.

'And you stayed too, after everyone else had gone. You stayed there – you were just sitting in your car. I was watching you, so what was that all about?'

I could have asked him where he was all that time, why he was watching me, but none of that matters. All that matters is that twenty-year old mystery and this new one too. And all I can think of is getting back to both in any way I can.

'Maybe for the same reason you were there. Maybe I was looking for answers.'

'What does that mean?'

'Jen was Penny's twin. I thought if I'd find her anywhere, I might find her there.'

Something crosses his face, something almost complicit,

shared. But then, suddenly, we both hear it. A car approaching, its engine whining as the driver changes into a lower gear for the climb to the car park.

Rory glares at me.

'I said, just you!'

He turns, staring wildly now towards the car park. But then he stops as we both hear the car drive on past the entrance, presumably making for one of the haphazard line of houses further along the lane. I turn back to him, and now it's my turn to try and make some sense out of what has for too long been the completely unintelligible.

'Why those messages?'

He looks at me.

'That message you left on my car; those were the same words I found in that book, after I first saw Penny.'

I hold his stare.

'I thought maybe it was there beforehand, that I'd missed it somehow, but I hadn't, had I? She wrote that, she wrote it for me, and you wrote the same thing.'

Rory hesitates a moment, a clear struggle going on inside, and I almost explode in an agony of frustration.

'Why?'

But, and not for the first time, he doesn't answer directly.

'That was all she was supposed to do. Make contact, but do it with lots of other people around. Then she was supposed to send you a message, see if you'd respond. If you did, she'd take it from there. If you didn't, she wouldn't; that was the deal, she promised.'

He stares at me again. 'But something went wrong, didn't it?'

His eyes are now burning into mine.

CHAPTER 77
PRESENT DAY

AND ONCE AGAIN, there it is. That same feeling. That I trust him.

Which is totally ridiculous in the circumstances, standing in front of a sheer drop with a man who's previously abducted me at knifepoint. But I do, just as I know that all this, and I still don't know what *this* is, is coming from a place inside him I know only too well, and that's a place of pain.

I lean closer, urging him all the while

'I don't know what went wrong; how can I? I don't know what any of it means – that message, why Penny wrote it – but you do, and if you tell me, then maybe we can try and work out what's happening here, maybe even try and work out where she is right now.'

He's still looking at me, his eyes guarded, but I can see something else there too. There's doubt now, and there's fear. Doubt that he may have got this wrong. And – maybe – fear as to the consequences if he has.

'It should have been simple.'

It's as if the words are being forced out of him, and perhaps they are. For whatever reason, he's now re-thinking all he's previously thought, and it seems to be terrifying him.

'It's you; it had to be.'

Then he tails off, hopelessly lost. About as lost as I'm feeling right now as well, but I stay silent, I don't crowd him, and after another moment he shakes his head.

'If it was, it would have been dangerous enough.'

Abruptly, he stops again.

'Dangerous to who?'

Rory takes a deep breath.

'It's all Penny knew. All she was ever told was that it was you, or someone close to you.'

I feel like I'm on some sort of switchback ride, jumping more and more erratically from rail to rail – making a brief connection, but just as I feel as if I'm moving forward, I'm thrown off course again. But suddenly, there's another distraction, another car approaching up the lane. This time we don't tense like we did a few moments ago. Maybe this one will simply drive past too. But as we both keep listening, our eyes now turned towards the lane, the note of this car's engine changes as its speed slackens, and we hear it slow to a crawl as it turns into the car park. Then there's silence as the engine is turned off.

Rory and I exchange wary glances. This is a well-known beauty spot. Whoever's in that car could just be some holiday-maker out on a jaunt or a local looking to stretch their legs, take in the view. But then, from the stile that leads from the car park to the approach to the folly, we hear a shout.

'Axel?'

I stare back down the hill as I recognise the voice immediately. And as he hears it too, Rory's face contorts in fury. Instantly, I hold up my hands, trying to calm him, but then I see Harry appear at the foot of the slope below. Rory turns back to me, and now the fear that first flooded through me when I saw him dropping down from that ledge a few minutes ago is back. I have absolutely no idea what he might do. By the time the advancing Harry can reach us, it's perfectly possible I might be taking that death-embracing plunge down to the valley floor after all.

But then Rory turns, starts to run down the hill away from the folly. From further down the slope on the other side, a breathless Harry keeps making his way up to me, but I just keep watching Rory as he crashes over a small hedge, his strong legs barely breaking stride.

And I keep watching, increasingly helpless, as he turns at the bottom of a small path, plunges on into a dense crop of trees and is lost from view.

CHAPTER 78

PRESENT DAY

A WARRANT CARD opens all sorts of doors. It was one of the first lessons Braith took away from her initial training. That training was conducted by a maverick officer who'd only lasted a few months in his new post before the authorities grew increasingly nervous about his determinedly unconventional approach to the coaching of raw recruits. But it was also one she's never forgotten, and it's advanced several investigations for her in the past. With luck, it will do again.

Braith eyes the on-site concierge as he moves from flat to flat in the complex, delivering the day's mail to residents. And as she does so, Braith lets her mind run on one of those residents, her senior officer, something – as she's already realised – she is doing more and more lately.

She's still deeply unhappy about the way Adams just let Axel go like that. Had it been left to her she'd have let him stew in a cell for the maximum time permitted and then applied to have him further detained for at least as long again. It was another of those lessons drummed into her by her maverick instructor. Another time-honoured tactic that has produced results many times too.

But lately, she's really begun to wonder about Adams. He was more heavily involved in the investigation into Cara's disappearance than she first realised. He'd even taken charge of it at one point when the original supervising officer had to go into hospital following a health scare. And Braith's forensic examination of the case notes identified several moments in that investigation where avenues hadn't been pursued and leads hadn't been exploited as aggressively as they could have been. Which could just be the benefit of hindsight, of course, but could be something else.

And then there was that phone call. That hissed one-sided exchange she heard from the other side of Donna Petersen's bedroom door as she spoke to someone on her mobile, followed almost immediately by the sight of her senior officer on his mobile too. Which could just be a coincidence, or – and again – could be something else.

Another aside from her maverick instructor floated through her mind as she studied those old case notes, well away from any prying eyes. He'd positively encouraged a healthy scepticism towards anyone and everyone involved in a case, and that included colleagues. No one, as he'd often point out, was ever in a better position to choke off potential lines of inquiry than the officer or officers supposedly pursuing them.

As the concierge posts Adams's mail through his letterbox, Braith pushes herself off the wall on which she was sitting and makes for the reception desk on the other side of the complex. A quick check among police property records has told her the concierge holds entry codes for all the flats for safety reasons.

All Braith has to do is find the one for Adams's flat.

CHAPTER 79
TWENTY YEARS AGO

CARA HADN'T DONE this since she was a small child.

Years before, she'd sit like this, at her mum's dressing table, in front of the mirror, opening the drawers, taking out the cotton wool balls and make-up brushes, applying lipstick, most of which went on her six-year-old cheeks rather than her lips, leading her indulgently watching mum to wonder if they shouldn't have christened her Coco instead, after the clown.

Since then, she'd used her own make-up on the few occasions she'd felt the need. Most times, she just didn't bother. But she was bothering tonight. And there was one particular part of that make-up she was struggling with.

'It's a disaster.'

Cara squatted hopelessly before the mirror, the arched wings she'd been attempting to ascribe above her eyelids, dark smudges of nothingness. Donna eyed her for a moment, her silence saying it all. Cara was right. Then she pulled a stool from across the room, straddling it so she was just a few inches from her daughter's face. She'd already volunteered her small car for Cara to drive that night. Now she had another task to perform.

'Close your eyes.'

Cara did as she was told, breathing in her mother's scent as she did so, realising, with something of a jolt, that she probably hadn't been this physically close to her for years. She felt a light brushing on her forehead as Donna got to work. And for a moment, even though her mum was there, she found herself missing her, along with her dad, who was away right now, overseas at yet another of his auctions.

'So, who's going tonight.?'

Instinctively, Cara made to open her eyes to answer.

'Keep them closed.'

Cara – her eyes still shut – hesitated, then shrugged.

'Everyone, really.'

'Everyone as in?'

'The whole year.'

'And Mark?'

Cara felt herself begin to tense.

'Of course.'

'And Jericho?'

Cara willed herself not to tense anymore, but it was already a losing battle.

'Why not?'

Silence descended. Briefly, Cara wondered if her mum was studying her handiwork.

But Donna wasn't. Her daughter's eyes might have been closed, but it really didn't matter. She was infused right now; there was no other word for it. She had a look on her face that Donna had to go back years herself to recall, but it was one she'd never forget. Back then, she'd looked much like her daughter looked right now.

In those early, heady days when she'd first met Axel.

CHAPTER 80
PRESENT DAY

'WHAT THE HELL do you think you're doing?'

Harry stares at me.

'Why weren't you picking up your calls or reading your texts? For God's sake, Axel, it was bad enough finding out from Patrick you're meeting some anonymous madman, but when I can't get hold of you too?'

Harry sweeps his arm around the open landscape, that sheer drop just metres away, plunging hundreds of feet down to the river and the valley floor.

'I was going to call the police. Then I thought, no, call, text, first. If I don't get a reply, find out what's going on.'

I look down at my phone and see his message on the screen.

'And who was that, for fuck's sake?'

Harry nods down the hill towards my now-departed companion.

'Rory.'

'Rory?' Harry stares at me again. 'The kid from the train?'

'Yes.'

'The one who abducted you?'

I struggle against the admission for a moment, then nod back.

'Who held you at knifepoint?'

Harry shakes his head, disbelief flooding his face. Maybe if our situations had been reversed, I'd be doing the same.

'You're an antiquarian bookseller, Axel, not some adrenaline junkie. Didn't you stop for a moment to think before you hared up here?'

But I'm not listening. All I can see is Rory once more, standing in front of me. What was he trying to say? And what was he still holding back? There was something he was desperate to tell me, something he was on the brink of telling me, and if Harry hadn't turned up like that he might have done. But somehow, I doubt it. There was still some hurdle he had to vault, some inner voice he had to silence before he could do that.

And what did he mean by saying people were in danger, that this was already dangerous enough? Who exactly was he talking about? And someone close to me; he said that too – but surely that could only mean one person now?

On an impulse, I hit the connect button on my mobile and hear Donna's number start to ring. Harry stares at me, increasingly bewildered, as my ex-wife's phone just keeps on ringing, but she doesn't answer. Still not really knowing what I'm doing or why I'm doing it, I cut the call as Donna's standard answerphone greeting kicks in, and I begin to run down the steep slope to my waiting car, yelling back over my shoulder as I go.

'We've got to find her, Harry. We've got to find Donna. Now.'

CHAPTER 81
PRESENT DAY

HER FAVOURITE POETS all used to do it. All the great Romantics: Coleridge, Byron, and Keats. They all enthusiastically embraced the opportunity to connect with nature, to nourish their creativity, garner spiritual inspiration, perhaps even experience the sublime.

The activity, if not obsession, back then was called Hydromania. Now it's called wild swimming, and Donna loves it. Not that she actually calls it that, because to her and to many similar devotees, it's just swimming. To call it wild always feels as if that's prioritising the urban and the municipal somehow over the rural and the natural. And around here she's spoilt for choice when it comes to the rural and the natural. Within a few miles of home she has a whole array of clear, deep water, from mountain lakes and river pools to old quarry sinkholes and lagoons. As well as the estuary and, of course, the sea. But today she drives to her favourite spot of all, a natural lake formed in a hollow half-way up one of the nearby mountains. And as she approaches, she lets her mind drift.

Urban dwellers seem more alienated from nature now than ever before. It's something she is noticing more and more. They travel to work on buses and trains, sit at a desk in front of a computer all day. Most of them live in small flats with no gardens and buy their food in supermarkets. If they pass trees out on a street, they're a relative rarity, and most of them wouldn't recognise individual birdsongs even if they could hear them above all the passing traffic. Humans are just not built to live that way. It's disorientating, alienating. And so it begins, just as it did with Donna, that latent hunger pulling them towards anything that feels like the great outdoors.

Donna parks her car, lines from Amy Liptrot's addiction memoir, *The Outrun*, now running through her mind as they often do at times like these:

By swimming in the sea, I cross normal boundaries. I'm no longer on land but part of a body of water making up all the oceans of the world, which moves, ebbing and flowing under and around me. Naked on the beach, I am a selkie slipped from its skin.

And that sudden immersion into freezing water, that immediate and instant shock to the system does something else of course. Something elemental takes over, a primeval instinct just to survive; it drives everything else out of your mind. Over the course of the last twenty years she's had cause to be grateful for that particular sensation many times. And on, or around, the anniversary of Cara's disappearance, she's even more grateful.

Changing, as she usually does, in her car, she's pleased to see that there's only one other swimmer in the lake that day. Conversation isn't encouraged, but there's always the odd one who seems to want to reach out and make contact. But this one, a woman, her head encased in a red swimming hat, is over on the far side by the reeds. She's just ploughing on almost mechanically and doesn't even seem to realise she has company, which suits Donna just fine.

But then, and just for a moment, just before she plunges in herself, she pauses as she looks at that red swimming hat, which is now turning as the woman bobs up and down across the lake. She has no idea why, but for some reason the movement reminds her of a circling shark. But then she puts that ridiculous notion out of her head, jumps in and gives herself up to the water.

CHAPTER 82
PRESENT DAY

I'VE no idea what this is. More paranoia? Another manifestation of the madness that seems to have totally claimed me in the last few days? The same madness that made me reach out like that towards a stranger on that train, that made me head back into a bookshop after a man who'd previously kidnapped me at knife-point. The madness that's claiming me right now as I dash back into Donna's house, our old home, the home where we raised our daughter, all the time yelling my ex-wife's name over and over again.

Harry certainly thinks so. He abandoned his car by the old folly and clambered into the passenger seat beside me as I started the engine to drive back down the lane. The expression on his face then and now says it all. So far as he's concerned, I've totally lost it.

But what if it isn't paranoia? What if this isn't any kind of madness? What if it's something else, some instinct telling me that something's wrong, badly wrong, and that Donna is now in danger? She has to be who Rory was talking about. And even if I can't explain it and certainly can't rationalise it, I can't ignore it and I can't not act on it either. It's as if I'm in the grip of some larger force propelling me along, and now I'm here, back in our old home, I'm becoming more certain, not less. I don't know how, and I don't know in what way, but right now Donna's in trouble.

I nod at Harry. 'She's not here – her car's gone.'

'So? She's probably gone shopping or something.'

I look round, wildly, as he tries and fails to calm me. On my instruction, Harry's been trying her mobile all the way down from my aborted rendezvous with Rory, but it's still going to answer-phone. That isn't that unusual, admittedly. Donna frequently forgets to take it with her when she goes out anywhere. That isn't just forgetfulness on her part, there's simply no need most times. She's cut so many people out of her life since Cara, has walled herself up so completely that few now try to reach out to her. She told me once that she can go days sometimes without a single call showing up on her display.

But today's different, this is different, and again I know it. It's something else telling me that Donna's at risk. I head into her bedroom, trying to ignore the always-closed door to Cara's old room. Then a sudden thought strikes me. Moving to a large chest of drawers, I open the second drawer down, knowing what she keeps there. One moment later I'm striding back to the car, Harry following yet again, increasingly mystified but still keeping pace with me. Because now I know where she might be.

It takes us just over ten minutes to get to the lake. Donna's car is on the bank, so whatever else I've got wrong lately, I've got this right at least. Her oldest, most favourite swimsuit, missing from that chest of drawers in our old bedroom, has led us to her, but it hasn't, because as I stand on the edge of the lake with Harry next to me, she's nowhere to be seen. There's one swimmer out there, a woman with a red bathing cap, but she's getting out on the other side, reaching for a towel hanging from the branch of a nearby tree, her clothes presumably stacked nearby. I don't know who she is, but she isn't Donna. Even from this distance across the water I can see she's at least twenty to thirty years younger than my ex.

I keep scanning the water. By my side I can sense Harry's own unease building as mine now approaches fever pitch.

Donna was here, of that there's no doubt.

But she's not now.

CHAPTER 83
PRESENT DAY

SHE'S TOTALLY FORGOTTEN what it used to be like. That brutal shock when your body first hits the water, the searing disbelief that anyone would choose to do this out of choice – and for pleasure! – the desperation to get back out as quickly as possible and to envelop yourself in the largest towel you can find. But then, and within moments, all that changes. Slowly but surely, something takes over that isn't pleasure exactly but is far from pain.

It's as if all the senses suddenly become heightened. Every nerve end seems to glow. Even sight and sound seem to shift onto a whole other plane. She feels connected to a world she's never known before, and it's all down to her. The woman she can see across the lake, slipping into the water just as she did herself those few moments ago.

She panicked when she first saw her. She was close to the bank when the woman pulled up, and it would have been disastrous if she'd actually tried to speak to her. But a couple of smooth strokes took her to the middle of the lake and then across to the other side, and even though she hasn't been wild swimming for a long while, she still remembers the etiquette. People come to spots like these to be alone with their thoughts, to escape from the everyday. So, she's confident that once she strikes out like that, the woman she can now see making her own strong strokes in the water won't follow.

But it's still so strange to be in such proximity to her after all this time. She felt close to her when she listened to the sounds of the house remotely, and she felt even closer when she slipped back into the actual house like that. But it was just her both times. Now there's the two of them, and it's almost as if they're alone in the world, which means she can do anything she wants, and no one will ever know.

And if she does what she feels like doing right now, then no one will even begin to suspect any sort of foul play. Donna is a late middle-aged woman swimming alone in an unsupervised lake with all sorts of hidden hazards under the surface. If anything happened, the police would investigate, but they'd probably just put it down to an accident waiting to happen.

She keeps watching as she sees Donna circling round in the middle of the lake. Right over the spot where the water must be at its deepest. Then Donna turns over and floats on her back, arms outstretched like a starfish. And even though she's many metres away, she can see that Donna has closed her eyes now too.

She could do it now. Right now. And as she thinks about it, begins to visualise it indeed, she feels the old familiar excitement begin to build inside.

CHAPTER 84
PRESENT DAY

'WHAT ARE YOU DOING?'

I hit buttons on my mobile, staring round the lake all the while, growing as cold as the water rippling out before us at the thought of what might have happened and where Donna might be. Then I bark out a one-word response as the voice on the end of the line asks which emergency service I want.

'Police.'

Harry keeps staring at me. Ignoring him, I tell the handler that I need police divers to attend the scene of a possible drowning, as well as paramedics.

The responder's calm voice modulates down the line.

'Did you see your ex-wife when she was swimming, caller? Did you actually see her go under the water?'

I don't hesitate for a moment.

'Yes, I saw her out on the water. Yes, I saw her get into difficulties. Yes, I saw her go under.'

Harry continues to watch me as the bare-faced untruth unfolds, but I'm way beyond worrying about that now. Only one thing matters and that's getting help, and whatever I have to do, I'm going to do.

Inspiration suddenly strikes me.

'The air ambulance.' I've seen it parked on one of the fields bordering a road I take from my cottage to the bookshop every now and again.

'It can land next to the cars; there's enough room here, I'm sure there is.'

Harry tries cutting in.

'Axel.'

I turn away from him, still speaking all the while. Reception can be hit and miss at this spot at the best of times.

'I'll stay on the line, but please, let me know what's happening, who's coming, how long they'll be.'

I feel Harry's hand on my shoulder and brush him off, but then he wheels me round. And now I stare at Donna, emerging from a large copse on the bank to our side, towelling her hair as she does so, before she stops and looks across at us. On the other end of the line the emergency handler, as calm and as cool as ever, gives the first of the updates.

But I can't take my eyes off Donna, who's now staring at us, a look of total bewilderment on her face.

CHAPTER 85
TWENTY YEARS AGO

THE FIRST HOUR was every bit as bad as Jools feared. The music was crap, the sound system was old and crackly, the only booze on offer was lukewarm white wine or even warmer cheap lager, and Cara was in a mood. In fact, Cara was in one hell of a mood, and the reason for it was obvious in the way her head would swivel towards the large double doors at the end of the hall each time they opened.

Mark had entered a short time before, shuffling as he always did, almost as if he was hoping no one would see him. And Cara, indeed, barely noticed him, and the reason was once again obvious.

Jools moved close to her friend as one song finished, and another started.

'I'll get him to dance.'

Cara looked at her best friend as Jools continued.

'He'll hate it, but he's too nice to say no. I'll keep him dancing for the next half hour. When he looks for you, I'll tell him you've gone to help out in the kitchen or something, that you'll be back in a bit.'

Cara didn't say anything.

'Just go and find out what's going on. You'll be a pain all night if you don't.'

Cara leant forward impulsively and kissed her. Then she turned and headed for the door.

———

A short time later, Cara let herself into the bookshop. It was quiet, almost sepulchral, and there was nowhere else she'd rather be. She moved on into the rare books room, calling out as she approached so as not to alarm its exotic lodger.

Then she stopped dead as she saw the empty room before her, Jericho and his meagre stack of possessions all gone.

CHAPTER 86
PRESENT DAY

BRAITH HAS no real idea what she's looking for. Adams is hiding something; she knows that much. But that's all she still knows. And Adams himself isn't exactly helping either.

Her mobile has already pulsed three times. She stole a glance at the display on the second call to see that her senior officer, of all people, was trying to get hold of her and that he'd made the first call too. Which is creepy given where she is right now. What he wants she has no idea – he can't know where she is, surely – but when the third call alert pulsed from the same number, she knew it had to be urgent, and that she couldn't ignore him much longer. Which made it even more galling that she still hadn't gained anything remotely useful out of this strictly unauthorised visit.

Then Braith's phone pulses for a fourth time and now she has no choice; she really does have to answer.

'DS Braith.'

Adams's voice crackles down the line.

'Braith, what's going on? This is the fourth time I've tried you.'

'I'm sorry, I'd nipped into a shop and left my phone in the car.'

She closes the doors on a chest of drawers she's just opened in the bedroom. Nothing of any interest inside there either.

'I need you to get over to Axel Petersen's place.'

Briefly, her pulse quickens. Has there been a development? Irony of ironies, while she's been pursuing this almost literal dead end, has something happened?

'Comms received an emergency call from him a few moments ago. It was the weirdest thing, some story about his wife getting into difficulties while she was out swimming. I've listened to the recording – he sounds frantic, then suddenly he cancels the call, saying he made a mistake. I want you to get over there and find out what's going on.'

'I'll do it straight away.'

'Report back to me the minute you've seen him. I'm in a briefing with the ACC for the next half hour but I'll be free after that.'

Then Adams pauses.

'Where are you anyway?'

'I'll be at his place in twenty.'

'I mean, right now.'

Braith opens the door, moving out into a communal corridor.

'I'm in town. Just picked up a pasty.'

Adams hesitates a moment, as if he wants to say something else, but then he cuts the call. Braith turns away, then stops. Further down the same corridor, the concierge from earlier is now eyeing her, suspiciously. But he isn't actually the problem.

The problem is a different figure she's just spotted moving down a path to another of the flats in the complex.

And Braith really – really – does not want him spotting her here right now.

CHAPTER 87
TWENTY YEARS AGO

'WHERE ARE YOU?'

Jools hissed down the phone line at Cara, and on the other end of the line, Cara's voice broke.

'He's gone, Jools. Jericho's gone.'

And that's all it took. That one crack in her best friend's voice that confirmed all she needed to know. She looked back across the dance floor and didn't reply for a moment. Mark was lovely. A real sweetie; he always had been and he always would be. Then Jools paused as she kept looking at him. At least, she'd always thought so. As the last hour had ground by and Cara remained a no-show, she'd begun to see a different side to him. Not that it mattered anyway. The world had shifted on its axis so far as Cara was concerned, and there was only room now for one boy in it. And it wasn't the one Jools could see across the dance floor staring mournfully towards the door. He didn't know it yet, but he was part of Cara's past. Someone else had taken his place.

Jools leant closer to her phone, quiet, urging.

'He's got no money, so wherever he's gone, how far can he have actually got?'

———

But suddenly, Cara wasn't listening. Because it wasn't strictly true that the rare books room was empty or that Jericho had left nothing behind. There was something there, pinned up on the wall.

Another sketch, but not of a leaf this time.

Of her.

Cara cut the call, snatched the sketch down from the wall, and dashed for the door.

CHAPTER 88
PRESENT DAY

THE POLICE ARRIVE despite my cancelling the emergency call. The divers haven't yet been alerted, so I'm spared the humiliation of specialist officers speeding up from their base some fifty or so miles away. But I still have to endure some very uncomfortable questions as well as Donna's confusion. She clearly can't remotely understand why I'd assume she'd suddenly got into difficulties on a swim she does virtually every day of the year. I don't answer because I can't. Maybe instinct has been eclipsed by paranoia after all.

Patrick calls later in the evening after Donna has left and Harry has returned home with her. Ostensibly he's called to update me on his search for information about Penny, but it's probably to check on me too.

So far as Penny is concerned, there's nothing to report. He's still hitting the same brick wall, meaning some sort of block may well have been placed on anything to do with her or her sister. Why that should be, he still has no idea.

A few moments later, I slip out of the rear door of the cottage and walk down to the beach. On the way I pass Aidan, mercifully without his pit bull this time. Briefly, I wonder what he's doing out here; he seems to be just hovering, almost as if he's keeping watch for something or someone, but I soon put him out of my mind. I have plenty enough to think about without puzzling over a neighbour I've always found slightly creepy, in truth.

I press on instead. Donna has her ritual, which is wild swimming. I have mine. In times of trouble, and at many other times too, I do what I'm doing right now; I walk. It's a ritual that began in the dark days and even darker nights after Cara disappeared. With tensions at fever pitch back home, I moved out for a while and travelled to another small seaside town, taking an out of season holiday let on the far western edge of the country next to a large park.

The walks were usually solo outings, but one night I had company. About a week or so into my stay, I became aware of a figure trailing me. I ploughed on and tried to ignore my ghost-like companion, until I suddenly turned and realised it was Mark. How my assistant had managed to trace me I didn't know. I assumed he was still opening the shop in my absence, but by then I frankly didn't care. For his part he didn't actually approach, just maintained his watching brief, making sure, like Patrick just now presumably, that I was OK, or as OK as I could be. Or maybe it was his way of trying to exorcise his own grief about the still-missing Cara. But then he seemed satisfied I wasn't about to harm myself and left me alone.

Out on this latest walk, I clamber up over some rocks to a path that leads around the headland. Idly, my eyes wander up to the castle high up on the hill. Then I look down onto a small car park where ice cream vendors ply their trade in the summer, and up again towards a small children's adventure playground, recently renovated with new equipment. It's become an instant hit with all the village children, their stressed parents delighted to deliver their hyper charges down here for a few hours each weekend.

Which is when, suddenly, I see him again. I see Mark, in my mind's eye at least. And what this is, again, I don't know. More paranoia probably. But for some reason a new and uneasy feeling begins to creep over me. Had all that been simple concern for me back then? Or something else?

Then, out of nowhere, another image flashes before my eyes, this time of Donna and Harry. And it's another of those strange associations, it can't be anything else, but they're twins too, of course. Like Penny and Jen.

But now my ex-wife, her brother and my assistant in the book-shop are all driven from my mind as I see someone else, and this is no figment of my probably over-heated imagination. This figure is standing on the beach below, staring up at me.

I hesitate a moment, then stand and walk down to the waiting Rory.

CHAPTER 89
PRESENT DAY

TIME ISN'T A PROBLEM. He has plenty of that. Distractions and interruptions aren't a problem either because no one is likely to disturb him. The problem is choice. Selecting just one from the dozens of photographs on offer before him.

At times in the past, he's tried to vary the background, selecting a snap from inside the house or a friend's house, then maybe the next one from outdoors, in a shopping centre or a park. But then he'd try to mix it up in other ways too. He'd choose one photo where she was alone and the next when she was part of a group. He thought it'd become harder to pick out new ones as the years passed, but actually it wasn't. Maybe he'd come to feel he now had a right to browse like this among personal family mementoes. As if he'd earned it somehow.

This time he chooses a photo of Cara on the beach outside the old family home. She's alone and walking towards the camera, the sun setting behind her, burnishing her hair an autumnal gold. Her eyes are cast down as if she's lost in thought. Which is when something suddenly strikes him, and he turns the photo over. They're usually annotated with the date they were taken, and sure enough there it is.

This particular photo was snapped less than a week before she disappeared. He turns the photo back over. Maybe she looked lost in thought for a good reason. Maybe she had a lot think about.

Briefly he considers another option, an interior photo this time of Cara sitting in her favourite chair, reading a book. She seems unaware the photo is being taken, which lends a natural quality to the shot. But in the end, he sticks to his original choice.

Then Mark takes the selected photo and lays it next to the other photos of Cara he's picked out over the last twenty years.

CHAPTER 90
TWENTY YEARS AGO

CARA CAUGHT up with Jericho on the platform of one of the local train stations, just as an east-bound train was coming in. This station was unmanned; he knew that and so did she. It would have been the reason he'd chosen it; so he would only have to navigate the guard on the train. But he wasn't going to get the chance.

Cara didn't speak as she approached, didn't need to. She just held up the sketch of herself she'd found on the wall. Jericho didn't speak either. He didn't need to either. The way he looked at her, and the way she looked back at him, told each other everything they both needed to know.

Cara moved closer, and Jericho just had time to mount an unconvincing protest.

'I'm trouble, Cara.'

She moved closer still.

'This is trouble.'

Cara whispered back.

'I know.'

Then she moved into his arms.

PART FOUR

PART FOUR

CHAPTER 91
PRESENT DAY

THE CARE HOME Open Day is part of a national initiative, according to the flyer that was thrust into my hand by the smiling helper as I arrived. It's a chance for the home in question to showcase what it has to offer to both potential residents and their relatives, in terms of its facilities, activities and services.

It isn't just about residents and their families though. Should I ever be inclined to give up the sometimes-dubious delights of life as an antiquarian and secondhand bookseller, the Care Home Open Day will also afford me a first-hand opportunity to experience working life in a care home and to talk to team members about how rewarding the sector can be as a career.

I look around at the milling residents and staff dotted around the lawns and open terraces as I arrive, more smiling helpers moving from resident to guest with trays of soft drinks and finger food. This was a regular event up to a couple of years ago, when the pandemic put a stop to it along with so much else. That was not only disappointing, but in some cases devastating, as residents became more and more isolated, with often-tragic results as end of life arrived with no family member present to hold their hands.

I keep looking around. Rory has provided me with a thumbnail description of the woman I'm searching for, but as luck would have it, the residents have each been furnished with badges proclaiming their first names in a gaily coloured font. So, all I have to do now is wander round the open lawns and terraces and hope that Beth isn't having one of her bad days and missing out on it all inside.

I look down at the flyer again and, as casually as I can, keep checking the different residents who are being helped or wheeled past me. There's a lot of creativity in UK Care Homes, apparently, so the flyer informs me, with teams in numerous homes supporting residents to express themselves via everything from painting to poetry writing, and drama to music making. And it's painting that's the theme of this Open Day, with the company who run this home challenging residents and staff to produce some special artwork.

A woman shuffles past, supporting herself on a stick. For a moment I think it's her, but a closer look at her nameplate revealed she's a Bee, short for Beatrice perhaps, but not Beth. A nurse looks at me, slightly curious, as I stare at the old and shuffling lady, so I look down at the flyer again.

In Suffolk, I discover, residents and friends of Cleves Place in Haverhill will be making the fun last all weekend, with music therapy on Friday, arts and crafts and a flower arranging workshop on Saturday, and a barbecue and art exhibition on Sunday.

Reading on, I find that in Surrey, the team at Appleby House will be unveiling the results of their ambitious community project, with five impressive all-weather murals put together by residents and local schoolchildren, from designs supplied by thirty different community stakeholders, from police to paramedics.

At Ferndown Manor in Dorset there's going to be beach-themed summer hat and bunting making, accompanied by holiday music from a DJ, while the Potteries in Poole is taking inspiration from the home's name with a Poole Pottery talk, exhibition and sale, with arts and crafts sessions.

And in Edinburgh, visitors to Lauder Lodge will be creating their own jewellery during a special workshop I discover, the motto of the day being Creative at Any Age.

———

The cautious thaw between myself and Rory is continuing. He was still holding something back yesterday evening down on the beach, but he does seem to have accepted that I was as frustrated by Harry's sudden appearance as he was. And he finally gave me some sort of lead.

'I don't know anything about her, not really. Penny only talked about her the once when I came across an old photo, but she's the only person from her past she's ever talked about, so it stuck.'

Rory paused, his brow creasing. I had a thousand questions. I wanted to know how he'd met Penny, why she'd concocted that crazy scheme to target me on the train like that, what that message in the Frame volume was about. But a semblance of trust seemed to be establishing itself, and once again the last thing I wanted to do was to spook him by pushing too hard, too soon.

'She might know something, I don't know.'

Rory struggled to control what were clearly raging emotions.

'But it's been days now. And if Penny's going to have made contact with anyone round here, it might be her.'

He gave me that name, the Care Home address, that brief thumbnail description culled from the old photo he'd once seen, and then, just as quickly as he'd appeared in front of me, he was gone again.

I look down at the flyer once more as I thread my way across one of the lawns, nodding at various passing residents and care home workers as I go. I skirt children, their presence paying testimony, so the same flyer informs me, to the host of intergenerational art activities that are also taking place to showcase the close personal relationship the home enjoys with local schools and nurseries. From one of the terraces a 1940s swing band begins playing.

Then, at the far end of the lawn, looking out over the estuary, I see a hunched figure in a wheelchair. I'm too far away to see the name on her badge, but something about her hair and build makes my pulse quicken. Of all the residents I've seen so far, she's the closest to Rory's description. One of the smiling helpers – perhaps a member of the care staff, perhaps a volunteer – passes, a tray in hand, stacked high with homemade scones along with small catering packs of clotted cream and jam. I stop her.

'Could I take two?'

I indicate the wheelchair-bound lady facing away from us, still just looking out over the estuary, and the helper or volunteer nods enthusiastically. Enthusiasm seems to be the order of the day.

'Of course. Beth loves them.'

Then my smiling companion nods at me as I pick up the two scones on paper plates complete with the accompanying catering packs and two wooden knives.

'Just make sure you do it right or you'll get an earful.'

This puzzles me, but she's already been commandeered by another eager scone hunter and the moment's gone. I look across at Beth, still facing away from me, then take a quick, deep breath and head over. There's a bench less than a metre away from her and I sit down, not attempting direct contact for a moment. Then I turn to her, indicating the scone.

'I picked up two by mistake. Would you like one?'

Nothing comes back by way of a response. She just keeps staring out over the estuary.

I hesitate, then decide to go for broke.

'Beth?'

She turns and looks at me and for a moment I'm surprised. I'd expected to see an elderly lady, but she can't be much older than me. But then I see her blank eyes and my spirits sink. She seems disconnected, as if she has no idea where or even who she is. At this moment, I can't imagine a soul less disposed to offer me any sort of help.

But then, as her features come more into focus, something akin to an electric shock courses through me as an equally sudden realisation dawns.

Because I know her.

We've met before.

CHAPTER 92
PRESENT DAY

FOR A FEW MOMENTS my brain refuses to kick into gear. Yes, we've met, but where, when? I definitely know her face, but maybe I just can't associate that face with the withered body that now seems to barely support her.

I've not seen her recently, I'm sure. Wherever our paths have crossed, it's from years ago. Swiftly I run through friends and acquaintances from the book trade, people I might have come across in book fairs or on my travels, but no names or faces spring to mind. Which means she must be from further back still, is maybe an old friend of Donna's; she definitely looks to be around our age. But still I can't place her.

'I'm looking at the care home for my mother.'

She just keeps staring at me, still blank, still uncomprehending.

'She's been living on her own for the last few years, but lately she's really found it a struggle.'

I struggle on myself, scarcely knowing what I'm saying now, barely listening to the fictions I'm inventing. My mind's racing all the time, searching for connections.

'When I saw the advert for the Open Day, I thought it was a good chance to come and see the place for myself, get a feel for it before I talk to her about coming here too.'

Still nothing from those uncomprehending eyes, and still nothing from my blank memory either. So, I plough on, much like those writers who give occasional talks in the bookshop, putting words down on a page in search of a story.

'How do you find the place? Have you lived here long?'

Briefly, there's something there as I look at her, but then it's gone. If that has stirred anything, it's vanished just as quickly.

'My old mum's a bit of a foodie. Well, she used to be – arthritis means she can't cook as well as she used to, but she still gives me what-for if the olive oil in the salad dressing isn't extra virgin.'

Mentally, I proffer silent apologies to my long-deceased mother for appropriating her preferences and prejudices like this. But I may as well have been talking about the man in the moon for all the response I'm getting. But then I stop. Because suddenly I know exactly where our paths have crossed.

Jools. That was her name. Cara's friend from school, her best friend in fact, the friend whose house I'd called at first after she went missing. Which is where I first met the woman now in the wheelchair before me; she's Jools's mum, and that's how I remember her. From that panicky morning as I searched for a daughter I wasn't destined to find.

That's one mystery solved – who she is, and how I know her. But it only ushers in a fresh one in its wake. What possible connection could there be between her and Penny?

For want of anything better to do I pick up a knife, take the scone I've brought over for her and split it into two, then open the small catering pack of cream, when suddenly she cuts in, speaking for the first time.

'Jam first.'

I look at her, my knife poised, but her eyes are fixed only on the catering pack in my hand.

'Then the cream.'

And a memory flashes in front of my eyes, as sharp as the colours out on the estuary below. It's of Cara, sitting at our old kitchen table, a scone in her hand too, patiently explaining to

Donna and me just why it had always had to be jam first and then cream and never the other way round. I knew Devonians swore by cream first and then jam, while their Cornish neighbours were equally adamant that the opposite was the only true way, but I'd never had any idea why my daughter should have elected for one rather than the other. Maybe this was the answer. Maybe it originated with Beth.

I hesitate. 'Cara wouldn't have it any other way.'

Beth's eyes focus on me as I attempt to smile.

'It was virtually a hanging offence if we even tried to put the cream on first.'

'Cara.'

Beth rolls the name around her tongue, almost underneath her breath, accenting each of the two syllables.

Then, abruptly, she turns back towards the estuary again, forgetting all about me, about the scone, and Cara, and the moment's gone.

CHAPTER 93
TWENTY YEARS AGO

MARK HAD LEFT THE DANCE. Jools didn't know where he'd gone. Cara still wasn't picking up her calls. But then, just as Jools was about to head home herself, her phone pulsed.

She snatched it up immediately, her friend's number on the screen.

'Cara?'

All she could hear for a moment was the sound of waves in the background.

'Where are you? What's happening? Did you find Jericho?'

Cara didn't speak for a moment, but then her voice, little more than a whisper, came back down the line.

'Yes.'

'And?'

Cara hesitated again as Jools heard another wave approach and then recede behind her.

'I need time to think.'

Jools looked back at the hall and the sweaty press of bodies still inside. Then she leant closer into her phone.

'What about Mark?'

Cara's voice came back louder now.

'That's what I need to think about.'

Then she cut the call.

CHAPTER 94
PRESENT DAY

His body isn't the worst she's ever seen, although given some she's encountered over the years maybe that's setting the bar a little low.

His face is probably his best feature. It's sort of crumpled and lived-in, but in quite a sexy way. She's heard the phrase before – tired eyes – without really understanding what it meant. But he has them. Eyes that look as if they've seen everything human beings have to offer and then more. Mysterious eyes too, which definitely elevates him above most of the punters she entertains in the front room of her small, rented terraced house with its private and very necessary side entrance, the main reason she agreed to rent it in the first place. It means men can approach and leave undetected from a side alley. This town is small, and no local wants to be spotted hammering on the front door of a well-known knocking shop.

As for the rest of his body, it's pretty well par for the course for a man of his age, which she estimates to be around his late forties or early fifties. A paunch, but not an excessive one. Muscles in most of the right places. But this one is different in another way from the rest of the flotsam and jetsam that pass through her side door and snort and thrust over her body five days a week, but never at weekends because that's when she has her eleven-year-old son to stay. This one likes to talk. In fact, sometimes he does nothing but talk, which was what he's doing right now.

She doesn't understand most of what he's saying; she never does. But she has the impression he's talking mainly for his own sake anyway, so she often drifts. As his voice rolls around the curtained living room, she wonders which of the local treats she might take her son to this weekend, be it a theme park or a local indoor climbing facility that has just opened and which she thinks he might like.

Briefly, some of what he's saying does register, though. There's something about his family, but that isn't all that unusual. Plenty of punters talk about wives, ex and present. Then she drifts again as she wonders if the indoor climbing facility has all its correct safety certificates and how she can check.

But then she realises it isn't a wife he's talking about today, ex or otherwise, but a daughter. And then she begins to tense, because there's something odd about the way he's talking about her too. And then it gets even odder as he starts talking about another girl, not his daughter, someone else. She doesn't know if she's hearing him right at first, or maybe she doesn't really want to. But he seems to be saying that he didn't even want to be in the same house as her – meaning his daughter – when she got to this other girl's age.

By now she's getting spooked, so she risks a glance at the clock on the side. He has ten more minutes before her next appointment. Giving a slight cough, she wonders if he might like to move on to some sort of happy ending before their time is up today. The way he's talking about young girls like that just feels wrong.

Which is when he looks at her almost as if he's seeing her for the first time. Then he looks at his phone as it beeps a text alert. Then the man she only knows as her 2 p.m. client, but who the rest of the world knows as DI Dan Adams stands, collects his clothes, dresses as quickly as he can and leaves by the side door.

CHAPTER 95
PRESENT DAY

HARRY HAS BEEN in a strange mood ever since they came back from the lake. Quiet, withdrawn, something clearly playing on his mind. But a lifetime's experience has taught Donna never to push too hard when he's in this sort of mood. All that would do would be to drive him deeper into what's become his habitual shell over the years. She just has to wait and hope that eventually he'll unburden himself.

Donna goes for a bath instead. She can hear Harry moving around the house, but it's comforting in a sense. Sounds outside the bathroom door hark back to days when there was always sound and movement here, be that Axel, or Cara with her friends.

But then, suddenly, everything goes quiet, and Donna, still soaking in the water, tenses. Has Harry gone home? She listens for the sound of his car driving away but hears nothing. And there's still no sound from inside the house either.

Donna, growing uneasy, climbs out of the bath and puts on a robe. She's no idea where this sudden unease has come from, but now she can't shake it off. Opening the bathroom door, she calls out.

'Harry?'

Nothing comes back. Donna looks towards the front door.

Maybe he's gone out for a walk, but now she can see the key still in the lock and the bolt in place on the inside too. So, Harry must still be in the house, but where?

Then, suddenly, from behind, her brother breaks in on her.

'Does he often do that?'

Donna wheels round, her breath suddenly coming in short gasps, but if he registers her new and sudden agitation, a brooding Harry gives no sign.

'Maybe you haven't noticed it, you must still see each other most weeks, but when you don't see someone for a while you catch things.'

Donna, calming now, takes a deep breath as Harry lapses into a troubled silence.

'Catch what? What are you talking about?'

For a moment she doesn't think he's going to say any more. That habitual shell again. But then, suddenly, he hunches closer.

'Some of the soldiers I used to go on ops with. They'd be fine – survive all sorts, come through every war zone, every tricky shout apparently unscathed.'

He tails off for a moment, lost in a memory.

'One squaddie, he was a real hero, carried five casualties out of a bomb strike in Homs. Four died in his arms, one survived. He's godfather to the man's new baby. Then one day – this is six months later – he's back home in his local convenience store and he's five pence short of the money he needs for his paper, just five pence.'

Harry's eyes are now even further away.

'He lost it. There and then, in that little store, the shopkeeper was going to give him his paper anyway, but he had a breakdown over one missing coin. Something just snapped.'

Harry keeps staring into the near distance as Donna watches him. There's something in his eyes now, something telling her that this isn't just a random memory. There's a rawness to his tone she hasn't heard before. So, is Harry talking about his own experiences here, something he's actually endured himself? Is he the man in that convenience store?

But before she can press him, Harry moves on.

'That girl. The one on the train. She was Cara's age, give or take.'

Then he looks back at her.

'Did Axel snap too?'

Donna doesn't reply and Harry doesn't elaborate. Five minutes later, he collects his keys, and this time Donna does hear his car as it starts up and he drives away. Quiet settles over the house again, but the rest of Donna's night is far from settled or peaceful.

Two things race through her mind. First, there's Harry's strange story and the window it has lifted on a brother who might have projected onto Axel details of his own breakdown.

But there's something else. When Harry's voice first broke in on her she'd turned to see Cara's bedroom door open behind him. Donna always keeps that door closed. Cara's space is always respected even if she hasn't occupied it for two decades. Everyone in the family knows better than to enter what they all know is less of a bedroom and more of a shrine.

Harry must have been in there while she was in her bath. That was why she suddenly couldn't hear a thing, and why she felt that strange unease.

But why Harry should have done that, and what he was doing in there, she has no idea.

CHAPTER 96
PRESENT DAY

I'VE PASSED the holiday park hundreds of times on the train and never given it a second glance. Occasionally I've heard fellow passengers pointing it out to their excited kids, some even identifying the one particular caravan they've booked, but that aside, it's just washed over me. Ours is a holiday destination. That's a holiday place. Nothing more to think about.

Until I see the photo.

———

I go back to Donna immediately after I leave Beth. My mind is in turmoil, but I manage to put on a reasonably calm front. I don't confide in her where I've been or why; I even manage to invent some half-plausible excuse as to why I want to look at Cara's old school photos, mumbling something about some possible new appeal on the police's part, using fresh images to the ones they've tried before.

Donna just leaves me to it. If she finds anything odd in the request, she doesn't show it. The news about that recently discovered body seems to have affected her powerfully, and now it's as if she's just waiting for the next blow to strike. The similar discovery of Cara's body, perhaps. Maybe that's why I want to keep going like this. My deepest fear right now is that if I stop, even for a second, I'll be sucked down into the same dark whirlpool that seems to be claiming my ex-wife. But I can't postpone it for ever, I know that.

Alone, I spread the photos out on the kitchen table in front of me. Most I discount, but as Cara progresses in school, Jools begins to feature more and more. I look at the pair of them, my daughter and her friend, at a sports day, out on a shopping trip in town, in the garden of this very house, down on the beach.

But then one photo in particular stops me. It's of Cara and Jools again, but this time they're outside a caravan. I place the setting immediately, and it sparks another memory, of the two girls spending part of a long summer holiday down there once, revelling in their new-found freedom, close to but far enough away from their respective homes. I also now remember Cara telling me that the caravan had been in Jools's family for years, that it was one of her mother's prized possessions, inherited from her own mother, and was just about the last thing she'd ever sell.

I don't know why that single photo lights the spark it does. I don't know why I feel my breath catch in my throat. Partly it's the girls, of course. They look like girls that age should look, happy and energised, in love with life and all its unfolding possibilities, worlds before them to conquer. And, by the look on their faces, with every intention of doing just that.

But then I begin to wonder. Does that caravan still belong to the family? I know there are several down there that families return to year in, year out. Will anyone be there who might still remember Beth and could tell more about her?

But above all, if there is a connection between Beth and Penny – and if that caravan is still in the family's possession – is that where Penny decamped to that night? Is this the answer to her apparent disappearance? Has she simply gone into hiding for some reason, and is she still there?

I arrive at the site half an hour later, the photo I've found still in hand. The whole place is pretty run down now, but I still identify the caravan in question within moments. I approach and tap on the door. I don't expect a reply from inside and I don't get one, so I push against it and the door swings open immediately.

Stepping inside, I stop, staring, as I see a gun pointing at me.

FOR A MOMENT the universe seems to shrink to that single, squat metallic barrel, held in what seems to be the steadiest of hands and pointing straight at my chest. My body sabotages me, fear robbing me of any thought of flight. All I can do is stand there and stare.

'Close the door.'

The gun is still all I can see. For a moment, I don't even register the fact that the command is barked out at me by a woman. But as I look up, it's not Penny, the girl I last saw walking away down that darkened lane. Rory's the only other person I've known in my life who has pointed any sort of weapon at me, but as well as being female, this voice is even harsher than his was that day, even more guttural. And while what I'm feeling is fear, what's informing every syllable of that curt, hissed instruction is simple, and it's hatred.

For a moment I don't recognise the woman holding the gun. Briefly, I wonder if we're in the middle of some massive misunderstanding, whether I've inadvertently stumbled in on an innocent holidaymaker, spooked by the sudden sight of an apparent intruder. But few innocent holidaymakers would bring a gun with them on a break to the seaside. Which is when I realise, for the second time today, that I know exactly who this is.

She's older, of course. And time hasn't been the kindest to her either; her hair's showing streaks of grey, and her face is lined. Crows' feet fracture the skin around her eyes, and she's a lot thinner now too. I may well have passed her in the street without realising who she was, but not here in this small caravan with the door now closed behind me. Just a few hours after I crossed paths with her mother, I stare at Jools, Cara's childhood friend, as she glares at me, that gun still in her hand.

I stand there for a moment longer, more lost than I've felt at any time lately, and given all that's happened these last few days, that really is saying something. Then I try and make some sort of tentative connection.

'Jools – please.'

Her mouth twists, rictus-like.

'You know who I am then?'

I hesitate.

'I wouldn't have. Not till an hour or so ago. But I saw you, and Cara. I was looking through some old photos. I never realised how many there were of you.'

Still that gun's being held steadily in her hand. Still it's pointing straight at me. At any moment I expect her to fire. In my mind's eye I run through those photos again, seeing once more the two girls, their arms around each other, laughing, joking, luxuriating in each other's company, the very best of friends.

'I never realised how close you were.'

Jools nods. 'Why do you think she came to me that night?'

I stare at her. 'That night?'

I flounder for a moment, then realise what she means

'The night she went missing?'

Jools snorts, almost contemptuously, the gun remaining rock steady in her hand.

'So far as you were concerned, maybe.'

Images from the dreadful day that followed flash in front of my eyes: my growing unease as the minutes ticked by, that first call to Cara's mobile, the first message I left, followed by another a few moments later, then more messages, a lot more, then the calls to her friends.

I keep looking at the adult Jools.

Then, driving out along the road leading to her house, that subsequent visit to Cai, scanning the lanes and nearby fields along the way in case she'd collapsed in a drunken stupor on her way home, trawling that beach. And then, finally, the recognition that something really was wrong and that call to the police.

I don't even see the gun now. While I was doing all that, had Jools known where Cara was all along? And Beth, her mum, had she known too? But why wouldn't she have said? She was a parent herself; she must have known the torment I'd be going through.

'Cara was with you that night?'

I stumble out the words, and Jools nods; only the slightest incline of her head, but a definite nod, nonetheless.

'But I came to see you. I talked to your mum.'

Jools shrugs.

'She was already pretty well out of it even back then, but she came through that night at least.'

Rage begins to build inside me.

'Came through? Kept our daughter's whereabouts from her parents – you call that coming through?'

'She wasn't going to. She was going to call you straight away, the minute she realised what Cara was doing, what was going on. And when she realised Cara wasn't going back she went mad.'

Each word is like a hammer blow. She wasn't going back? My own daughter? Up to now I've been convinced she must have been abducted by someone, held against her will somewhere. But is Jools saying that all that was her choice? That everything that happened that night was her own doing?

'Call your mum and dad – it's all she kept saying. Whatever's happened, talk to them, work it out.'

Jools eyes flash.

'Cara lost it, and I mean really lost it; I'd never seen her like that before. She was yelling at her, didn't she understand?'

I cut across, desperate.

'Understand? Understand what?'

'The danger she'd be in if Mum did pick up that phone.'

My confusion grows. This is the second time I've heard something like this, the first time from Rory, and I'm no closer to understanding what Jools means by it either.

'I thought I had problems with my dad. It was such a relief when that bastard left us – at least then I only had Mum to worry about.'

Jools's eyes flash. 'But he was a walk in the park compared to you, wasn't he?'

I try to wrestle back some sort of control.

'What did Cara tell you? What was I supposed to have done?'

But she doesn't answer directly.

'She could hardly think straight as it was. No wonder, not after everything that had happened with Jericho.'

I seize on the name, like a drowning man clutching at a lifeboat.

'Jericho? Was all that something to do with him?'

She looks at me with something almost approaching pity.

'It's all she said. You can't ever know.' Jools snorts, contemptuous. 'Her own mum and dad, and your own daughter couldn't even tell you.'

'Tell me what?'

Her eyes never leave mine, and all of a sudden, it's clear as I see them again in my mind's eye, as I see Cara and Jericho. But this makes no sense either.

'Was Cara pregnant?'

She just keeps looking at me, the granite in her stare my all too obvious answer, and I stare back in mounting disbelief.

'Are you saying that's why she went away, because she was pregnant and didn't want to tell us?'

But this is crazy. Cara was always able to tell us things; whatever happened, she was always able to come to us. And how bad would something like that have been anyway? I didn't realise she and Jericho had become that close, but it wouldn't have been a problem. It certainly wouldn't have merited all that happened next.

'So, the child – did she have the child?'

'Children.'

I stare back at her.

'She had twins.'

Jools shakes her head, almost more in sorrow than anger as my world explodes again.

'For a man who spends his days surrounded by all those books, you really can be totally fucking stupid sometimes, can't you?'

The feeling of dropping into that void continues to grow.

Penny is Cara's daughter.

Penny is the surviving twin.

Meaning Jen, the soul who plunged from that bridge... But then I stop, simply can't take this in. And suddenly, I'm not seeing Jools anymore and I'm still not seeing that gun either. Question after question is swimming around inside, each one piling on top of the other, but all I can see now is that girl on the train. I'm reliving that moment when I looked up, looked into her eyes, believing for an instant that I was looking into Cara's eyes, my own daughter's eyes, and now I know why, because in a way I was.

Jools's voice cracks.

'She saw you. She told me.'

I cut across again.

'What? What did she see?'

But she doesn't even seem to hear me. She just takes a deep breath and raises the gun towards my head.

CHAPTER
NINETY-EIGHT

ANY JOURNEY REQUIRES ADJUSTMENTS. And a twenty-year journey's going to require more than most. You can't anticipate every bump in the road, can't know when some unexpected event is going to hurl a curve ball your way, so you have to stay alert.

It sounds exhausting, as if your guard must perpetually be up, but you'd be surprised how quickly it becomes second nature. It becomes relegated to your peripheral vision. You get on with the everyday but keep a weather eye out for the unexpected. And then you deal with it.

It helps that you've always got what you might call the ultimate sanction. That you can simply make a problem go away. That might cause other problems because disposing of a human body is really not that easy, but around here there's plenty of deserted lanes and tracks, as well as acres of uninhabited land and plenty of tributaries and water courses running directly out to sea.

There's another option, of course, which is to let the problem solve itself. Everyone around these parts has seen the picture of those two fishermen who stumbled upon that giant sturgeon that day. But what's often missed in the story is that they could no more hook that giant creature out from its depths than sail to the moon. They just ran as it leapt up out of the pool and beached itself on the bank. It killed itself, in fact. It created the conditions that led to its own demise, which is a powerful lesson. Those fishermen didn't have to do anything, save taunt a creature they didn't even know was down there.

And once those unknowing hunters did that, their prey effectively embraced its own destruction.

CHAPTER 99
PRESENT DAY

I BRACE myself waiting for the explosion, or maybe not even that. Would you even hear it? Just a flash of light maybe, and then what? But I never find out. Because nothing happens.

Jools lowers the gun. Then she looks at me, and for the first time there's something in her eyes I haven't seen before. Fear's now flooding her face. Because she can't do it. She can't pull that trigger, and now she's scared.

'Jools – please.'

Then I duck as she hurls the gun at my head, striking me a glancing blow, and I crash to the floor. She dashes past me and out of the door. I struggle to my feet to go after her, but by this time she's already almost out of sight, haring away as if her life depends on it, maybe because in her mind it does.

Reeling, and not just from that close encounter with a gun, I stand there for a moment, trying and failing to take in all I've just been told. For a moment I even wonder if I've just hallucinated it in some way; whether my overheated brain, assailed on all sides by all that's happened in the last few days, has finally given way.

But then I see the gun lying where it fell by the door, and I know this is real. I pick it up, place it back on the table, then exit, retracing my steps to my car and trying desperately not to think of anything for at least the next few minutes, so I can work through all I've just been told.

I can't go home, I know that. And I can't go to Donna or my place of usual retreat, the bookshop, either. I need to go somewhere I've never been before; I need a blank space to inhabit and then maybe – maybe – I can start filling in the blanks inside my head, as well as working out what I have to do next. I need time and I need space and I need lots of it.

The problem is, I'm not destined to get either.

CHAPTER 100
TWENTY YEARS AGO

CARA BARELY KNEW where she was going, but that didn't matter anyway. Her dad did it all the time and now she was doing it too. She was just walking, giving herself space and time to think.

It had been a month since the night of the school dance. She'd split with Mark straight after. She'd seen Jericho almost daily but there was still that massive Tamerlane-shaped cloud above their heads. So, and while she waited for it to clear, however that might happen, she walked along beaches and streets. She climbed grassy hills. She stared out at the sea. Then she walked back along the streets that led to her dad's bookshop.

Which was when, suddenly, it was back. The strangest feeling that someone was watching her again.

Cara wheeled round. There were people passing on the pavement opposite, some other people coming out of a nearby pub. But there was no one she knew, and no one seemed to be taking any particular notice of her as they went on their respective ways either. But still she had the same feeling she first had as she stood with Jericho by that pop-up food stall that day. That someone was out there, and that they were keeping tabs on her.

Further down the street, a police car parked in shadows cast by the slowly setting sun caught her eye. For a moment, she thought about walking over there, relating all this to the officer whose dim shape she could see inside, but what would she say? It all sounded ultra-strange in her ears; it would sound even stranger if she actually said it out loud.

But then she realised that something else was staying her hand, and now she knew she was being ridiculous. Because as she kept looking down the street towards the police car, the officer – still just that distant shape inside – started the engine. The car drove away, probably having been summoned to some incident somewhere. But as it disappeared from view, so did that strange sensation. She'd felt like that once before, when that vehicle that looked like a Jeep disappeared too, and now it was back again. Cara didn't feel as if she was being watched anymore.

She turned away, shaking her head as if trying to physically banish thoughts that had to be little more than flights of fancy. But then she stopped again as she saw something else across the same street.

Cara stared across at a busy car wash. It wasn't Jericho's car wash; the one he worked in was in the car park of a large super-market on the other side of the town. But the sight of all those young men – all quite clearly from overseas and working like demented beetles – still brought him back before her eyes.

But that wasn't why she was standing there, feeling her breathing quicken as what was obviously their well-worn routine unfolded in front of her.

Because as she kept watching, she had it.

She had the answer to all this.

All of a sudden, she knew what must have happened.

CHAPTER 101
PRESENT DAY

A WRACKED Jools is back where she was all those days ago. High above Freshwater, Cara's old home village, looking out from the ruined castle across the estuary to Red Roses, her own former home village on the opposite side of the water.

When she was here a few days ago she was exultant as she watched Axel being subdued by that taser. Now, she's experiencing contradictory emotions, and it's all down to him, to Axel again.

She'd never really been able to work him out. She never saw too much of him of course, even when she visited Cara. He was away a lot, attending those strange book fairs of his, touring all those creepy houses, buying up libraries. But it wasn't just that. To appropriate a phrase from his field rather than hers, she just couldn't read him. With most people she met back then, she was able to get a handle on them pretty well straight away. Living with a mum like hers she'd developed what you might call adult skills at a very early age. But Axel, Cara's dad, had eluded her in ways she'd never really understood.

It didn't help that the terrified Cara wouldn't tell her the whole story. But in a way, her just being terrified was enough. All she'd say was that she couldn't stay there, not at home, not for a single moment longer, and Jools had to help her, and so, of course, she did. She tried pressing her, she couldn't help herself, but all Cara would say was that she was in danger, and from just about the closest person in her world. She knew she was because she'd seen at first-hand what he could do, and if Cara told Jools what she'd seen then she'd be in danger too. There was no time to probe further back then. The only thing that mattered was keeping her best friend safe, and so she did.

Part of her wishes that Axel himself had filled in some of those missing pieces in the caravan. That she might have trapped him into doing that, but he hadn't, of course.

Jools met Cara just the once after her friend came to her that night. Cara always insisted that the lack of contact, excruciating as it was for both of them, was for Jools's own safety, even though she'd never say exactly why. So, Jools knew there had to be a pressing reason why Cara suddenly wanted to meet up after all that time. But she was totally unprepared when she found out why.

It was when the iron really entered her soul. And what happened since only fused it, ever harder. And so she returned to a village she hadn't revisited in twenty years. To extract payment for a two-decades-old debt.

Seeing Penny on that train, watching her take that seat opposite him, was a bolt from the blue. She recognised her immediately, of course, even though she'd only seen the odd photo of her now and again. It was those eyes. Cara's eyes. Looking at her was like looking at the mother. Jools just hovered there, in the train vestibule doorway, watching, transfixed, which meant she saw everything, of course. Axel reaching out like that, putting his hand on Penny's arm, the instant furore it provoked. But even then, he still wasn't easy to read. He actually looked lost and confused in the aftermath of it all, and she almost felt sorry for him.

That soon vanished though. The moment she followed him out of the station and saw him head for his car, before he hesitated, then turned back to Penny and approached her. She was going to intervene, but things happened so quickly. The next thing she knew, Penny was getting into his car while she just stood there, rooted, the double-whammy of seeing just about the last person in the world she expected to see getting into a car with the last man she should ever have gone near in her life. It simply robbed her of all resolve.

Jools paces the open space, the walls of the ruined battlements on all sides. So why didn't she act as she'd wanted to act just now? It was what she'd come back to do, so what stopped her? Was it talking to him like that? Was she having the same doubts she had on that train? Is that why she hadn't been able to pull the trigger?

Or is this what Axel does? What he's always done? Has she just been manipulated, played? Maybe as he manipulated and played Cara all those years ago too?

CHAPTER 102
PRESENT DAY

IT STARTS within five minutes of my pulling out of the caravan park.

For the first four of those five minutes my mind's still racing, a succession of images flashing in front of my eyes, all involving Cara at the time she disappeared, searching for moments I should have seen, clues I should have picked up on, changes in behaviour I should have spotted. But I spotted none, of course. And maybe if I had registered anything particularly untoward, I'd just have put it down to a girl surfing sullenly, in common with so many of her peers, through her teens.

I turn on the radio, desperate for distraction. I channel hop for a few moments, unable to even settle on a station of choice. Music washes over me; voices dance from the speakers without my hearing a single word. A couple of drops of rain splatter the windscreen. Still on automatic pilot, still barely realising what I'm doing or even where I'm going, I put on the windscreen wipers, switch stations, change gear, accelerate, slow down, accelerate again.

But then one face above every other swims in front of my eyes, and it's not Cara now, it's Penny. The girl on the train who I realise now is my own flesh and blood.

Which is when I also realise that I'm being followed.

CHAPTER 103
PRESENT DAY

I WAS DIMLY aware of the car in my rear-view mirror for a mile or so without really taking any notice. Then again, I'm not taking any notice of anything much right now. But as the quiet road I've been driving along gives way to a dual carriageway that leads to the larger towns and cities down the coast, I catch a quick glimpse of an indicator light being switched on just a moment or so after I switch on mine, and a car behind me swinging down onto that same dual carriageway.

For a moment I'm angry with myself. With all I've got to deal with right now, the last thing I need is a persecution complex. Who would be following me, for God's sake? I drive on for a mile or so, trying not to even look in the rear-view mirror, but when I do the same car's still there, maintaining what looks like a steady speed behind. I can't see the driver; he or she has the visor pulled down even though there's no sun shining in through either of our windscreens. At this time of the day it's high in the sky above. As a test I accelerate, pushing up to just over the speed limit. The distance between us remains the same, meaning the driver behind must have increased their speed to match.

And now I am beginning to get spooked. A junction's coming up and I indicate to leave. Behind, the following car does the same. I cancel the indicator and stay on the dual carriageway as if I've had a last-minute change of heart. The driver behind does exactly the same.

And now I know it's not my fevered imagination. For whatever reason, someone is following me, and different possibilities flash in front of me. It could be Jools, of course, but the last thing she did was run away from me, so why would she do that? There's Rory too, but again, why would he? We seem to have moved way beyond that sort of sport on his part. I stare into the rear-view mirror for as long as I dare, but I still can't make out anything beyond a dim shape behind that sun visor. So then I focus on the car itself, but it's just an anonymous saloon that, for some reason and I don't know why, puts me in mind of a police pool car. But why would the police be following me?

This ushers in a new thought. Should I drive to the nearest police station and report this? And should I tell Adams or Braith all that Jools has just told me too? But I don't, and for now anyway I don't know why. Maybe it's just another in a fast-lengthening list of things I have to work out.

I turn off the dual carriageway at the next junction and slow for a set of lights just after a roundabout. The car behind follows, but then another car appears round the roundabout and pulls up immediately behind me, putting itself between me and my apparent pursuer. The lights remain on red, but I can see nothing's coming towards me. Suddenly, I accelerate, the rear of my car fishtailing as I hurtle down the single lane carriageway in front of me. The driver behind stands on his horn, presumably by way of an angry waring to an overly-impatient idiot. But he stays where he is, with the car that had been following me trapped behind him in turn.

There's a petrol station with a car wash a few hundred metres down the road, out of sight of the lights. I swing in and park at the entrance of the car wash, kill the engine and wait. Sure enough, a few moments later the car I'd sped away from drives past, the driver clearly visible. But as he does so he's being passed in turn on his right by the car that was following me, blocking any clear sight of the driver inside as the car races to try and catch up with me again.

I stay there for a moment before another beep behind me sounds. I look at a car now waiting to go into the car wash itself, put my car in gear, then swing back onto the road, heading away in the opposite direction.

CHAPTER 104
PRESENT DAY

I CHECK into the anonymous chain hotel twenty minutes later.

I wasn't even aware there was a hotel in the area until I saw a sign displaying the symbol of a bed and an arrow pointing to the left. I turn off the road and travel down onto an old reclamation site, now hosting shiny new purpose-built restaurant units, complete with the new, and seemingly ubiquitous, multi-storey apartment blocks towering above them on all sides. Then the hotel comes into view and it looks antiseptic and soul-less. It also looks to be largely devoid of people either inside or out, making it more than fit for my purpose right now.

I don't even register the name of the chain above the front entrance as I pull into the car park, choosing a spot in the corner with a view of the main entrance. I check out the other few cars in the car park in case my pursuer has somehow levitated himself or herself there before me. Then I remain in my car for fully five minutes waiting to see if that anonymous-looking saloon reappears. When it doesn't, I open the door, tensing suddenly as the automatic door to the main entrance to the hotel opens ahead and a male, middle-aged, comes out, looking around. Then, spotting another chain outlet, an eatery across the car park, he heads over to it. I take a deep breath and walk into the empty reception.

Ten minutes later I've registered and have an electronic room fob in my hand. My room's on the first floor at my own request. I don't want to risk getting into a lift only to find my pursuer getting in too and the pair of us trapped inside. If the young receptionist was surprised that I'd walked in with no luggage she didn't show it. Maybe it's that kind of place.

Coming up from the stairwell, I walk down a long corridor with doors every few metres on either side. It's empty again. Locating my room, I hold out the fob and a green light on the door sanctions my entrance. Moving inside the small, box-like space, I check the corridor behind me one last time, but it remains empty, and the door to the stairwell I accessed at the far end stays closed.

There's silence inside the room, but I go into the bathroom anyway and quickly check it out. Returning to the bedroom, I even drop to my knees and check under the bed. Suddenly remembering, I go back to the door and flip on the security latch, checking the fish-eye view of the corridor through the peephole at the same time. But there's still nothing and no one outside.

Too late, I remember that I haven't any food or, perhaps even more importantly right now, any wine with me. I try and remember if I saw any sort of in-house restaurant as I came into the reception area but know I won't head down there anyway. The thought of sitting in some open space surrounded by strangers, watching the door to the car park opening and closing, admitting more strangers all the while, makes me break out into a sweat. And the idea of straying further afield to that chain eatery I saw as I parked almost makes my heart go into palpitations.

I sit on the bed, heavy. That strange rigmarole with the pursuing car has only postponed the inevitable. And any panic I've been feeling over who that might be and why they were following me is now quickly banished.

Because if all Jools was saying is true, and for the life of me I don't see any reason why she should have lied, then my world and Donna's world have just been blasted apart again. Cara was pregnant. That's why she vanished like that, according to Jools, only that wasn't the only reason. So, what else was there? And why did Cara turn to her best friend and not us? She'd clearly felt she was in danger, and Jools equally clearly felt that it was from us, from myself and Donna, or maybe only from me, but what sort of danger could I – or we – possibly have posed to our own daughter?

I stay where I am, staring at the red dot on the TV, the remote control next to it, picking out more details of the room as I do so: a small kettle on a tray with tea and coffee sachets next to it, an iron on a shelf along with a hairdryer, an open-sided wardrobe, a small selection of hangers fixed in place inside. I stay there, not moving, hoping my mind will begin to work all this out on its own if I just give it time.

But then I move on from one overwhelming puzzle in Cara to another in Penny. Given all that Jools has just told me, it was definitely no accidental meeting that night. She couldn't have anticipated that I'd reach out to her like that, but all my previous suspicions were correct. She'd deliberately seated herself opposite me, so at some stage she obviously intended to make some sort of contact herself. That also explains why a young girl would accept a lift from an apparent stranger who'd already made an exhibition of himself in that way, and it explains her curious manner in the car, those clear and obvious nerves that may now be nothing to do with any fears she might have had about me. Was she going to come straight out and tell me who she was? But if that was the point of her taking that train journey in the first place, why didn't she just do that?

And then I think of Rory. He obviously knows some, if not all of this, but, equally obviously, he wasn't about to talk to me directly about it either. So, does he share Jools's dark suspicions about me? Does he think I was the architect of Cara's disappearance in some way too? Is that why Rory was so reluctant to open up to me, because he still saw me – maybe even still sees me, despite what seems to be that recent thaw – as a clear and present threat? And did Penny feel the same? Or did she simply not know? Did she travel on that train that day to try and solve a mystery? To lay to rest a twenty-year old ghost?

I look out of the window again, staring unseeing across the car park for a moment. Then I still as I catch sight of something in my peripheral vision. Looking down at my car I see something that wasn't there before.

Another note on the windscreen.

I STAND THERE, frozen for a moment. I can't see anyone outside, but someone was there – that note didn't just float down from space. I can't hear anything either. Nothing from out in the corridor or anywhere in the rest of the hotel. It's as if I'm alone in the world, but I'm not. That note's telling me that.

Standing to one side of the window, I keep scanning the car park, which looks pretty much as I left it. I can still see the chain eatery in the near distance, but no one's going in or out. Everywhere I look, it seems as unremarkable and as largely deserted as it did before.

But then, on the other side of the car park, in the shadows, as if someone's deliberately parked in the one spot where it won't be immediately visible from the hotel, I see an anonymous saloon, much like the one that tailed me a few minutes ago. It's impossible to tell if it's the same one, of course, but I checked that car park out when I arrived, so surely I'd have spotted it if it had been there then.

Suddenly, I turn for the door. Without stopping to think – because if I did, I know I wouldn't do this – I retrace my steps down to the car park and pick up the note, knowing what it will say. Sure enough, it's those same four words again.

Can I Trust You?

I look round. Now I'm closer I can see that there's no one in the anonymous saloon I just spotted from the hotel window. I scan the windows of the chain eatery again as best as I can but can't see anyone looking out from there either. Cautiously, I head back inside, note in hand. No one appears in front of me as I return to my room.

I look at my phone, which I'd left behind on the bed, half-expecting there to have been some sort of message while I've been outside, but there's nothing. And now I want it – I want a message, I want contact, any kind of contact. I stare at the screen for a moment, like a junkie desperate for a next hit.

Then I wheel round as there's a knock on the door.

CHAPTER 106
TWENTY YEARS AGO

CARA DASHED FOR HOME. She had absolutely no time to lose; she knew it. Jericho's fate – his whole life maybe – was now in her hands.

She burst through the front door a few minutes later. She knew that only Mum would be there right now, Dad was away on business, but Mum should still be able to tell her what Cara now desperately needed to know.

Briefly, she stilled as she hared inside, even though she didn't know why. Some instinct made her pause, but then, like a wave, all she'd come to do, to say, washed over her again. She had to tell Mum what she'd just seen. Mum had to tell the police, and they had to tell Jericho too. They had to get all this out there before it was too late.

Cara called out for her, but then, and without even waiting for an answer, she approached and opened Mum and Dad's bedroom door.

Which was when everything changed.

CHAPTER 107
PRESENT DAY

I FREEZE AGAIN, just staring at the door all the while.

Was I followed? As I came back inside, was someone walking up those stairs behind me? Then the knock sounds again, and this time it's sharper, more insistent, as if my visitor's growing impatient.

Suddenly, out of nowhere, a memory returns, of another time I stood inside a room, listening like this, but when that was, and who was on the other side of that door, I can't remember. Another of those strange blanks.

I keep staring at the closed door in front of me. It could just be some member of the hotel staff out there, of course. A solicitous manager or receptionist come to check that all's OK with the room perhaps, although while the establishment might score adequately for location and economy, I really didn't have it down as a trailblazer in customer relations. It was as much as the bored operative manning the front desk could do to direct me towards the stairs. Taking a deep breath, I cross to the door. For a moment I'm tempted to just get this over with and fling it open, confront directly who's out there. But then the memory of Jools with that gun returns as I reach out for the security latch.

I lean forward and peer through the spyhole, taking a moment to orientate myself to the distorted version of the outside world that presents itself. Sure enough, someone's standing close to the door, but they're standing too close and all I can see is a head that seems to be bowed, as if whoever's there is trying to conceal themselves from view. Then I realise I'm actually looking at the back of a head, because the figure slowly turns round.

And now I can see clearly who it is.

What the hell?

Swiftly, I flip the security latch and stare out at my ex-wife, standing in a corridor outside a hotel room I didn't even know I was going to be occupying myself up to half an hour or so ago.

'Donna?'

She pushes past me and heads on inside.

CHAPTER 108
PRESENT DAY

SLOWLY, every nerve end feeling as if it's on fire, I close the door. For a moment neither of us speaks. Donna looks as tense and wracked as I've ever seen her. And there's something else going on now too – she looks haunted. And out of all the questions racing through my head, out comes the one I perhaps least want the answer to.

What I really want to know is, what the hell is she doing here? Was she the mystery driver in that car? Did she put that note on my windscreen? Was she responsible for those other notes, maybe even that inscription in the Frame collection, and if so, how and why? But I don't come out with any of that.

'How did you find me?'

Donna's mouth permits her face a smile that's no smile at all.

'Always were a creature of habit, weren't you, Axel? The only person I know who's kept the same password for more than twenty years.'

I gaze at her, blank, as she takes out her mobile and shows me an image on the screen, the location of my own mobile clearly displayed along with accompanying geographical co-ordinates.

'All I had to do was activate your find-my-phone software. It led me straight to you.'

I keep looking at her.

'Is that how they did it too?'

Donna doesn't reply, her expression blank.

'Is that how they tracked me like that?'

'What are you talking about?'

I hand over the note left on my windscreen, the mystery of how my pursuer in the car knew where I was, after I thought I'd lost them much less of a mystery now. But it's a different one that's claiming Donna as she stares at it for a moment. Then she looks back up at me.

'This is all about Cara, yes?'

And twenty years of bitterness are fired out at the world inside that one simple question, and I can't blame her. She's suffered more than her fair share of the flat accusations underneath the stilted exchanges, the whispered conversations that stop the moment she walks into a shop, is spotted on a local street.

She shrugs her shoulders. 'I suppose we should have expected it. Yet another anniversary.'

'It's more than that.'

She looks at me as I take another deep breath, because now this is not about some troll, some internet persecutor. We've moved way beyond that.

And then I tell her. I tell her everything. I tell her about Jools, and I explain who she is, that she was Cara's school friend, but I can see she remembers her immediately; she has no need to dredge her memory as I had to do.

I explain about finding Jools in the caravan. I explain about the state she was in. And I reprise, word for word, or as close as I can, the bitter accusations she hurled at me even if I didn't fully understand them, and still don't. And, along the way, I explain all about the circumstances Cara found herself in before she walked out on her home, her parents and a life that had quite clearly turned irretrievably alien to her. I tell her that our daughter was pregnant and that she gave birth to twins. I tell her about the death of Jen, one of her two girls. I tell her the real identity of Penny, the mystery girl from the train. The one thing I don't tell her, because I still don't know, is where Cara is now or what's happened to her.

Donna sinks, slowly, onto the bed. I sit beside her, knowing only too well how she feels. Even with the limited time I've had to absorb this, saying it all again out loud has drained me. Some part of me still can't take this in. Maybe part of me never will. For another few moments Donna stays silent. I'm half-expecting her to just get up and walk out as she tries to assimilate yet another hammer blow in a life that's endured too many already.

But then she looks up at me.

'So, it wasn't me?'

I stare at her.

'All these years, I've been so sure it was.'

'What are you talking about?'

Donna looks towards the window, a woman on the clear brink of a personal Rubicon, unsure, even at this late stage, if she can actually take that last, fateful, step.

Then she turns to me again.

'Why do you think I'm here? Why do you think I tracked you down like this?'

I realise I haven't asked her that. She's explained how she's found me. What she hasn't explained, is why.

'I've been on the brink so many times and pulled back every time – but tonight...'

'On the brink of what?'

Donna's voice is steady, her eyes clear.

'I've come to confess.'

CHAPTER 109
PRESENT DAY

'YOU REMEMBER what it was like back then. Not just when Cara went missing, but before as well?'

Donna doesn't elaborate. She doesn't need to. It was the only time we'd really hit a serious problem in our marriage. Before Cara, it had briefly become the single biggest threat to a relationship I truly believed was indestructible.

It was the nineties, the economy was booming, and a whole breed of aggressive new collectors had suddenly appeared. With their new money they wanted – no, demanded – all sorts of rare and beautiful objects, from paintings to cars and books. Many of the older collectors found the new demand too enticing to resist, and volumes that had previously vanished from the market suddenly surfaced again. Records were smashed, which only encouraged more collectors to look again at their collections and wonder at the prices they might achieve in what had become over-heated times.

'This is no excuse, I know.'

She hesitates, really struggling now.

'But we barely saw each other back then, and there were reasons, I know. I'm not blaming you for that either.'

Those reasons were simple and, at the time anyway, overwhelming. A window of opportunity had arisen to build exceptional libraries, with a flood of disposable income suddenly available at the same time. The auctions that sprang up to service that new income quickly became the stuff of legend, and the prices paid quickly became legendary too.

Nearly 40 million dollars was secured for the Estelle Doheny collection, just under a fraction of that for the H. Bradley Martin, and it wasn't just books that were swept up in that seemingly unstoppable flow. A Japanese businessman paid over 160 million dollars in one week for just two paintings, a Van Gogh and a Renoir. It was clearly the time to make money, and I did so by the simple expedient of working day and night as the effects of those starry, market-leading auctions filtered down through the food chain. At the time I saw it as securing our family's future. I know now that the opposite was true.

I clear my throat. She's no need to say anymore.

'Who was he?'

'That doesn't matter.' Her eyes are pleading. 'I'm serious, Axel. That's all long gone, and so much regretted too – please believe me. It would just have been one of those things. Something I'd catch myself remembering from time to time and wonder how I could have been so stupid.'

Donna falls silent and I supply the prompt.

'But?'

She takes a deep breath; pictures I can already see she'll never be able to banish forming in front of her eyes.

'Cara found out.'

I stare at her, a tell-tale red glow now beginning at the base of her neck.

'She didn't actually catch us, not…'

Donna tails off.

'But it was still pretty obvious what was going on. She just stood there for a moment, looking at me.'

Donna falters. 'Then she turned, and walked out.'

I wasn't thinking about Donna. All I was thinking about was

the police. Time and again they'd asked me, had asked the two of us, if there'd been anything upsetting Cara at the time that might explain why she could have vanished like that. I said no, so far as I was concerned there wasn't, but as that all flashes through my mind, Donna cuts across, clearly already anticipating what I'm just about to say.

'I told them, Axel. I told the police everything just in case it had any bearing on what had happened.'

For a moment she pauses, as if on the verge of saying something else. But then she moves on.

'I thought maybe it was payback at first. I'd put her through hell, having to walk in on something like that, so I thought maybe she was doing the same to me.'

Donna stares, bleak, towards the window again.

'Then one day became two, then a couple of days became a week and then it was obvious this was something else.'

All I can think is, a stupid, short-lived, affair. It seems so trivial compared to all that's happened since. If you'd told me when we first married that Donna might stray like that, I'd have been incandescent beyond words. Now everything she's saying is just washing over me, and it's not because I don't care, it's because it just seems so unimportant by comparison.

Now it's my turn to struggle.

'You were right. That wasn't why she went.'

Donna nods, looking bleaker by the moment.

'And she might have told us exactly why if she'd still trusted me. Whatever it was, she might have come to me. She had before with all sorts of things – not anything like that, but things that were still important.'

She doesn't say anything else for a moment, but then she looks at me again.

'But I'd fractured that, hadn't I? I'd fractured that trust, so she didn't.'

For a moment neither of us speak. Then I do what I've wanted to do for so long, what I should have done in those endless days after Cara went missing, but we were both buried so deep in the black hole into which we'd suddenly been plunged that I didn't. I reach out my hand and take hers.

Donna hesitates, then looks at me. Our eyes meet, connecting after what feels like almost a lifetime. Then I move closer, and she doesn't move away.

CHAPTER 110
TWENTY YEARS AGO

CARA STUMBLED away from the house, telling herself that it didn't matter. Only one thing still mattered right now and that was Jericho. They had to sort this out and they could do that themselves; they didn't need anyone else's help.

But as she turned the corner at the end of the street leading to the bookshop, she stopped dead. Because suddenly he was there, meaning he had to have followed her, but how could he have known where she'd go? But there was no time to think about that either, because Jericho was her only priority. Dimly, she was aware of someone else approaching from behind, but she pushed on, all but running into the bookshop.

Jericho was where he always was, in the rare books room. Putting everything else to one side – trying not to even think about what she'd just seen – she concentrated on the one matter of the moment, the other thing she'd seen that evening that might now change everything too.

'Did Mum and Dad ever come to the car wash?

Jericho stared at her, puzzled. Of all the things he'd have expected them to talk about right now, this had come from way out of leftfield.

'I don't understand.'

'Please – I'll explain, but just tell me?'

Cara stared at him, silent eyes entreating him to say that they had. But Jericho shook his head.

She persisted. It was the only explanation that made any kind of sense out of all this.

'You're sure? Absolutely sure?' She tried again. 'Or even just one of them?'

Jericho just smiled wryly.

'They'd have got the VIP treatment if they had.'

CHAPTER 111
PRESENT DAY

I WAKE up alone a few hours later. For a moment, as I surface out of sleep, a feeling takes hold of me. I can't work it out at first, but I feel at peace. As if the world, so massively out of balance for so long, has somehow re-orientated itself.

And it's all down to Donna, of course. And last night, the two of us together again after so many years apart, back as a couple once more, for however long that might last. Will it just be the one night, or longer?

But then I shake my head as I lie there, getting way ahead of myself as ever. Why can't I just be grateful for small mercies, if that's what this is? Why start complicating things already? Then I see the note on the small table beside the bed.

I sit up instantly. For the last couple of moments, I've imagined Donna to be in the bathroom, or maybe gone to pick up coffee or some breakfast, but a note left behind tells a different story. I pick it up and read the message, which doesn't take long. It comprises just the one word.

Sorry.

I calm myself again, our conversation from last night replaying inside my head, as well as her tortured face as she confessed her long-dead affair. Still, nothing happens inside when I think of that.

None of the rage I imagined I'd feel, none of the anticipated bitter sting of betrayal. It still just feels so petty compared to all that's happened since, and so sad, too, in a way. The fact that Donna's carried this round all these years just makes me feel hollowed out. If only she'd said something at the time, we could have worked it through. Lots of other couples have had to, and we'd have been strong enough to put it behind us, I know we would. But neither of us was exactly thinking rationally back then, I suppose. And after Cara went missing – compounded by Donna's guilt as to what may have led up to it – perhaps that was always going to be a step too far.

I sit on the bed, Donna's note still in hand, trying to put all that out of my mind, trying to recapture that unaccustomed peace I felt when I woke up just a few moments ago, but now I can't. In fact, I'm beginning to feel unsettled again, but can't work out why. I type a quick text to Donna, telling her that it's OK and to send me a text to let me know she's OK too, then I head into the bathroom and turn on the shower.

But all the time, I'm still mulling over that note.

Sorry.

It has to be an apology for all she's told me. There can't be anything else. But then images begin to flood back as I stand under the pounding water – the drive over here – the car that tailed me – that note on the windscreen – that knock on the door – then Donna standing outside on the corridor.

I shake my head as I reach for the soap because I'm doing it again. Haven't I got enough of real-life conspiracies to contend with without conjuring fresh ones in their wake? Last night was about one thing and one thing only, and that was putting old demons to some sort of rest, not re-casting my ex as a new one, the kind who follows me in cars and leaves notes on my windscreen before messing with my head even further by pouring out her heart and taking me to bed.

Coming back into the bedroom, the towel wrapped around me, I see immediately that the text symbol on my phone is illuminated. Donna must have seen my text and replied. I dry my hands quickly. I've ruined more than one phone in the past that way.

For a moment I just stare at the message on the screen.

Can I Trust You?

At first I don't know what to do. I cross to the window and look out, but again there's no one out there, just a couple of business types heading for their cars, and a delivery driver ferrying trays from a van to a side door that I assume must lead to the hotel kitchens. I turn back to my phone and almost before I realise what I'm doing, I type a reply.

Is this Penny?

For a few excruciating moments, nothing happens. I hesitate, desperate to send a follow-up text, but maybe I'm learning something at last, because I don't. Then, suddenly, there's a one-word reply.

Yes

PART FIVE

PART FIVE

CHAPTER 112
PRESENT DAY

LESS THAN ONE minute after receiving that text I'm down in the car park, pushing past another perennially tired looking businessman on his way to his identikit car. Maybe it's the diner from yesterday evening I saw heading for the chain eatery. In truth, I barely see him, barging him out of the way as we both head for the revolving swing doors. If he makes any sort of protest, I don't hear it.

I almost hurl myself into my car and fix my phone to the cradle on the dash. Fingers fumbling all the while, I input a postcode I was sent a few seconds ago. It's the only other text I've had since that one-word confirmation that it was Penny on the other end of the line.

Or the seeming confirmation, of course. Like everything that's happened these last few days, I can't be anywhere near sure.

The postcode's local. Maybe if I was more tech-savvy I'd be able to pull up the exact location before I set off, but that's going to waste precious moments I don't have. The automated voice tells me to begin the journey and I put the car into gear and swing it out of the car park, nearly wiping out the same businessman now crossing the car park. The look on his face as he stares after me says it all. It's not exactly been the best of starts to his day. How mine will turn out, the next half hour or so will tell.

As I head back onto the road, I realise that the anonymous-looking saloon I saw from my hotel window last night has gone, but there's no time to ponder the significance or otherwise of that right now either.

I start to suspect where I'm going long before I get there. And, once I drive past the station and take the road that leads to my beach-side cottage I know for a fact. I'm being led back to the place where all this started, in a sense. Back to the lane that leads down to those few houses where Penny alighted that night. The lane I returned to the next morning and saw that uniformed copper who turned my world upside down.

Sure enough, the automated voice on my phone tells me I've reached my destination as I pull up. I look round but can see no one. So, do I go down the lane itself, start banging on doors again? Or do I just wait for whoever might now appear? Does someone in one of those houses know Penny after all? Has she even been there all this time? It's a crazy thought, I know, but it seems to chime with the craziness of all that's been happening lately, so I can't discount anything anymore.

I check the phone, get out of the car, look round. Still nothing and no one in sight. Then I turn back to see if any more texts have come through, but before I can do that, I see someone appear at the top of the lane.

Harry.

CHAPTER 113
PRESENT DAY

BETH CAN'T SETTLE. For the last hour she's been wheeling herself up and down inside her room, from the bed to the door, from the door towards the window, then back to the bed again.

The Care Home staff think it's probably the result of the Open Day. Even though most of the long-term residents enjoyed it, it was a break from the usual routine, and that does have this sort of effect sometimes. For a few days after such events some of the residents can be unusually agitated. Some would go off their food, refuse to take their medication; some would even become aggressive when asked to do the simplest of tasks. Some, like Beth, just couldn't seem to stop moving. But they all calmed down, eventually. Only Beth is going to break something of a mould here, because she isn't going to settle for days, and it isn't the disorientating effect of a break from a comforting routine that's the problem.

It was him, her visitor. She still doesn't know who he was or what his visit was all about. All she does know is that he's dredged things up, things she'd banished to the back of her mind for so long she thought they'd never return, only now they have. And now she's sensing what she sensed all those years ago, before the drugs claimed her at least, and that's danger, a malevolent force at work. And, once again – and this is another all too rare moment of lucidity – it's all to do with Cara.

But then she slips back again. Back into the more usual fog inside which she moves for most of the time, and she forgets she ever even knew a girl of that name.

But, and slowly, an image does begin to form.

She only saw him the once. It was a fleeting glimpse from a distance, outside Cara's father's bookshop, but it still chilled her. There was something in the way he was standing there, watching. He just seemed so calm, so collected, so controlling, and in charge. As if he could do anything, and he knew it.

She tried talking to Cara about him, but the young girl just flipped. There was nothing she could do, nothing anyone could do, didn't she understand that? He held all the cards! He could make everything, and anyone, simply disappear, and no one would ever be any the wiser!

Then Cara fulfilled her own prediction. Cara disappeared, and Beth took refuge in the substances that had been her crutch and comfort for too long. And the downward spiral continued, exacerbated now by the certain knowledge she'd let another young girl down.

First, her own daughter, Jools, by her habitual omissions over more years than she ever wanted to remember.

Then the young girl she knew had turned to her for help, even though she'd told her not to help at all.

CHAPTER 114
PRESENT DAY

HARRY ADVANCES TOWARDS ME, looking more threatening with every step. Thirty years in the Tigers – the colloquial name for the Prince of Wales's finest – had always given him a menacing air. He's never looked as menacing as he does right now.

I raise my hands, a pacifying gesture. I don't know what the hell is happening here, but from the look on Harry's face, I can see I may have just seconds to find out.

'Harry—'

He cuts across, instantly.

'I know, Axel.'

I just stare at him.

'I fucking know.'

Harry holds out his mobile, a message – indistinct – on the display.

'Donna texted me.'

I keep staring at him.

'What did you do? Threaten her? Fuck with her head like you've always done. Or just lie?'

'What are you talking about?'

'It's you, she told me. She still doesn't know about Cara, but this latest girl – she knows, Axel.'

I hold out my own mobile, fingers scrabbling to bring up my last message on the display.

'She's here, Penny's here.'

Now it's Harry's turn to stare at me.

'I had a text from her, a few minutes ago, not long after Donna left.'

Harry cuts across again.

'What do you mean, after she left?'

'She's been with me. She was with me last night, all last night. She didn't tell you?'

Something's beginning to shift now in Harry. I plough on.

'Penny's here in one of these cottages; maybe she was here all the time.'

But even as I'm saying it, I'm faltering. Because something's staring both myself and Harry in the face. For a moment neither of us speaks, then Harry gives voice to what we're both thinking.

'We're being played, aren't we?'

But all I'm looking at is the phone in his hand. That text from Donna that can't have come from her.

So, where is she?

And what's happened to her?

CHAPTER 115
TWENTY YEARS AGO

CARA WAS SPENDING LESS and less time at home now. Every time she walked in, the air was so dense with the weight of what wasn't being said she felt as if it might crush her.

So, night after night she'd go across the estuary to Jools's house, and at weekends they'd spend time together down in the caravan park too. Fortunately, Dad was still away and so he wasn't around to pick up on the atmosphere. Or to witness Mum's occasional and painful stumbling attempts to explain the inexplicable.

Days passed like that, then a few weeks. She was walking more now too. And more and more, Cara's steps took her past the car wash where Jericho worked, or where he used to work. She knew in her heart of hearts that he wouldn't be going back there. Much as she knew, despite everything that had happened between them, that her persuading him not to board that eastbound train on the night of the dance was a temporary reprieve at best. As time went on, he was becoming more and more terrified what the future might hold, with that theft charge hanging over him. At some point, and it could happen at any time now, she knew, he'd be gone and for good.

And every time Cara thought about that, she grew frantic.

Jericho could not leave, not like this. But she also knew she wouldn't emotionally blackmail him into staying either. There had to be a way of resolving this and she knew it had something to do with this place.

Cara paced the pavement outside the car wash. She listened to the shouts and calls of young men – other immigrants or refugees – who'd been Jericho's workmates. She witnessed once again the careful routine that had exploded like a blinding light inside her head when she'd first seen it.

Once again, she watched as yet another car was checked in for cleaning. She barely gave the driver a glance as he walked away, to do some shopping perhaps or grab a coffee. Instead, she watched the small army of young men swarm around the car, opening the doors, removing the few possessions from inside, before storing them in a portacabin office across the yard, ready to be returned once the interior of the car had been vacuumed and cleaned.

Cara kept watching. That had to be how Jericho's prints were found inside their house. She had no idea why that framed print and book – or her own old diary – would be inside either her mum's or dad's cars, but they must have been, and Jericho must have taken them out prior to starting the cleaning.

But he kept insisting that neither Axel nor Donna had ever been there, so now she really was at a loss.

Until something else caught her eye, reflecting off the fading sunlight. Cara looked up at the winking light of a CCTV security camera. She stood, rooted, for a moment longer. Then she turned and made for the office across the small yard where one of the young men was already storing the possessions he'd just removed from inside the latest car they were preparing to clean.

CHAPTER 116
PRESENT DAY

I DIVE BACK inside my car, Harry doing the same behind me, and pull out from the lane onto the road down to my beachside village just ahead of him, heading for mine and Donna's old home.

But as I swing back out onto the road my mind's working overtime. Because is it possible I've got this all wrong? Have I got Donna wrong? Was I too hasty in dismissing all this as anything to do with her? And all the time I drive, too, those earlier uneasy suspicions regarding my ex-wife return. Could she be behind that strange pursuit last night and this latest text too? She certainly knows about the inscription in the Frame collection, because I told her.

But she's not the only one. Rory does too, of course, and so do the police, but why would Rory or the police play these kinds of charades? Then again, why would Donna? Once again, I seem to have a million questions and no answers. Although, and like Harry still following, maybe I now have a way of finding one answer at least.

I drive on, down the winding lanes, hugging the coastal road all the way down to journey's end. Pulling up outside our old home, I see Donna's car parked outside. Another car is parked close by, but I don't recognise it. I call out her name as I get out and approach, but there's no reply. I knock on the door, but there's still no reply from inside. And suddenly that all too familiar surge of anger erupts inside me, even if I don't know why or who I'm angry with, and I hit the door hard. Then I stop as, like the door of that caravan yesterday, it suddenly swings open in front of me.

But it doesn't swing fully open because something's blocking it, on the floor just inside the hallway. And now the door's partly open at least, I can smell something, a thin, acrid, almost metallic smell coming from inside, and I hesitate, some instinct stirring, warning me of danger.

Pushing the door against the obstruction, I feel it give slightly. Then, pushing harder all the while, I stop and stare as a human arm suddenly flops into view.

CHAPTER 117
PRESENT DAY

FRANTIC, I squeeze through the small gap in front of me, one thought and one only now in mind.

Is this Penny? Have I finally caught up with her only for someone to have got to her first? I mutter a silent imprecation to the Gods, promising I'll never ask for anything in my life again, but please let her be safe. One second later I stop again, staring down as I see Donna lying on the hall floor.

She's on her side, curled in an almost foetal position. Blood is seeping from underneath her, staining the rug that covers the wooden floor dark red. She's not moving and, at first glance anyway, doesn't seem to be breathing either. I drop to my feet, scrabbling fingers searching for a pulse in her neck, and for a moment I can't feel it but then, suddenly, it's there. It's weak – way, way too weak – but blood is still pulsing inside her.

But Donna still isn't moving, and even to my untrained eye it's clear that while she may be with me for now, my ex-wife is slipping away fast. I raise her head, taking in the wound to her skull that seems to have caused all the damage. Then I dash for the kitchen, pick up a whole roll of paper towels and start pressing them against her head, trying to stem the bleeding, whispering to her all the time.

'Hold on, Donna, hold on. I'm getting help – it's on its way.'

I pull out my phone, wiping the blood, Donna's blood, from my fingers as I do so, and hit 999. The call connects almost immediately, and I gabble out Donna's name and address, tell the operator I need an ambulance, that my ex-wife has been attacked.

Smooth and professional, the operator responds.

'Is the attacker still in the house?'

I pause and look round. I hadn't even considered that.

'I don't know. I don't think so.'

'If you're in any immediate danger then you must leave the property, wait outside.'

'I haven't heard anyone.'

I look round again, but then shake my head as I hear a car pull up outside.

'I haven't checked, but I'm sure we're alone.'

'And it's just the one victim?'

Then, suddenly, I stop again. Because a hand has just grabbed my arm. I look down to see Donna's now-open eyes staring up at me, her mouth struggling as she tries to speak. I drop the phone and fall to my knees, gripping her hand in return. And from somewhere, using strength she probably didn't even know herself she possessed, her spirit prevailing even as her body is giving way, she manages to force out just the one word.

Or, more accurately, just one name.

'Penny.'

And a new suspicion assails me. Is Penny not the innocent victim? Has this been part of some elaborate plot right from the start? Is all this down to a twisted young girl on some sort of revenge kick?

From my phone, still on the floor where I dropped it, I can hear the operator calling out my name, but my eyes are only on Donna, struggling to force out something else. I lean closer, just managing to catch two further words.

'Help her.'

Then she lapses back into unconsciousness.

I turn back to my phone, cutting the call. There's nothing more to say to the operator right now because there's nothing more I know. She has all the information she needs to dispatch help, and that's all that matters. Then I stop as I realise another text has just been delivered.

My hands are stained with more of Donna's blood, and it smears the keys and the screen again as I open it up. The text takes a moment to appear, and I soon realise why, because there are no words this time, just an image.

Once again, I wipe the screen clear of the blood that's momentarily obscuring it, to see Penny, standing in the hermetically sealed rare books room in my bookshop, looking back at me.

CHAPTER
ONE HUNDRED EIGHTEEN

A BODY on the hallway floor.

The body of his estranged wife.

The DNA of the ex-husband present at the scene.

There's only one conclusion, isn't there? It's inescapable. The events of the last few days have tipped him over the knife edge on which he's been balancing ever more precariously for years. On the anniversary of the disappearance of his own daughter, he did something to another young girl. And then turned his attentions to his ex.

Whether it's true or not doesn't matter.

What matters is whether it's taken to be true.

Because history, as all military men will tell you, is only ever written by the victors.

CHAPTER 119
TWENTY YEARS AGO

CARA FOLDED herself back into the shadows as she saw the on-site concierge move past, a few packages in his hand.

She watched as he opened the first in a series of letterboxes on the ground floor of the flat complex, before disappearing up a small flight of stone stairs to more maisonettes and apartments on the floor above.

Scanning the numbers on the doors in front of her, she moved towards the one she wanted, praying no one was watching, but reassuring herself that she shouldn't look overly suspicious even if she was spotted. There were plenty of apartments in this complex; people were coming and going all the time. She could be just an innocent visitor.

Apart from the fact that she was now quite obviously checking the windows of the apartment she was now standing outside, trying to see if any were loosely latched, but they weren't.

Cara stood back, frustrated. But then, above her head, she saw another window, frosted glass this time; the bathroom, she assumed.

And that was slightly open.

CHAPTER 120
PRESENT DAY

CHAPTER 119
TWENTY YEARS AGO

A BEWILDERED-LOOKING Aidan is standing guard outside Donna's open door. I managed to gasp out to my neighbour that Donna was hurt, that help, an ambulance, was on its way, that he just had to stand there till they arrived.

I'd dashed outside to find Aidan standing by his car a few metres down the street. There was a big teenage party taking place on the beach apparently, and the road outside Donna's house was the closest he could park to home. But I barely heard him as he stumbled out his explanation. All I could think was, where's Harry? Why isn't he here, and why isn't he taking care of all this? But there's no time to pursue that. Now, I'm speeding down the lane towards the main road that will take me down to the bookshop.

As I hurl the car around the first of a series of bends, I catch the approaching siren of an emergency vehicle before I turn and speed off even faster in the opposite direction. But I push that to the back of my mind too. They've their job to do. Now I have mine.

As I drive, I hit a speed dial button on my phone, Mark's name coming up on the display. He won't be in the shop at this time, but he lives close by; he can get there a lot quicker than I can. But the call just rings out, not even diverting to answerphone, so I can't leave a message. I hit the phone in frustration, but then still as a sudden thought strikes me. Because how could Penny have even got in there? And if she didn't get in there of her own accord, how could anyone have taken her in there when only Mark and I have got a key? Mark, who's now not picking up his phone.

But then another face swims before my eyes, and this time it really is from out of nowhere. Because I see DI Adams. And now I'm back at the start of all this, to that uniformed officer banging on the door of the bookshop that day with Rory and me inside, and my sudden realisation that he probably wouldn't remain outside for long, because police officers have keys for that sort of eventuality; I'd read it somewhere, I was sure I had.

Then I shake my head, growing more frustrated, because if Adams does have anything to do with Penny, that means he probably had something to do with Cara as well, which is madness. Then I pause again. But he was on that case all those years ago, of course. Just as he's been leading the investigation into what might have happened to Penny too.

And I must be getting more and more paranoid all the time, because I suddenly remember that it's not only Mark and I who have keys to the rare books room, but Donna as well, as back-up in case I was out of the country, and she couldn't reach him. And while this obviously can't be anything to do with Donna, given the violent assault she's just suffered, Donna having that key meant others would have access to it too. Like Harry.

Which is when something else flashes through my mind. Because I've just realised that, as I swung away from the village a few minutes ago, I didn't hear a single sound from the nearby beach, despite Aidan telling me some big party was taking place down there, the large gathering that had forced him to park next to Donna's house.

Then my phone rings. I reach over to answer it but, my fingers fumbling again, I don't manage to hit the connect button before the answerphone cuts in. I listen to my standard greeting message coming out of the speaker in an agony of impatience. Is this Mark? Has he seen my missed call and is returning it?

But the voice I hear next isn't Mark.

'Mr Petersen?'

I hit the answer button before Adams gets chance to finish his message.

'Yes, I'm here.'

He barely breaks stride.

'You made another emergency call?'

'Yes, my wife, she's been attacked.'

'And you're with her now?'

'No.'

I tail off, and his voice, clipped and suspicious already, acquires an even more brittle edge.

'You've left her?'

I don't reply for a moment. What do I say? How much can I, should I say? Suddenly, I cut the call and replace the phone on its cradle; I simply can't handle all this right now.

Then I activate the original text message delivered earlier, and then that photo of Penny in the rare books room. Which is when I pick out something I haven't seen before. Because she's wearing the scarf, the kaleidoscope-coloured scarf I saw hanging up that day in the shop, the scarf that Rory must have taken away with him. I keep looking at it as I drive on. So, has this photo been mocked up? Is this an old photo, not from today at all? Am I going to dash down to the bookshop to find I'm on the end of some elaborate practical joke and the rare books room is empty?

Or am I plunging headlong into a trap?

CHAPTER 121
TWENTY YEARS AGO

CARA SEARCHED THROUGH DRAWERS, rifled through cupboards, but so far, she'd found nothing.

There was just a small selection of clothes in the bedroom, in the spare bedroom not even that. She drew a blank in the kitchen and the bathroom too, utensils, soap and a single toothbrush aside. Moving back into the sitting room – the first room she'd searched – she looked round, desperate to spot anything she'd missed.

Which was when, suddenly, from years before, Cara recalled a story she'd once read, one of many she'd devoured in those tunnels and passageways inside her father's bookshop. The title and the author escaped her for now, but she could recall the tale clearly enough, and for a moment she reflected on the irony. Because it was something her dad had always said to her. That books would always lead you through.

Cara looked up at a small bookshelf, a collection of titles on open view. She ran her hand along the spines. And now she remembered the author and the name of the story. The author was Edgar Allan Poe. The story was *The Purloined Letter*. And it dealt with a theft that had been concealed by hiding the object of that theft in plain sight.

And Poe was the author of the volume Cara now prised out from the shelf as she stared at the title.

Tamerlane.

Cara kept staring, her breath quickening all the while, much as it had when she'd managed to persuade the owner of Jericho's car wash to let her view their old CCTV tapes and had then seen a driver – a driver she knew well – pull up in his car those couple of months before.

Then she wheeled round as she heard the flat door opening behind her. Panicked, Cara pushed the volume back in place and retreated into the spare bedroom across the small hall. Pressing herself into an empty wardrobe, she realised she couldn't now totally close the door, but that partly open door also meant she could see everything that was about to unfold.

As not one but two men appeared from the hallway and then faced each other in the sitting room in her direct eyeline.

CHAPTER 122
PRESENT DAY

I DASH INSIDE THE BOOKSHOP. There's no need to disable the alarm as it's already been switched off. And once again all those names and faces I saw on my drive over here swim in front of my eyes. But this can't be anything to do with any of them, I'm convinced of it. Yet someone's here – that disabled alarm is telling me that only too clearly – and maybe more than one person too. Penny certainly, if that photo on my phone is genuine, either of her own volition, or with someone else if that someone else has forced her.

'Penny?'

I yell out her name as I head inside, but there's no answer. But something's changed, I can feel it. There's an unmistakable atmosphere inside an empty shop, but I can feel a presence strongly now. I plunge into the tunnel that leads away from the main reception room.

'Penny!'

I yell out again but there's still no reply. I head for the rare books room and hit the light switch, but no light comes on. For a moment I just stand there, disorientated in the darkness; my eyes are unable to penetrate the gloom, unable to see if there's anyone inside or not.

What I should be seeing, in the very middle of the room, is the capsule, constructed of mahogany beams with acrylic walls that can breathe but are as strong as tungsten. It took a whole team of specialist carpenters to bring it inside over twenty years ago and fit it out. It's where I store the most valuable books in the shop, the ones that require a constant temperature to preserve them, their dust jackets wrapped in custom-fitted acrylic cases, all ready for the most serious of collectors to be ushered in to inspect.

I stare into the dark, my eyes still not yet adjusting. Remembering my phone, I scrabble for it before recalling that in my haste I left it back on its cradle in the car, so I can't even summon up the dim illumination from the screen to light my way.

'Hello?'

I call out, straining my ears. I don't expect a reply, but maybe I can pick up the sound of someone breathing. Again there's nothing. Apart from that certain knowledge that I'm not alone.

I take another step inside, sensing, if still not seeing the capsule now just a couple of metres in front of me. Now I'm closer I can hear the faint hum from the motor that empties and replenishes the air. I take one more step and then another, and within a few seconds I'm standing by the wall of the structure, breathing in its all too familiar smell.

Which is when I hear it. A sound behind. I wheel and can now make out a faint glow; not a light exactly, something else, but I don't know what. And then I hear a footstep and then another.

I call out again.

'Hello?'

Momentarily, the footsteps stop, but then there's a loud click. The glow begins to burn brighter as if someone has turned up the wick on a candle, but whoever's there is behind the glow and all I can now make out is a dim shape.

'For fuck's sake, who is this? What do you want?'

From the capsule, I think I hear something too, as if someone inside is stirring, but I keep my eyes fixed on the apparition in front of me. The glow burns brighter again, and now I can see a hand holding some kind of portable light, not a candle. It's something gas-powered, because now I hear a hiss as the pressure's increased and the light illuminates some more.

Then, suddenly, I see who it is.

CHAPTER 123
TWENTY YEARS AGO

'CARA CAME TO SEE ME.'

Now all but holding her breath, Cara stared through the crack in the partly open wardrobe door. Jericho was facing her, but he couldn't see her. All he was looking at was the man in front of him.

'She asked me if Axel – or Donna – had been to the car wash. I told her they hadn't, but a couple of days ago ...'

Jericho tailed off, uncertain. His companion remained silent as the young man took a deep breath and struggled a conciliatory smile.

'I suddenly remembered that you'd called in.'

Still, he was being met with that same silence.

'I just wondered. Did you have anything in the car? Anything of Axel's or Donna's? Something from the house?'

Jericho spread his arms wide, almost in a surrender gesture, his tone still mild, his manner as pacifying as ever.

'You probably didn't think about it at the time, but if you did and I'd touched anything when we cleared the car...'

Jericho paused again, clearly trying to quell his nerves, and no wonder. A whole world, his whole world, was hanging on the answer.

'That would explain those prints.'

The other man's gaze swept around the room, as if he was struggling to remember. Cara pressed herself further back in the wardrobe, irrationally fearful that he'd spotted her. Then, suddenly, he swooped down and picked something up from next to the fireplace. The next second Cara saw a flash of light reflect off a metallic surface as whatever he'd picked up slashed across his young questioner's throat.

Then Jericho collapsed, choking horribly, onto the floor.

CHAPTER 124
PRESENT DAY

FROM THE OPEN DOORWAY, Harry stares at me. The man I last saw on the lane leading down to that small collection of houses. The man who followed me to Donna's house, but never arrived.

And now, maybe I know why.

He's looking at me much as he looked at me at the top of that lane too, but then I realise something's wrong. Now he's coming more and more into focus, his eyes seem glassy, the pupils enlarged. It's as if he's staring, but not seeing me. I take a step towards him, when suddenly he crumples and falls to his feet, and for the first time, I can see that someone's behind him.

And there's something in the hand of that figure behind, something I don't recognise at first, although maybe that's some kind of defence mechanism kicking in, because I don't want to.

Slowly, and for the second time in as many days, a gun rises before me until the barrel points straight at my chest. At the same time, I hear a voice.

'Hello Axel.'

I stare into the dim illumination in front of me, barely daring to even breathe.

I make to speak, but then I stop, can't go on. I feel dizzy, as if I'm about to pass out, and as bile burns the inside of my throat, I blink, almost as if I just need to clear my vision and then this trick won't be played on me any longer.

But the same figure still stands there. As composed and calm and in control as ever.

And still holding that gun.

CHAPTER 125
TWENTY YEARS AGO

THE ATTACKER now had his back to her; Jericho was still on the floor. Blood was pooling out underneath his prone body, his precious life draining out of him, courtesy of that single slash to his throat, which Cara could now see had been inflicted by what looked like some kind of ornamental fireside poker.

All Cara wanted to do was run to him, hold him, offer him comfort, try and help, even though she knew already he was probably beyond all help. But something stopped her, and it wasn't cowardice, and it wasn't fear at what that attacker might do to her if she did reveal herself like that; it was the sudden lurch in her stomach.

Later, when she realised she was pregnant, Cara would initially dismiss what had happened as she stood there. She was too early into her term for any life inside her to make itself known in that way. But she felt it, nonetheless. An instinctive, almost atavistic reminder of the stakes she was playing for. Something telling her that she didn't have only herself – or even the father of her child – to think about now. Her body telling her she had someone else to think about as well.

Jericho gasped up at his still-silent attacker, and there was no attempt on his part to pacify now; the scales had well and truly fallen from his eyes, the depth of his assailant's mendacity laid bare.

'You won't get away with this.'

But Cara could hear it in Jericho's voice. The crushing realisation that he was wrong. Given the circles his attacker moved in, he could get away with anything.

CHAPTER 126
TWENTY YEARS AGO

THE TRAIN GUARD SMILED, that's all she did, a simple smile as she checked her ticket, and Cara almost broke down in tears. Immediately the guard's kindly face creased in concern.

'Are you OK?'

Cara looked out of the window, taking a moment, struggling to compose herself. Across the estuary, to the right of her window seat, the seat she always chose on these sorts of journeys, the castle came into view, the ruined castle she'd seen every day of her life, the castle she'd played in as a child, as well as partied in years later. But now – and how that realisation pierced her – it was a sight that would not, could not, be there for her from that moment on.

'Can I help?'

The train guard was still standing by her seat, the same concerned look on her face, and Cara hesitated again, but only for a moment.

'Sorry. Miles away.'

The guard hesitated in turn, not totally convinced by the young girl's slightly too brave smile, but they were coming into the first halt on the line and doors had to be opened, passengers had to alight, others had to board, so she just gave a quick, half-assenting nod before giving the young passenger back her ticket and heading away.

Cara looked back out of the window again. Now, across the estuary and squatting in the shadow of that same castle, she could see the house, her home, at least up till an hour or so ago, something else she was now leaving behind, a house that would be a home no more.

Getting away hadn't been difficult; the party had been the perfect smokescreen. They'd expect her back at some point the following day, but they wouldn't expect her too early, not after an all-night party. Those texts she'd sent asking if it was OK for her to stay with Jools should help too.

Dad would probably go down to the bookshop without worrying where she was. Mum might assume, at the start anyway, that she'd gone into town with a friend for a coffee. She should have plenty of time before any sort of alarm was raised. Plenty of time to get as far away as she could.

Cara looked out of the window at the beach. Years before, she'd taken countless innocent strolls there, a chance to lose herself in daydreams and imaginings. But lately, those solo walks had become a necessity. A release from doing what she'd had to do for the whole of that time, putting up a front, putting on a face, something she could simply do no more.

She'd told no one why, not even Jools, not really, and that had been one of the biggest wrenches of all. Her best friend had known something was badly wrong. She'd badgered and badgered her to talk, and finally, last night, and badly spooked, she'd cracked, and no wonder.

In the space of one single day and night, she'd witnessed one life end, and she now knew another life was growing inside her. But Cara didn't tell her best friend everything. She told her about the baby. But she didn't tell her about Jericho and what had happened to him. She didn't tell her that he'd escaped one war zone only to find himself in a very different one, but it had wreaked the same result. Now he was gone. And she couldn't tell her how or why, because then Jools would have felt impelled to do something about it and Cara couldn't risk that. Now, there was only one thing she could possibly do, and this was it. Put as much distance between herself and her former home, as much distance between herself and what had turned into her darkest nightmare, as she could.

The train began to slow for the next request stop on the line. They'd just passed the myriad collection of holiday caravans grouped around a small inlet that – and although she would never say as much to Jools, and even though they'd spent a lot of time there lately – had always seemed to her to be the grimmest of places. It said something about her state of mind right now that she looked out on their corrugated roofs and peeling paint with another piercing stab, knowing she wouldn't be seeing them again either.

Cara turned back as the train slowed and then came to a halt. The female guard who'd provoked that sudden hot flush of emotion by her concerned question was visible through the window, checking the platform for any more arriving passengers. Then she moved back into the carriage as the doors slid open and the only passenger who'd embarked, a lone male, appeared, further down the same carriage.

Cara felt her heart lurch up into her mouth.

In fleeing one nightmare, had she just plunged headlong into another?

CHAPTER 127
PRESENT DAY

A FEW HOURS before learning of Axel's emergency call about Donna, Adams looked up as Maya appeared at his shoulder, sliding a slim report along to him as she did so.

'As promised.'

Adams glanced down at it, then up at the pathologist.

'Headlines?'

'Male, age still to be determined. He wasn't killed at the spot we found him; the soil samples we've managed to retrieve make that clear enough. He was killed somewhere else and then moved there, possibly quite recently.'

'Why would anyone want to do that?'

'Maybe whoever killed him was worried he might be found where he was originally buried.'

She paused. 'Or whoever killed him moved the body to a spot where they knew he'd be more likely to be found.'

Maya looked down at the report too. They'd already established there'd been heavy rain recently; there'd even been a couple of landslips in the area, so it was possible this body had been disturbed somehow. But somehow, Maya doubted it. There seemed something almost theatrical in all this.

'We do have a match on the database though.'

Maya permitted herself a small smile as Adams's head jerked up and he stared at her. She'd always believed in saving the best till last.

Maya slid another report, one from two decades before, across to him.

'A young man who'd been picked up in connection with the theft of a rare book.'

She nodded at him.

'You were involved in the original investigation, according to the notes.'

Adams didn't reply for a moment as he stared at the face before him in the second of the reports, and Maya paused again as she eyed him, now growing increasingly curious.

She'd hadn't expected profuse and fulsome thanks. She didn't expect Adams to perform a victory lap to celebrate what had to be counted as something of a breakthrough. But she was seeing nothing right now, no reaction at all.

In fact, as he kept staring at the face of the young and long-dead man in the report in front of him, Adams didn't even look surprised.

CHAPTER 128
TWENTY YEARS AGO

CHAPTER 129
PRESENT DAY

SHE'D ALWAYS TALKED to him. Confided in him, in a way. He was like some kindly uncle, always willing to listen, never to judge.

All that changed of course, and like everything else, it changed on the day Cara walked in on him and her mum.

But maybe they could have got over that. It was like that age-old analogy Donna was always quoting about relationships and plates. It wouldn't ever have been the same between the two of them, but they could have maybe put it behind them. Everyone's entitled to the odd mistake.

Until she saw what happened that night.

What he did to Jericho.

CHAPTER 129
PRESENT DAY

FOR A MOMENT longer I just keep staring at the gun.

Then I look up again.

But this is no trick.

Across the rare books room, Patrick's eyes are fixed on mine.

CHAPTER 130
TWENTY YEARS AGO

He seated himself on the train seat next to her. Cara was frozen, couldn't move, couldn't even speak. Last night, she'd had to double back from the beach party, convinced she was being followed, fearful it was him. And now he seemed to have caught up with her anyway.

Looking round, he did a quick check, making sure no one was in earshot as she tried to stay calm, telling herself he was going to talk about her walking in on him and her mum like that, that he couldn't know she'd been there in his flat, that he couldn't know she'd seen what he'd done.

And she was right, because he didn't talk about that. But he didn't talk about himself and Mum either.

He talked about her and him instead.

CHAPTER 131
PRESENT DAY

I TRY TO SPEAK, then stop. I can't.

Images flash before my eyes: birthday parties, Christmases, family celebrations.

And Patrick.

Always Patrick.

Always there.

Not just as our solicitor, but as our oldest family friend.

But he wasn't.

Was he?

CHAPTER 132
TWENTY YEARS AGO

HE TOLD her he hadn't realised, not till that moment when she saw them together. How he had thought Mum could leave, could set up with him, that Cara would go with them and how they'd all be together, just as they should be.

But when he saw Cara, standing in that doorway, that was when he realised. This wasn't about Mum at all. It wasn't about the three of them, setting up a new family together. It was about the two of them. Her, and him.

He told Cara how sorry he was. How confused he'd been, how something had happened between them without either of them knowing, but they knew now, they both did, so maybe this was a good thing. It could all be out in the open from now on; there'd be no need to pretend anymore.

Because they had a connection; he knew it and so did she. And now they could stand before the world and tell everyone what they knew in their hearts already, even if they'd never been able to acknowledge it, maybe even to themselves.

This was meant to be. They were meant to be.

They had to be together.

Then he leant closer as he told her that this wasn't just talk.

Because he'd taken steps, practical steps, to make sure that this new future of theirs wasn't just a pipe dream, that it really could happen.

He paused. He couldn't go into the hows or the whys. But recently, he'd come into some money.

CHAPTER 133

PRESENT DAY

'It was too much for her to take in, I know that now, but it didn't matter, because I was thinking for the two us; she just had to understand that, accept it, and she would have done, in time, I know she would.'

It's all pouring out of Patrick now. It has been for the last few minutes. More and more insanity assaulting my disbelieving ears.

'I told her we could do anything, go anywhere, that all we had to do was move away, start somewhere fresh.'

And I can actually see it, just as he's saying it. I can see Patrick, and I can see Cara too, staring back at him much as I am right now, feeling as I do right now too, as if she'd just landed on some alien planet. It must have been bad enough walking in on her mother and our oldest family friend like that, but this was so much worse. Now that same family friend was telling her that nightmare was just a stepping stone to an even worse one.

'You couldn't ever understand, how could you? Donna couldn't either. And Cara was still so young back then; that's why she had to trust me.'

He pauses.

'But it did things to her. I can see that now too. Finding her mum and me like that. The shock stopped her thinking straight. She wouldn't have tried running away otherwise.'

Suddenly, I launch myself at him, fingers scrabbling for grip around his windpipe. Momentarily disorientated, he falls to the floor, the gun skittering away a metre or so. But as I press down on his throat, his own fingers scrabble in turn, reaching out for and picking up the gun before smashing it against the side of my head. I crash away, momentarily stunned. I'm aware of Patrick dashing across to a nearby wall, fixing something back in place, then my eyes clamp shut as a blinding light flashes on overhead. Slowly, I open my eyes to see Patrick, the gun back in his hand, staring at me, his breath coming now in great gasps.

Then I still as I see Penny, inside the capsule, staring eyes swivelling wildly all around, looking traumatised beyond belief.

CHAPTER 134
TWENTY YEARS AGO

CARA STILL HADN'T SPOKEN, hadn't even moved. Patrick's words were continuing to swirl all around her.

But then, out of the window, she caught sight of another smaller, ruined castle in the distance and she knew they'd be coming into the next stop along the line in just a few moments time.

Struggling to keep her voice under control, she turned back to him, told him she needed to go to the toilet; that this was all so overwhelming, she needed time to think, to take it all in, and he smiled back. Then he told her to take all the time she needed. They had all the time in the world.

Cara stood, remembering something as she did so, and for a moment, she almost ruined everything by asking him. Because he wasn't even supposed to be in the country right now. He was supposed to be thousands of miles away at some auction, bidding on some book for her dad. But then she paused. Because clearly, she hadn't been the only one preparing an exit route. He'd been busy putting his own in place as well. And any bidding he'd been doing, or had been planning on doing, would have been courtesy of an international phone link.

Cara moved down the carriage. The kindly guard who'd smiled at her earlier was standing by the door, the train now coming into the station. And smoothly, not looking behind herself once, Cara glided past her as the train slowed to a halt, then slipped down onto the platform and moved away.

I WAS WRONG. Now I can see her more clearly, it's obvious that Penny isn't traumatised, she's drugged.

I turn back, gasp at him.

'What was she, bait? Or just some sick kind of insurance policy? Here in case you needed her?'

For his part Patrick can't seem to tear his eyes away from her. She seems to draw him in like a magnet as I rail on.

'If I got too close to the truth, she was there, was that it? Ready to set me up? Let the police draw their own conclusions.'

But Patrick's still just staring at Penny. For a moment I'm tempted to launch a fresh assault, but it would be near-suicidal, and I know it. His attention might be all on Penny but I'm still very much in his peripheral vision, and he's still got that gun.

My breath continues to come out in gasps, each word almost having to be squeezed out.

'So, what's next? Kill me, then play what you've been playing all along? Act the concerned family friend? There's enough evidence you've been worried about me for a long time now – all those phone calls, and all those visits. If you checked up on me again here in the shop no one would think anything of it.'

Behind us, Penny shifts position slightly, looks over at the two of us, but I can see she has absolutely no idea where she is or what's happening to her. For his part, Patrick keeps staring at her and I realise just why she's drawing him in like that. And once again, it's those eyes. The eyes I first fell inside that night on the train. The eyes that, all too briefly, convinced me my long-lost daughter was back with me again, sitting just a metre or so across the carriage. Cara's eyes. The eyes staring out from that capsule at us.

And it's like a signal. Penny's still totally uncomprehending, of course, but there's something flashing down through the generations, a silent, almost telepathic call to arms. Without thinking, because, and for the second time in as many days I know that if I do think then I'll never do this, I launch myself at Patrick again, uncaring now of the consequences. I take him off guard momentarily once more, smashing him to the floor as I roll on top of him.

But I've overplayed my hand again and I don't trap him as I should have done, as I would have done if I'd had a second longer to think about it. He's not even winded; he's on his feet in an instant and he brings the heel of his shoe down hard on my outstretched hand, crushing some bones. I can hear them crack and I feel a lacerating pain as they do so.

Inside the capsule, I see Penny's head flop in front of her as if the effort of just looking over at us is already proving too much. And in that instant, I know that she'll take none of this in. She'll retain no memory of this or of anything else, probably from the moment she alighted from my car, if that's when Patrick first got to her. She'll come round as if from some sort of coma to find she's in that capsule – and her apparent captor will be outside, seemingly killed by his own hand, the balance of his mind hopelessly disturbed, a man driven mad by guilt and grief.

Out of the corner of my eye I now see a syringe in Patrick's hand. I'm still bent double, clutching my own shattered hand, but I know if I stay here just a moment longer the contents of that syringe will be washing inside me and I'll be powerless, like Penny. Patrick will have total freedom to rearrange my death scene in any way he wishes to serve the fiction he intends to create.

I stagger to my feet as he approaches. My back's against the wall and there's nowhere to hide and nowhere to run, only towards Patrick and that syringe. Patrick stares at me, like a butcher assessing a carcass. And I can almost see him now, nodding along sadly as the police outline their all too obvious conclusions.

I've nothing to lose now. I launch myself forward again. A second later, I feel the most savage of punches. I see the brightest of lights illuminate my eyes. I feel the air being almost physically sucked out of my lungs by the strongest force I've ever felt in my life as I raise my hands to the skies, almost in silent prayer, and I see a syringe plunge into human flesh.

Then I feel the blackness descend.

PART SIX

EPILOGUE

CHAPTER 136
PRESENT DAY

THE HOLIDAY SEASON hasn't started yet, so there are just a few locals on the beach along with their dogs, including Aidan, of course. The ever-present Aidan with what looks like yet another new pit bull. Once the season does start, his dog, along with all the others, are barred from using the beach, so they're all luxuriating in their short-lived freedom.

Florries, the local fish and chip shop, isn't open for business yet either, but the small beachside shop is serving the usual teas, coffees and ice cream. But we haven't called in up to now, and something tells me we're not going to call in today either. For now, and just like every other day for the past few months, all Penny seems to want to do is walk. It's an activity she shares with her grandfather, of course, although I haven't told her yet about my own addiction to Beachcomber-like treks across deserted headlands and cliffs.

I didn't even know if she wanted company at first, but the way she hung back before she was about to set off suggested otherwise. And she didn't protest as I pulled on my boots and set off with her down the small path to begin the first of what's turned out to be dozens of different explorations.

We're living back in the old family home for now. Penny's sleeping in her mother's old room, surrounded by all Cara's things; her books and posters and the like. I hesitated over even showing all of them to her at the start, but she's spent hours in there since she arrived.

In the confusion of that confrontation back in the rare books room, Patrick's syringe hit one of his own veins rather than mine. After he was discharged from hospital – the same hospital that treated me for what turned out to be a not-so-minor heart attack suffered at the same time – Patrick folded pretty quickly in his first police interview, which, by all accounts, resembled more of a vicious interrogation on the part of DI Adams. After all this time a small-town country solicitor was never going to stand between him and finally wrapping everything up. Patrick was charged with the murder of Jericho, the attack on Donna and Harry and the abduction and imprisonment of Penny.

Almost as an aside and under the same heavy pressure from Adams, he also confessed to the anonymous phone call regarding my taking Penny away from the station in my car that night, a call I'd always assumed had been made by Rory. Another part of this story that I'd got wrong.

There've been no formal charges laid against him in respect of Cara. Illness claimed her life as we all now know. But how I wish there could have been.

Just how long Penny and I will stay here in the old family home, I don't know. Maybe when Donna is herself discharged from hospital, we'll have to make some sort of decision. According to the doctors. Patrick had left her for dead and it was only by a miracle he hadn't succeeded. And the fact that help had been at hand with my arrival, of course, which had been a happy accident. One of the few strokes of luck we'd had over the previous twenty years. But perhaps we both deserved some good fortune for a change.

Penny still hasn't spoken much about anything – her mum,

even her sister. Once she'd been checked over and the drugs with which she'd been forcibly injected had been flushed from her system, I did expect to be bombarded with dozens of questions from a young girl desperate to fill in a lifetime of gaps. But none of that happened. So, I made a cautious offer for her to stay in her mum's old house with me while she worked out what she wanted to do next, and after a few moments thought, she nodded back. And that was that. We both moved in and here we've stayed ever since.

Rory's been a regular visitor, but again she doesn't seem to talk too much to him either and he's been largely silent on these visits too. Maybe they're both doing the same right now – getting used to a halfway-normal life at least, after too long enduring an existence that's been anything but. Maybe that's what we're all doing.

But this morning, our walk's interrupted. One of the local dogs has always made a beeline for Penny for some reason, and he's doing the same right now. Depositing a small ball at her feet, tail wagging furiously, adoring eyes imploring her to pick it up and throw it for him. Penny's done it each day too, brushing aside the owner's apologies with her customary good grace. But this morning she just stands there, the ball in her hand, looking down at her furry disciple as he barks and yelps up at her. For a moment I don't think she's going to do anything, but then she bends down and gives her canine acolyte a quick pat on the head before reaching back her hand and throwing the ball towards the water.

Then she looks back at me.

'I want to go somewhere.'

I wait for her to expand, but she doesn't. A hundred or so metres away the dog's splashing happily through the small waves coursing in from the estuary, nudging his ball ahead of him all the while.

'After next week.'

I tense. Next week is something else we haven't talked about yet. The start of Patrick's trial.

Slowly, almost shyly, she reaches out her hand and loops her arm through my arm. She hasn't done that before either. Up to now there's been no physical contact at all.

'Let's get that over with first.'

CHAPTER 137
PRESENT DAY

A FEW MONTHS EARLIER, and two days after Patrick's arrest, Adams was back on the bridge, resting his arms on the stone parapet, looking down at the water once again.

Braith was standing by his side again, but this time she wasn't an unwanted presence, an unwelcome irritant. This time she was there at Adams's invitation.

'It's all I could see back then, every time I looked at her. I'd stand by the side of her bed, watching her as she was sleeping. I'd even keep watch from the window sometimes when she was playing out in the garden or walking down the street to school. It was though if I took my eyes off her for a moment, then it would happen to her too. My daughter would disappear as well.'

Adams struggled as Braith watched him, the ghost of the original Cara case extant in his eyes.

'It was as if there was only one way to save her, and it became this crazy fixation. It wasn't just a normal case anymore. It was like some kind of deal with the devil. Find Cara. Then I keep my own child safe.'

Braith felt her own mind returning to that same time, seeing herself as she pored over all those reports in the papers even though she was too young to take in most of what she was reading at the time. Hiding behind half-open doors, listening to news reports on the TV, positively drinking it all in. To the point where she was seeing just that one face too.

'Looking back, it was inevitable I suppose. I was living inside some kind of madness; it was only a matter of time before it started to infect everything else. And then it became this giant self-fulfilling prophecy. And I lost her – and everything else – anyway.'

Adams looked down at the spot where decades earlier those unknowing fishermen had landed their giant catch.

'Then Penny disappeared, and it was like it was happening all over again, as if I was back in the middle of all that, and I've started doing it again too. I've started watching her, parking up outside Suzy's house at night, watching her from my car, swearing to her, even though she can't see or hear me, that I'll do it this time – I'll find Penny even if I couldn't find Cara, that it'll be OK, that this time I will keep her safe.'

Braith, still staying silent, looked down at the water too. His story wasn't her story. But in one respect it was the same. Adams was painting pictures of shadows and connections, the shadows and connections that had twisted his life out of shape. But similar connections and shadows had changed the course of her life too, and that, again, was all down to Cara. Adams's quest may not have been her quest, but she'd been on a parallel one ever since that first story broke, ever since, as a six-year-old sucking on a lolly, she saw Axel standing in the doorway of her old home.

All that happened to Cara might have exploded the most forcefully in the lives of others, but the ensuing ripples had ensnared so many more too.

CHAPTER 138
PRESENT DAY

DONNA'S finally discharged from hospital as Patrick's trial begins, but she still isn't well enough to attend. So, Mark picks her up from the hospital instead. He immediately turns towards the coast road leading down towards her house, but Donna tells him she wants to go to his flat first.

As Mark pulls up outside, he tenses as he sees the waiting Harry, but Donna reaches across, laying a comforting, if frail, hand on his arm. The last time Harry was here he'd been intent on a white-hot confrontation. This visit is to be anything but confrontational.

Harry had last called in on Mark at the same time as Axel was calling for help for Donna. He didn't waste time on pleasantries such as waiting for Mark to answer the door. One second after he'd hammered on it, Harry just kicked it down instead.

When he received that second text, following Axel on the drive back to his sister's house, he was going to ignore it at first. But then he stood on the brakes as the image screamed out at him from the screen on his phone. It was Cara, but not as he remembered her. This was an older Cara, and he knew exactly where it was taken too. He'd gone with Donna once to the home of Axel's strange and withdrawn assistant and remembered well the utterly

anonymous character of the flat occupied by its similarly anonymous occupant.

A moment or so before, his sister had been all Harry could
think about, but Axel was on his way there now. So, he turned the
car round, frantically trying to remember exactly where Mark
lived. If there was a chance – even the slightest chance – that this
latest text was a summons of some kind, then he had to respond
to it.

Pulling up outside the flat a short time later, he launched
himself at the door. There didn't seem to be anyone inside, but
that wouldn't have stopped the enraged Harry anyway. Within
moments he'd checked the flat from top to bottom, but there was
no sign of his beloved and still much-missed niece. But then Harry
saw the trap door let into the ceiling, and it was hanging open.

Grabbing a chair, Harry hauled himself up and inside. Scrabbling round for a switch, he couldn't find one, so he dragged out
his phone, accessing the torch. Looking round, he couldn't take in
what he was seeing for a moment, but then he slowed his breathing, calming himself down, an old trick from days witnessing
similarly inexplicable scenes in the Army.

Harry looked round at photo after photo of Cara tacked up on
the walls, including the photo he'd been sent of the older Cara.
And Harry stood there, rooted and bewildered, as he took in
every detail of what was obviously some kind of shrine.

And then he felt it. A sharp pain as if someone had just
stabbed a needle into a vein. And now, of course, he knew who.
Followed by a slow descent into what felt like oblivion.

Now, Donna is led by Mark inside that self-same flat, and
Harry can see those same photos, now assembled on the sitting
room table. Donna takes a moment to leaf through the precious
collection, curated and chosen by Mark, for her. It was another of
her rituals as the anniversary rolled round. One more photo
would be added, by Mark, at Donna's request, to what became
known as the Cara wall. Another way of keeping the faith, of

promising her daughter that she was not forgotten and that one day she'd return to see all these photos for herself.

Axel didn't know about it. No one did, apart from Donna and Mark. And Patrick, of course. She'd made the mistake of telling him. And she knows now that he stored that information away, all ready to use one day. A ticking bomb, all ready to be detonated.

And he did that, by diverting Harry to Mark's flat, using one of those photos to lure him there, ensuring Axel would make that dash down to the bookshop alone.

Donna picks up one of the last photos in line, the one of Cara artificially aged by a computer program, an approximation of how she might look twenty years on from her disappearance. Then she brings the photo to her lips, kisses the imagined image of her daughter and tells Mark that it's time to stop this annual ritual.

They know now what happened to Cara. It's time to put her, and all this, to rest.

CHAPTER 139
PRESENT DAY

AT THE SAME time as Donna is with Harry and Mark, I'm standing with Penny outside one of the most famous courts in the world.

Above us, the statue of Lady Justice is where she always is, perched on top of the capital's Old Bailey, along with the stone sculptures of Fortitude, Truth and the Recording Angel, draped in her ominous heavy robe. The huge wooden doors and black gates stand wide open, the equally famous words carved into the stone above clear for all to see. *Defend The Children Of The Poor & Punish The Wrongdoer.*

Penny looks at me and I squeeze her hand. Then she walks inside the old building, a police officer checking her ID before removing her personal possessions to be returned later. She waits in a featureless room at the end of an equally featureless corridor before being called up to give her evidence. From the public gallery I watch as she blinks in the artificial light streaming in through the large window, burnishing the dark panelling lining the courtroom, lending a soft lustre to the green leather upholstery.

In the raised dock, and behind a glass screen, alone as defendants always are, is Patrick. Directly opposite is a judge, with the prosecution and defence teams along with the clerk of the court occupying the centre of the room. And they all listen, intent, as she gives her evidence.

A few days later, we're both back there again, waiting along with everyone else, but not for much longer. Five minutes ago, we received word that the jury are returning, having reached their verdict.

Today, the concluding day of his trial, has played out pretty much as everyone expected. The prosecution and defence barrister made their closing speeches to the jury before the judge provided the usual summing up. The jury were then excused to consider their verdict. It wasn't expected that they'd be out long, given the overwhelming nature of the evidence, in the light of which Patrick's decision to plead not guilty was simply incomprehensible. But his reaction to the closing speech of the prosecution barrister was even more so.

The barrister borrowed a speech from a famous old play. It was all part of his closing argument that nothing could ever be really consigned to the past. In fact, and borrowing further from the playwright in question, he argued it was wrong to even call it that.

Because whatever you've done before, it's always there. However you've acted, you must live with it, and not just then but now too. You might hide whatever it is you've done for most of the time. Your friends, family, even your partner, be that wife, husband or lover, may never suspect a thing. You might even forget about all that yourself from time to time. But you can't erase who you are. You can't undo what you did, and even more importantly, it always catches up with you, often when you least expect it.

Which was when, suddenly, Patrick started to splutter, then laugh. No one could quite believe it at first. Even the prosecution barrister himself faltered a couple of times, but he continued, professional to the end.

I kept staring at Patrick as the closing speeches concluded. Had the events of the last twenty years finally unhinged him? No one in that courtroom was finding a great deal to laugh about right now, so that seemed the only possible explanation. The odd thing was that this wasn't the cackling of a madman. He seemed genuinely amused by all the barrister was saying, and not even the direct intervention of the judge could stop his shoulders shaking. We could all quite clearly see that there looked to be tears of mirth in his eyes as well.

Then, the jury return. The clerk stands and asks if they have reached a verdict upon which they are all agreed. Almost as one, the eleven seated members of the jury nod, obviating any need for the foreman to actually speak, but he delivers their one-word verdict anyway.

Guilty.

I look across at Patrick again, his head bowed, staring now into a future that's no future at all; imprisonment with no prospect of parole or release. When he's led away from that dock it will be to a cell that will be home for him forever. And now there is no laughter. Now there is no mocking challenge, if that's what that was, no metaphorical and defiant two fingers up to the peers that have just judged him for the events he instigated and the horrors he carried out. Now the last laugh has sounded. And it belongs not to the perpetrator of his crimes, but to its victims, past and present.

Patrick is led away, and I reach out my hand again, just like I did on that train. Then I lead Penny away too.

But there's still one more ritual left to observe. And all the major players in this story – myself, Penny, Rory, Donna, Mark, Jools and Harry – as well as the two police officers, Adams and Braith – are going to be there for it.

And one other visitor as well.

CHAPTER 140
PRESENT DAY

THE DAY after Patrick's trial concludes, Jools joins forces with a family she believed she'd hate for all time.

Jools couldn't do anything about Cara's death. No one could. And she couldn't look after Penny or Jen either, even though she'd begged to be allowed to do so. But Cara insisted she could not, that it was still too dangerous, even though she still wouldn't say why.

Everyone knows that now too, of course. She still feared Patrick. She still dreaded what he might do if he found out where she was. She'd seen what he was capable of at first hand, and she still felt much as she'd felt all those years before. For the sake of a family she loved, she had to keep the truth about him a secret.

But Cara did want her oldest friend to keep tabs on Penny and Jen. To watch over them, albeit from a distance. And, as far as her oldest and best friend was able – and Cara knew she was already asking the virtually impossible – to try and make sure they stayed safe.

Cara had no idea that by contacting Jools like that, she'd guaranteed the opposite. Patrick hadn't been able to find Cara all those years, but he'd kept close tabs on the unknowing Jools, just in case. And when Cara finally contacted her, he monitored her every movement. With Cara's passing, his surveillance passed onto her daughters in turn. Which meant that when Penny boarded that train that night, Patrick knew exactly where she was going, what she was doing, and why. And he also knew he had to stop her and put an end to all this once and for all.

Jools led Axel, Donna and everyone else to Cara's grave. Previously, only she and her girls knew where it was. It was another of Cara's mysterious instructions as she neared the end of her life, all part of her overwhelming desire to protect those nearest and dearest to her.

The service is simple. There's already been a funeral, but once the local church was informed of the circumstances, they had no hesitation in arranging another farewell for those unable to attend the first time. And all the family and extended family are there this time too, as are Adams and Braith.

But there isn't just the one funeral taking place today. Adams released Jericho's remains to the care of Axel and Donna, after enquiries overseas had revealed that his former family in Iraq were all now deceased. But Mark made some additional – and characteristically forensic – enquiries, and two days ago, he managed to find Jericho's brother, Omar, still living in Germany, now with a family of his own.

Omar is the unexpected visitor today. Tears welling in his eyes, he's finally able to say goodbye to a brother he hasn't stopped thinking about for twenty years. And as the coffin containing Jericho's remains is lowered into the grave, he steps forward and caresses a single leaf down onto the coffin lid, the Snow Leaf he's kept air-dried and preserved for the whole of those twenty years too.

Axel, Donna, Penny, Rory, Omar, Harry, Jools, Mark, Adams and Braith all stand before the graves that have been lined up side by side, paying their own silent tributes.

Then everyone turns and makes their respective ways home

CHAPTER 141

PRESENT DAY

I'VE no idea what to expect when Penny comes back with me from those two funeral services. I half-expect her to walk out again, unable to settle. But for a few days she just stays in the house and helps look after Donna, who is still convalescing.

Then she tells me – again – that she wants to go somewhere. Suddenly, the memory of that walk on the beach, and the encounter with her regular canine friend with the ball comes back to me and I half-expect her to take the train and revisit the animal rescue centre. But she doesn't. She asks me to take her to the book-shop instead.

When Penny walks in, it's like history repeating itself, as if I'm stepping back decades with her mum. Like Cara, she wanders the winding labyrinths, almost breathing in the old books before her, and like her mother too, she trails her hand across what must look like acres of exposed spines. I think of repeating what I said before to Cara, trying to explain that in their own way each and every one of the books she's seeing and touching possesses a soul. But I don't. Like her mother before her, Penny seems to know that already.

Then she asks if she can work here from time to time, along-side the ever-present Mark, and of course, I agree. It could turn out to be another form of withdrawal, or it could be a first step in re-engaging with the world again. As with so many things in both our lives right now, only time will tell.

As for my own re-engaging with the world, once my work in the bookshop is over for the day, I've taken to retreating to what used to be my old study in the eaves of the house, once Penny has gone to bed. After a lifetime surrounded by other people's writings, I've started writing myself. I'm putting down on paper the events of the last twenty years, beginning with that first and life-changing encounter with Penny on the train. I don't know why I'm doing it, or how it will turn out, but I know what the book's going to be called. It's the only thing it can be called.

Can I Trust You?

I also don't know how long Penny's going to stay here, and in a sense it doesn't matter. All that does matter is that while the past may have caught up with us, none of us is trapped in it anymore. We're looking forward now. Into what, I don't know. But for the first time in more years than I care to remember, I'm looking forward to finding out.

ACKNOWLEDGMENTS

Grateful thanks as always to the wonderful editor, Sue Davison, the great cover designer, Jayne Mapp, and the two inspirational powerhouses behind Hobeck Books, Rebecca Collins and Adrian Hobart.

One of the great joys of writing this novel was spending time in the company of booksellers and book collectors, sometimes face to face, sometimes remotely, sometimes simply courtesy of their excellent books. I'd like to acknowledge the research debt I owe to, among others, Nicholas A. Basbanes, Shaun Bythell, Martin Latham, Jeff Towns, Louise Boland, John Baxter, Emma Smith, Lucy Mangan, Rebecca Lee, Andrew Pettegree, Arthur der Weduwen, Chris Paling and Rick Gekowski.

Many a happy hour has also been spent in dozens of book-shops across the UK and abroad while writing this story, but two stand out in particular. First, there's the legendary Shakespeare and Company in Paris, from whom I transplanted my very own Tumbleweed into this tale. Secondly, there's Peter Harrington in London, founded by Peter in 1969 and continued to this day by his son, Pom. The Peter Harrington website has also been a hugely useful research resource.

ABOUT THE AUTHOR

Rob Gittins is a screenwriter and novelist. Rob's written for almost all the top-rated UK network TV dramas from the last thirty years, including *Casualty*, *EastEnders*, *The Bill*, *Heartbeat* and *Vera*, as well as over thirty original radio plays for BBC Radio 4.

He's previously had six novels published by Y Lolfa to high critical acclaim. This is Rob's third novel for Hobeck. He is also the author of a brand new series set on the idyllic, if occasionally sinister and disturbing, Isle of Wight. The first book in the series, *I'm Not There*, published in September 2022. Rob has also written a psychological thriller, *The Devil's Bridge Affair*, which published in October 2022.

Visit Rob's website at: www.robgittins.com

I'M NOT THERE

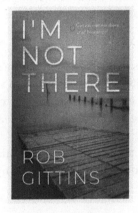

'Everything is cleverly brought together in a thrilling climax.'
Sarah Leck

'It has the feel of one of those books that gets a plug and takes off
to be a top ten bestseller.' Pete Fleming

'Dark, gritty, well-crafted characters and some gut-punching
shocks, first rate crime writing'. Alex Jones

Two sisters abandoned

It was a treat, she said. An adventure. A train journey to the mainland. Six-year-old Lara Arden and her older sister Georgia happily fill in their colouring books as their mum pops to the buffet in search of crisps. She never returns. Two little girls abandoned. Alone.

Present day

Twenty years later, and Lara is now a detective inspector on her native Isle of Wight, still searching for answers to her mother's disappearance.

A call comes in. A small child, a boy, has been left abandoned on a train. Like Lara, he has no relatives to look after him. It feels as if history is being repeated – but surely this is a coincidence?

A series of murders

Before Lara can focus on the boy's plight, she's faced with a series of murders. They feature different victims in very different circumstances, but they all have one thing in common: they all leave children – alone – behind.

So who is targeting Lara? What do these abandoned souls have in common? And how does this connect to the mystery of Lara's missing mother?

THE DEVIL'S BRIDGE AFFAIR

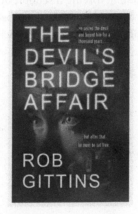

'I literally had shivers running down my spine!' Monika Armet

'So well written I was completely drawn in to this tale.' Lynda Checkley

'A pacy thriller that will challenge many of your preconceptions.' Angela Paull

Lightning splits the sky, night somersaulting into day And in that moment, a life is lost...

The name of the Devil's Bridge derives from a local legend, telling the story behind a bridge that was built centuries before for the town, built by the devil himself. But there was a price. The devil vowed to return at different times and in different guises with dark consequences for those who live in the bridge's shadow.

Most in the town believe it to be just a colourful local story; a flight of fancy. Dark deeds can happen anywhere – and there's no such thing as the devil.

Then a massive scandal, involving a schoolboy and his English teacher, hits the community, and even the most die-hard of sceptics begin to wonder if a devil-like figure is walking in their midst.

OTHER CRIME AND THRILLERS BY ROB GITTINS

A crime series set in the hidden world of witness protection.

Gimme Shelter
Secret Shelter
Shelter Me

What's a wife, husband or partner like when you're not watching?
A psychological thriller exploring the dangers waiting to ensnare
those who try to find out.

Investigating Mr Wakefield

PRAISE FOR ROB GITTINS

'Rob Gittins is a highly acclaimed dramatist whose work has been enjoyed by millions in TV and radio dramas.'
Nicholas Rhea – author of the Constable series, adapted for TV as *Heartbeat*

'Visceral, strongly visual and beautifully structured... powerful, quirky characters.'
Andrew Taylor – Winner, Crime Writers' Association Cartier Diamond Dagger

'Gittins introduces the reader to a dangerous and troubled part of society, and his murky, damaged and at times violent characters are as vividly (and disturbingly) portrayed as those of Elmore Leonard.'
Susanna Gregory – crime author

'Unflinching... as vicious and full of twists as a tiger in a trap.'
Russell James – crime author

'The definitive interpretation of 'page turnability' ... characters that step effortlessly off the page and into the memory.'
Katherine John – crime author

'TV writer Rob Gittins .. hits hard from the start.'
Iain McDowall – crime author

'Visceral realism doesn't come much better than this. Brilliant.'
Sally Spedding – crime author

'Noir at its most shocking.'
Rebecca Tope – crime author

'Terrifying and suspenseful, non-stop jeopardy. Just be glad you're only reading it and not in it.'
Tony Garnett – TV Drama Producer, *Kes, Cathy Come Home, This Life*

'Gittins is an experienced and successful scriptwriter for screen and radio ... startling and original.'
Crime Fiction Lover

'Well-plotted and superbly written.'
Linda Wilson, *Crime Review*

'Full of intrigue and narrative twists ... powerfully written and uncompromising in its style.'
Dufour Editions

'Corrosive psychological consequences which match those in the best Nicci French thrillers.'
Morning Star

'If there's one thing you can be sure of when it comes to Rob Gittins's literary output, it is that he's not afraid of a scintillating pace ... this has all the hallmarks of a cult classic and I couldn't recommend it highly enough.'
Jack Clothier, Gwales

'Well-drawn characters and sophisticated storytelling.'
Publishers Weekly

'Unputdownable ... this deserves every one of the five stars. I would have given it more if I could have.'
Review on Amazon.com

"Uncomfortable, taut, brutal, it will hold you gripped right to the end. A wonderful piece of writing.'

Cambria

'Fast action, convincing dialogue, meticulously plotted through-out. Every twist ratchets up the sense of danger and disorientation.'
Caroline Clark, Gwales

'Thrilling … bloodthirsty.'
Buzz

'Gripping and exciting, fast-paced. There is something a bit different about Gittins's writing that I haven't come across before.'
Nudge

HOBECK BOOKS – THE HOME OF GREAT STORIES

We hope you've enjoyed reading this novel by Rob Gittins. To keep up to date on Rob's writing please do look out for him on Twitter or check out his website: **www.robgittins.com**.

Hobeck Books offers a number of short stories and novellas, free for subscribers in the compilation *Crime Bites*.

- *Echo Rock* by Robert Daws
- *Old Dogs, Old Tricks* by AB Morgan

- *The Silence of the Rabbit* by Wendy Turbin
- *Never Mind the Baubles: An Anthology of Twisted Winter Tales* by the Hobeck Team (including many of the Hobeck authors and Hobeck's two publishers)
- *The Clarice Cliff Vase* by Linda Huber
- *Here She Lies* by Kerena Swan
- *The Macnab Principle* by R.D. Nixon
- *Fatal Beginnings* by Brian Price
- *A Defining Moment* by Lin Le Versha
- *Saviour* by Jennie Ensor
- *You Can't Trust Anyone These Days* by Maureen Myant

Also please visit the Hobeck Books website for details of our other superb authors and their books, and if you would like to get in touch, we would love to hear from you.

Hobeck Books also presents a weekly podcast, the Hobcast, where founders Adrian Hobart and Rebecca Collins discuss all things book related, key issues from each week, including the ups and downs of running a creative business. Each episode includes an interview with one of the people who make Hobeck possible: the editors, the authors, the cover designers. These are the people who help Hobeck bring great stories to life. Without them, Hobeck wouldn't exist. The Hobcast can be listened to from all the usual platforms but it can also be found on the Hobeck website: **www. hobeck.net/hobcast**.

OTHER HOBECK BOOKS TO EXPLORE

Silenced

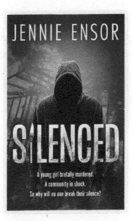

Silenced is the compelling and gritty new thriller by British author Jennie Ensor. A story of love, fear and betrayal, and having the courage to speak out when the odds are stacked against you.

A teenage girl is murdered on her way home from school, stabbed through the heart. Her North London community is shocked, but no-one has the courage to help the police, not even her mother. DI Callum Waverley, in his first job as senior investigating officer, tries to break through the code of silence that shrouds the case.

This is a world where the notorious Skull Crew rules through fear. Everyone knows you keep your mouth shut or you'll be silenced – permanently.

This is Luke's world. Reeling from the loss of his mother to cancer, his step-father distant at best, violent at worst, he slides into the Skull Crew's grip.

This is Jez's world too. Her alcoholic mother neither knows nor cares that her 16-year-old daughter is being exploited by V, all-powerful leader of the gang.

Luke and Jez form a bond. Can Callum win their trust, or will his own demons sabotage his investigation? And can anyone stop the Skull Crew ensuring all witnesses are silenced?

Pact of Silence

'What an emotional rollercoaster! Darkly addictive and packed to the rafters with secrets, I was flipping those pages, desperate to see how it unravelled.' Jane Isaac, psychological thriller author

A fresh start for a new life

Newly pregnant, Emma is startled when her husband Luke announces they're swapping homes with his parents, but the rural idyll where Luke grew up is a great place to start their family. Yet Luke's manner suggests something odd is afoot, something that Emma can't quite fathom.

Too many secrets, not enough truths

Emma works hard to settle into her new life in the Yorkshire countryside, but a chance discovery increases her suspicions. She decides to dig a little deeper…

Be careful what you uncover
Will Emma find out why the locals are behaving so oddly? Can she discover the truth behind Luke's disturbing behaviour? Will the pact of silence ever be broken?

Milton Keynes UK
Ingram Content Group UK Ltd.
UKHW042303060923
428183UK00004B/96

9 781915 817228